RISE OF THE HAUGENBERRYS

A NOVEL

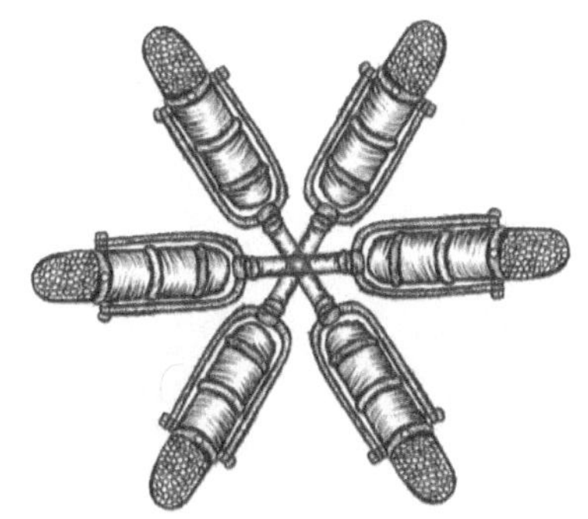

ZACH BODDICKER

ILLUSTRATED BY CHARLY FASANO

DAISY DOG PRESS
JOES, COLORADO

FOR THE REAPER

I'm AJ Washburn: spinster, fag-hag, amateur comedy emcee. People like groups of three. Here's another: *Doer of Stuff*. That's what I've settled on, that's what I tell people, bippity boppity boo.

One thing I like to do is receive a free college education. I have one paid-for embossed and watermarked diploma, and maybe a dozen of the paperless variety. How do you do *that*, you ask. Easy—you work nights, live near a university, and simply *don't stop* going to classes. Professors don't even notice in the big ones. Once they get to know you, and you prove to be a perspicacious student, then you can request to "audit" a class. That'll get you a ticket into the smaller upper-division courses.

I've been doing this fairly consistently for fifteen years. All the professors know me, or know of me. Never has a single prof or administrator taken me aside and drawn attention to my excesses. I assume some of them feel pity for me. That's a fair trade.

Night classes during the summer term are sparse, so I usually take summers off. But when Professor Becker announced he'd be teaching an Existentialism & Contemporary Culture seminar, I couldn't resist. A test-run of a new curriculum, he told me. He actually e-mailed *me* about it. That's how much of a free-loading institution I've become around the University of Denver campus.

And so it was, the end of June, still early in the course. There were twelve other students, most of them dudes half my age. I knew some of them from other classes. The ones I didn't were easily melted by my cougar jokes and general irreverence. Becker always ends his lectures with a profound question or concept to take home. That night's offering: *who you are gets in the way of who you could become.*

I ruminated on this as I drove to my apartment, and on the short walk to the Lo-Ball to meet Rikki. Did my rumination change anything? Did it lead to any plans for self-improvement? Of course it didn't.

The night's headliner was a band from Nashville. I knew nothing else about them, and it didn't matter. I ordered a vodka cran and claimed a spot near the stage where I'd be easy to spot. I'm found-family-oriented, and Ricardo Montoya is the closest thing I have to a domestic partner, though we've never lived together. He's the least flamboyant uncloseted thirty-something gay man one could ever expect to meet. I tended bar at a mostly-gay lounge for over a decade, so I feel like I'm really saying something here. I like to keep things positive, so I'll say Rikki excels at deferred punctuality. He has a way of arriving after I've written him off as a no-show and my disappointment has passed.

There's no backstage area at the Lo-Ball. The only path onto the stage is a small staircase at the front suitable only for the fully able-bodied. I had set my drink on one of the steps, oblivious, like a teenager stopped mid-crosswalk checking a text message. As I scrolled on my phone, I felt something heavy on my left shoulder.

"Excuse us."

I turned and found myself eye-level with an acoustic guitar

attached to a giant man from a fictional time and place. Over seven feet in stature, I estimated. Just behind him was another giant. I apologized, embarrassed, and removed my drink from the step. The giants climbed onto the stage and began a quick survey of the small, cluttered performance space.

The house lights and sound faded as they tuned their instruments. I expected one of them to say something banal, baritone, a brief introduction or tired expression of gratitude. No.

> *Oh hummingbird*
> *Mankind was waiting for you to come flying*
> *along*

Angelic tenor harmonies from both giants; their vocal range at odds with their stature. Loose ends of conversation ceased, and people began to gather near the stage. The men approached their microphones after a few more phrases, and began strumming their guitars. Both instruments looked like toys in their hands.

The song sounded familiar, but I couldn't name the artist. I thought it might be a Simon & Garfunkel tune I was unaware of. I'd have to ask someone.

The song played out, and they ended it abruptly. Both men froze, looking out at the crowd as though they were waiting to hear a pin drop. Someone shouted and clapped, then everyone shouted and clapped. Both giants smiled.

One of them curtsied. Yes, curtsied. He then approached the microphone. "I'm Abe," he said. "That's Dan. We're the Haugenberrys. Happy birthday, George."

Abe started another song. Dan eventually joined in, smiling once he recognized it. These guys didn't play their instruments like other players, maybe due to the mismatch between their hand sizes and instrument sizes. The act of fretting and strumming didn't look like it came naturally to either one. The awkwardness was sort of endearing, like the tinge of pity one feels while encountering a piece of "folk art."

The song's first chorus passed, and Dan stopped playing, appearing either distracted or as though he'd just had a minor epiphany. He approached Abe and stole his microphone and stand. Abe, who'd been singing with his eyes closed, looked annoyed. Dan then began singing and strumming a different song. Abe crouched and had a drink from a water bottle, then stood and joined in—another vaguely familiar tune.

They made it through the first chorus and another verse before Abe walked behind Dan and pulled the cord out of his guitar, producing two violent pops in the PA speakers. Abe approached the other of the two vocal mics and began yet another song while Dan plugged his guitar back in, producing another pair of loud pops.

I knew this one—"The Air That I Breathe" by the Hollies, a childhood favorite that I played hundreds of times on my beige and orange Fisher Price record player. I still see the red and black 45rpm label spinning in my mind every time I hear it.

They allowed the song to play out in its entirety, to my great satisfaction. Abe and I made eye contact for the first time as the crowd applauded. I just happened to place my hand over my heart at the very moment he looked at me. *Oh great*, I thought. *There goes my wall. Just massaging a scar. Don't mind me.*

Rikki arrived at my side right then, having managed to cut through the dense crowd. "Who are these lumberjacks?" he shouted into my ear, his breath ripe with gin and tonic.

"Abe and Dan Haugenberry," I said. "They don't seem to get along. It's someone named George's birthday. That's all there is so far."

Abe started another song. Dan smiled and yelled *hell yes* toward the ceiling once he recognized it and joined in. They seemed to have a special affinity for the tunes they were play-ing, like each one was a surprise gift. They didn't use a set list as far as I could tell, and seemed to have a disregard, if not contempt, for mics and mic placement. Their instruments were at times too loud for the vocals, and vise-versa. I imagined Jill at the sound booth had gone through half a box of tea tree toothpicks already.

Again, I recognized the song but couldn't identify it, so I asked Rikki. "Someone needs to reposition the stage lights," he said. "Seeing a lot of chest, not a lot of face."

Dan started singing "Muskrat Love," mischief in his eye, as though he were trying to taunt Abe. It worked. Abe didn't strum along. He began looking around the dark edges of the stage for something, eventually picking up a half-full bottle of water. He walked behind Dan and poured it onto Dan's head.

Dan stepped away, muttering, running his hand through his hair. By the time he had his eyes clear, Abe was into another song. Dan looked at Rikki and me for a moment, like he expected us to tell him what to do next. Abe was a few verses in when Dan began strumming all the open strings on his guitar, random, out of tempo, out of key. He reached into his front jeans pocket for something and walked behind Abe.

He flipped open a Zippo lighter, lit it, and placed the flame at the bottom seam of Abe's untucked plaid western shirt. It took a few seconds before Abe noticed. His eyes opened and he stopped singing. The flame was now self-sustaining, so Dan backed away. Abe reached his hands around his back to extin-guish the flame.

While everyone's focus was on Abe and the fire, Dan grabbed someone's full pitcher of beer from the edge of the stage and tossed its contents at Abe. It seemed the beer toss was just another antic rather than an attempt to put out the flame. Abe turned his back to Dan at this point, and Dan gave Abe a boot to the ass, causing Abe to fall forward onto a stack of amplifiers.

Dan stepped down from the stage into the crowd. He handed his guitar to me and began gesturing for everyone to make room. When a maybe ten-foot diameter area was cleared, he turned to address Abe, who'd removed his guitar and shirt and was approaching the stairs.

"Let's see some hustle!" Dan shouted, his hands cupped around his mouth. Abe charged at him as soon as his feet hit the dance floor, stopping just short of tackling. Both crouched slightly like wrestlers and began a slow counterclockwise rotation around the edge of the clearing.

"One of you kick the other one's ass!" Rikki shouted. I backhanded him on the shoulder.

I don't know the first, second, or third thing about wrestling terminology, but Abe made the first attack, aiming low. Dan was now on the defensive, struggling to avoid being flipped onto his back. Abe had a good enough hold on Dan's legs that he was able to lift him and carry him closer to the center of the room before letting him down—not a full-on smackdown, but not gentle. Dan tried to scramble away, but Abe had him pinned on his stomach and his legs locked up. Within a couple more moves Dan's shoulders were flat on the floor—the most freakish biomechanical sculpture I'd ever observed up close.

Abe slapped the floor with his free hand and released his hold. He was the first to stand up, bowing his head and lifting one fist into the air. He then went for the front door of the venue without a word. A few high-fives were given. Dan stood, brushed himself off, and followed.

The crowd exploded—whistles, whoops, chanting for *more more more, fight fight fight.* This went on for a solid minute until the lights came back on and some old-school country music began to play on the PA.

Everyone looked around at everyone else, as if to ask *what did we just see?* It was—in almost every way—the opposite of the typical Lo-Ball act. It was raw, audacious, chaotic, dangerous. One didn't get the sense these men had mood-stabilizers in their diets.

I found myself near the back of the room, having been shuffled about during the wrestling match. Dan's guitar was still in my hands. Jill was behind the soundboard, looking frazzled and uncertain whether she or the venue was safe and secure. I handed the instrument to her.

"What the hell was that?" I asked.

She grabbed the guitar and placed it behind her. "Never again," she said.

I wandered the crowd looking for Rikki, until I found myself back at the sound booth. Josh, the Lo-Ball's talent buyer and a long-time friend of mine, looked to be consoling Jill. He saw me and we had a brief hug.

"Where did you find those guys?" I asked.

"Behold the Fightin' Haugenberrys," he said. "Just moved to the neighborhood. From out east somewhere. Eastern Colorado. Forty miles from one town I've never heard of, and forty from another town I've never heard of."

I asked how they got the gig, since the Lo-Ball was a fairly exclusive venue.

"They gave me a VHS tape," Josh laughed. "Remember those? That was their audition. I had to buy a VCR at Goodwill to watch it."

I asked him what was on the tape.

"Pretty much what you just saw, except thirty years ago in a high school gym."

This was intriguing. I had to see this tape, but before I could inquire further, Josh was whisked away by some emergency outside the venue. I wondered if the Haugenberrys had moved their brawl out onto the sidewalk, and so headed in that direction.

Some bro had wrecked his crotch rocket a half-block north of the venue. A wheelie-gone-awry apparently, minor injuries, likely DUI, a routine Friday night eye-roller. There was no sign of the brothers, so I walked around the building to see if I could find them. No luck, so I went back inside. No sign of Rikki either. Had I been ditched? I checked my texts. Nothing. Time for another vodka cran.

I noticed legendary Denver hipster Oliver Brown standing near the back of the room, surrounded by a small crowd. He'd lost his right arm at the shoulder in an auto accident a couple months previous, and hadn't been seen out in the wild since. My friend Gary was speaking with him. I approached and got Gary's attention, just long enough for him to invite me to an after-party.

I didn't get a turn with Oliver before the headliner took the stage. I assumed he'd witnessed the Haugenberry act, and I was anxious to get his take on it. Oliver's first big concert was the Beatles at Red Rocks Amphitheater, to give you an idea of how long he's been around. He's owned a record store since I was a single cell. Don't quiz him on all the artists he's seen. You'll become fatigued, dehydrated, disoriented.

The headliner began their first song, all the members extremely well-groomed and a bit too fashion-heavy to pass as a country band. Mormon missionaries in pastel custom-tailored western wear. They looked like they were coated in whatever shit they used to put on food in cookbook photos from the sixties. Rikki emerged from the back hallway. He'd been in the basement talking to some of them.

"I think someone got off the Lawrence Welk Expressway a few exits too soon," he said.

We gave them a chance, but despite having some fantastic musicians, they just weren't doing it for us. Having to win over a room after the Haugenberrys wouldn't be on my to-do list. After a couple songs we moved to the very back of the venue where the band's merch tables were set up and some amount of visiting was possible and acceptable while bands played.

We explored the majesty of the band's lavish spread of color-coordinated vinyl records, T-shirts, embroidered button-up work shirts, glittery decals, lip balms, coffee mugs, etcetera etcetera. The entire spectrum of pastel, like a fully-stocked tray of wedding mints. It was a trust-funded band, without a doubt, and their artistic director, if not the whole band, had to be gay. Rikki confirmed this. "Nothing on this table was conceived by a straight person," he said.

Where were the Haugenberry brothers? I turned a few corners looking for them. They'd be easy to spot, impossible to miss. They couldn't have gone far if they wished to get paid. I ditched Rikki and headed past the sound booth toward the stairs to the basement green room.

No Haugenberrys there either, so I reversed course and turned the corner to the sound booth. There they were, standing shoulder to shoulder, listening to Jill. Abe held his guitar at his side like a tennis racket, the duo blocking the narrow hallway to the main room. I crept up behind them, and though I couldn't see Jill's face or hear very well, there was no doubt she was venting. I crept closer, until I was within a foot or so from Abe's back. There was a faint odor of burnt hair.

Jill gave the brothers a run-down on what never to do again, which amounted to a nutshell description of their entire act. The brothers nodded after each of her outbursts, not arguing or asking questions. It was clear to me which of the involved parties needed a career change.

One of the musicians onstage asked for more of something in their monitor speaker, and this ended Jill's rant. Pretty sure I got crop dusted as the brothers walked away from the sound booth. I followed them nonetheless, and this led the three of us out onto the sidewalk in front of the venue.

Abe reached up to adjust a letter on the marquee, then

pulled a pouch of roll-your-own tobacco out of his rear jeans pocket and began his ritual. I stood a few feet away, pretending to look aloof. Dan stood at the curb, shirtless, facing the street, his guitar resting on his shoulder. Abe noticed me once his cigarette was lit.

"You were in the front row," he said. "Not the safest place to be. What did you think?"

I took a few steps toward him, extended my fist, and we bumped. His fist was approximately twice the size of mine. I introduced myself.

"Not what anyone was expecting, if I may speak for everyone here."

Standing right there in front of him, I had a chance to get a better estimate of his vitals—seven feet, give or take a few inches, early-to-mid-forties, a little gray in the sideburns and scruff. Thick, but not fat. No beer bellies on either. All of their physical features looked to be consistent and normal in proportion.

"I'm starving!" Dan shouted.

"Go put a shirt on," Abe said. "This isn't the Kremlin."

And with that, Dan jogged across Broadway, headed north. That famous black and white photo of Bigfoot came to mind.

"Christ," Abe said. "I'd better make sure he gets back okay. He's just not himself today."

I asked where they lived, and Abe told me the cross streets. It was in the direction of Gary's house, so I invited them to the after-party.

"I'll introduce you to some people."

I offered to text him the address. He said he didn't have his cell phone. I offered to write the address down for him.

"Just tell me. I'll remember it."

I did. We fist-bumped again, and he was off.

"I'll make it over, at least," he said, walking backwards for a few paces. "Should we bring anything?"

I thought a moment. It wasn't my party, and I just planned on bringing myself. "Your A-game. Just bring that."

A brief stop at my apartment was necessary to freshen up and hit the reset button. Let me tell you what I look and feel like after four drinks, after being tossed around the edge of a wrestling match, after having been up since five o'clock, after an eight-hour workday and Existentialism class:

Picture a deflated sex doll caught on a chain link fence behind a small town Elks Club, flapping in the wind.

Of course, I haven't looked my best since I was probably twenty or twenty-two, when I was at the very peak of average-looking. I brushed my teeth, clawed at my hair in a couple spots, re-upped the lipstick. I wouldn't have turned down an amphetamine, and I wouldn't have ventured back out, but didn't want to miss an opportunity. This had the makings of a grandiose project, which I was very much in need of. I made a deal with myself: if they didn't arrive by midnight, I'd leave the party.

It's a ten-minute walk to Gary's from my place. My mind was racing with possibilities. A large showbill hung in my mind that read *The Fightin' Haugenberrys with the Colorado Symphony Orchestra at Red Rocks Amphitheater.*

Oliver, Gary, and another dozen people were already at the party, having skipped out on the rest of the headliner's set. I invited myself in, and Oliver came straight for me, gesturing for a side-hug, mentioning that his ribs were "still falling into place."

"I stopped by the shop today," he began, addressing the entire crowd. "So, I'm going through a box of records, cleaning them, and it occurred to me that I've become—in my heavily modified, one-armed state—a physical manifestation of a turntable."

He stepped back from the circle that had developed. "Imagine a giant vinyl record hanging from my neck." He stiffened his left arm, lifted it slightly, moved it slowly to his right, and then back towards his body, mimicking the movement of a tonearm and stylus being placed on a record. "It's grotesque. Like I'm at the center of a David Cronenberg plot."

Oliver was back in full force, likely in better health than ever due to a hospital diet.

I got some one-on-one time with him sooner than expected. I assumed he'd grown tired of discussing the accident and recovery, so I asked him what he thought about the Haugenberry act.

"Marx Brothers anarchy mixed with some old-school wrestling, to an oddly-curated soundtrack of 8-track era soft-rock. Who woulda thought. Sign me up!"

I asked if he recognized any of the songs the brothers had played, and he produced a quick list of artists—Seals & Crofts, America, Gordon Lightfoot, plus a few other names that weren't familiar to me. "All hits during the Nixon presidency, which suggests something clandestine," he added.

My attention turned to the street-facing windows of the front room. I could see Dan sitting on the stone-and-concrete ledge of the front porch, eating a slice of pizza. Oliver gestured toward the front door.

"Oooh! Here's your chance," he said. "Go figure those dudes out before someone else does."

I made for the porch, nervous, as though I were about to ask one, or both, of them to a Sadie Hawkins dance. Abe sat on the steps using a multi-tool to tighten the leg screws on a metal patio chair. Dan stood and introduced himself, then returned to the ledge.

"I see you found something to eat," I said.

Dan held the slice up. I knew exactly where he bought it, how much it cost, and who made it.

"If *I* were Al," Dan said about the slice and its maker. "I wouldn't be proud enough of this to put my name on it. Name it after an ex-wife, maybe an abusive priest. C'mon, Al. Keep your eyes on the ball."

Abe finished with the chair and set it upright. "There," he said, before sitting on it and shifting his weight around to assure its structural integrity. Then he went for the other of the two patio chairs. "Always got to worry about what we sit on," he said, lifting the chair and checking its screws.

I sat on the newly repaired chair.

"How often do you guys perform?" I asked.

"Pretty much never," Abe said.

The Bee Gees started playing from Gary's porch speakers, mid-song. Dan started laughing. Abe begin to smile and hum along.

Dan looked at me. "I'm gonna guess you've been to Georgia on a fast train."

It took a fraction of a second for this to register with me. He was referencing one of my dad's favorite country songs. I didn't know a world without it, and I could crush it at karaoke without looking at the words.

"I've never been to Georgia, actually," I said. "*But*, I *have* been there on a fast train."

"Okay, good," Dan said. "Our dad was a large animal vet. Self-taught. One day we were helping him. He was shoulder-deep in a cow's uterus and out of nowhere he started singing..."

How deep is your love? How deep is your love?

Abe joined in on harmony immediately

> *I really mean to learn*
> *Cuz we're living in a world of fools*
> *Breaking us down, when they all should let*
> *us be...*

They were both laughing by then.

"Oh fuck," Dan said, standing and going for the steps. He looked choked up suddenly. Abe continued with the chair as Dan walked past him toward the sidewalk. I didn't know what to say, so waited for Abe to speak.

"Don't mind him. Our dad passed a couple months ago," Abe said, turning the chair upright and sitting on it.

"I'm sorry to hear that," I said.

Abe sat back and looked up at the ceiling. "Dear George Haugenberry," he said. "Wrote an insult for everyone—just like that old Creedence song."

An insult comic, large animal vet, and probably also a giant —to imagine a more fascinating person would be asking too much of the universe.

"No one was safe," he continued. "Old ladies, newborns. Hell, he'd come out of surgery and have one for the anaesthesiologist, any doctor or nurse within striking distance." He snapped his fingers. "Just like that. It was pathological."

A few people I didn't know walked out on the front porch, breaking our line of sight. They complimented Abe on the show, then headed across the street into the darkness. More Bee Gees played over the speakers. All the questions I'd arrived with had faded, for the time. *Stop with the agenda,* I told myself.

There was much laughter and merriment inside the house. I asked Abe if he wanted to go in and meet a few people. He declined but didn't appear too anxious to leave. The silence became comfortable after a while, but I couldn't just *not* talk.

"Just moved to town?" I asked.

"We're renovating the old family house," he said, mentioning the address. "So, we'll be around 'til that's done."

Certain homes in the neighborhood are known solely by their address. All of them rentals, usually once-glorious large homes long-since split into apartments. I knew the address. I'd been there in various states of disrepair, many years ago, of course. I mentioned this.

"Stop by whenever," he said, standing and stretching. "I'm spent. What time is it?"

We had a few parting words, another fist bump, and he took off. I felt like I hadn't quite made the impact I'd hoped, but at least they knew I existed. I said my goodbyes to Oliver, Gary and the rest and headed for my apartment, satisfied that I'd achieved at least *something* by attending the party. I'd gotten some alone time with the brothers without coming off as too pushy or awkward. I knew where to find them and scored a personal invitation to visit them whenever. *Gold.*

The wheels were spinning when I reached my apartment. I stripped down, sat on my couch, and began writing on a notepad—ideas, sketches, the beginnings of a strategy. I had visions of the Haugenberry brothers on a national stage, mingling with the stars, while I pranced around the margins with my little magic wand, making it all happen.

The thing is, I know better than to think up this kind of shit.

My fitness regimen is simple and consistent: one casual half-mile walk to the Golden Spork for breakfast at least every other Sunday. Rikki usually meets me there, but I'll go alone. I order my food right away, as Rikki is never on time, and certainly never early.

I scored an outside table without having to wait and began flipping through the *Westword*—Denver's weekly arts and culture rag. I needed to familiarize myself with their current roster of writers and editors. Rikki arrived within a couple minutes. "How are we this fine morning," he said, standing beside the table as though he were pretending to be a waiter.

"Oh, you know. Who I am is getting in the way of who I could become."

He scoffed. "Only a privileged, straight white chick would say something like that at ten in the morning. You should have an IKON pass hanging from your neck."

"Why don't you sit down? Hemorrhoids?"

"I just don't feel like sitting."

"Jesus. Sit the fuck down already."

And so he did, without showing any sign of discomfort. I'll never know why. He just does that kind of thing sometimes. Talk turned immediately to Gary's party, and I told him about the brothers, and some of what I'd learned. I moved my coffee out of the way and placed both of my palms on the table.

"So, Rikki," I began. "This is what I'm thinking."

"Whoa whoa whoa. You know what I think?"

"I haven't even said anything yet."

"You're getting way ahead of yourself. I can tell you that already."

I had a sip of coffee.

"These dudes could be a big deal," I said. "And they have *no* idea. They're not dumb—I'm not saying that—they just don't seem to recognize the potential."

Rikki sat silent, his arms folded.

I gave him a run-down of the little research I'd done earlier that morning. They had no social media presence whatsoever, as individuals, or as an act. No video footage online, no recordings, nothing at all. I mentioned their VHS audition tape, and his eyes lit up.

"Now that is *quaint*," Rikki said. He asked some basic questions—where were they from, what do they do, why they're in Denver. I told him what little I knew.

"Our conversation didn't get too far," I said. "There was Bee Gees, a cow's uterus, some fixing of chairs."

"*What?*" I knew I had Rikki's attention at this point. My ability to draw him into even the most hare-brained of ideas is uncanny. His coffee arrived, and I could tell his mind was now focused on the brothers.

"Do they *want* to be a big deal?" he asked.

"That's sort of a downer question. Rikki."

"I'd say it's of central importance."

I conceded, cementing my plan to drop by the brothers' house sometime later that day.

"One more question," he said. "Why you?"

"What do you mean *why me?*"

"Why are *you* the person for the job," he said, both finger pistols drawn and pointed at me. "Last I checked, you have no experience managing musicians or sideshow freaks."

"How many times have you watched *Star Wars*, Rikki?"

He began doing the math.

"I don't remember Luke Skywalker ever struggling with that question," I said. "*Why me? Why me?* And, I know for damn sure no one with their legs crossed and pinky in the air ever asked him that over coffee on a Sunday morning."

He smiled and nodded. "I'm just curious."

"Why me? Why this?" I said. "*It's there to be done*, that's why. And, I'm not getting any younger."

He clapped his hands. "Go for it then," he said, returning some levity to the conversation. "Start small, don't overwhelm the dudes with commitments and business stuff. Keep it fun. You know how you can get."

"Oh, really," I said. "How can I *get?*"

"You know."

"Oh, *I know* I know. I'm the most self-aware idiot in the asylum."

We stopped at Panopticon Records after breakfast. I hoped Oliver would be working, as I wanted to get his advice and anything else he'd have to offer regarding my nascent plans for the Haugenberrys. He was in his usual spot behind a glass display case, cleaning a record with a damp rag. He noticed us and removed his reading glasses.

"I'm going to have to suck it up and buy a record cleaning machine," he said. "This is a task for a two-armed man."

Rikki pulled a record from a wall rack and inspected it. "This cover art really speaks to me," he began. This is one of his regular gags.

"Please tell us," I said.

"It says, 'Hello, Rikki, my name is Ozzy Osbourne, and I like to dress up like a figure skater some days and a vampire on others. Today I have chosen both.'"

Oliver wiped his eyes and set a small stack of records on the counter between us. "Here you go. Since you asked about it. This is the Haugenberry set in a nutshell."

I flipped through the stack, recognizing most of the cover art.

"I could probably dig up all of these on 8-track if you want a more authentic experience," he added.

I set the albums back on the counter, having no intention of buying them, and Oliver seemed to sense this. "Take 'em," he said. "It would be a lesser sin to charge you for a stack like that."

I thanked him, and figured I'd buy something else to offset the exchange. I thumbed the "New Jazz" bin pretending to have some idea of what I was looking at.

"I need your opinion, Oliver."

"I don't do opinions, AJ," he said. "Opinions are for assholes."

Rikki spoke up. "I thought the saying went 'opinions are *like* assholes', etcetera, etcetera."

Oliver is careful with his words. Rikki knew this, so I gave Rikki the side-eye. "Both statements can co-exist."

He thought a second. "You could get all Valley Girl about it, I suppose—*opinions are, like, for assholes.*"

Oliver smiled. "Now you've created a statement completely devoid of substance. Some statements aren't meant to inter-mingle, I guess."

"That sounds like Wittgenstein," I said, while it actually made me think of the one time Rikki and I had tried to make out.

"Oh, shut up with the name-dropping," Rikki said.

"Wrong Wittgenstein, dude," I said. "*Chet* Wittgenstein, from Arvada."

"Oh, of course," Rikki said. "Chet. He's always talking stupid shit."

We had Oliver shaking his head, a bit rosy in the cheek. "You two are a trip," he began. "You're like Vladimir and Estragon from *Waiting for Godot.*"

"My god!" Rikki groaned, head tilted back, eyes wide. "Would you people stop with the humanities references already. You're going to make me puke all over these Carpenter's records."

Oliver and I looked at each other and winced. Rikki eventually noticed the silence.

"What now?" Rikki asked.

One thing I learned too late in life is *never* explain to someone why a comment he or she made was offensive, especially when pure, innocent ignorance is the cause. Just let it ride, and let someone else do it.

"So," Oliver said, attempting to get things back on track. "You want my opinion about something?"

I extended my index finger toward him in a wait-just-a-second gesture and closed my eyes. "I'm trying to enjoy this awkward moment. This is my elusive, ideal comfort zone."

Rikki made some comment about having a staring contest with a Judy Collins record.

"Ollie," I began. "I need to make these Haugenberry brothers into international superstars. What do you think? Yes? No?"

He laughed. "What's stopping you?"

"Oh, you know, just the usual stuff," I said. "Self-doubt, finances, reality."

He asked if I'd ever managed a band or had any managerial experience whatsoever. I didn't like the direction the conversation was taking.

"No," I said. "I'm mostly looking for a pep talk right now. You've been around a while. Do you think these dudes have what it takes? Do they have that *thing*, whatever it is?"

"Absolutely," he said. "You can't look away. It's bizarre,

physically uncomfortable, sonically beautiful, seems strangely authentic, and dare I say *wholesome*."

"My thoughts, exactly."

"Do they *want* to be international superstars?" Ollie asked.

"We haven't discussed that yet."

"Run with it," he said. "What's the worst that could happen?"

"We certainly don't need to go into that right now!" I said.

A paper mâché eyeball hangs from the ceiling at the center of the store, attached to a rotating mirror ball motor. I found myself staring at it, feeling some combination of relief and renewed ambition. I now had two pillars of my support system on board. That was two more than necessary, but it was comforting. I grabbed the stack of soft-rock albums and thanked Oliver.

"Okay, fellas," I said. "I'm going to do this."

I backhanded Rikki on the ass as I walked past him, headed for the front door. He set the Judy Collins record back in its bin, losing his staring contest.

"Whatever you do," Oliver said. "Study up on the history of organized crime. The academic stuff, not Hollywood. The entire structure of the music biz is based on mob hierarchies."

THE FRONT DOOR to the Haugenberry house was open when I arrived early-afternoon, mentally prepped for a high-stakes job interview, managing my anxiety with some mindful breathing, astral projection, and other lovely-sounding shit I know nothing about. The cringe-y shiver that the sight of the house had brought out of me for so many years was gone. The brothers had transformed the exterior enough that it seemed like an entirely different place.

A power tool of some kind was being used in a distant upper-floor room. I knocked on the open door and shouted a couple times before Abe emerged from the rear of the house carrying a canvas tool bag. He looked surprised to see me.

"I was just taking my afternoon walk," I said, attempting to sound like I hadn't arrived with world domination on my agenda.

"We're a bit short on furniture," he said, looking around the rooms and through the gaps in the wall studs. Most of what I remember of the first floor was now just pipes, beams, and partially knocked-down walls. He managed to find a pair of metal folding chairs that he brought out to the front porch. He suggested we sit out there to get out of the dust.

"Time for a break," he said. "I've been at it since six."

I felt compelled to get straight to the point, but I had to

contain myself, so I asked about the house. Their great-great-grandfather had it built in 1893, and it had been lived in by one descendant or another until the mid-sixties, eventually broken up into apartments in some awkward legal agreement between their father and uncle. "George was the last to go, and we're the end of the line, so here we are, wondering what the hell to do with this place when we're done."

The end of the line. Now there's something we could talk about later.

Dan emerged from the house, holding a pocketknife and one of those foot-long logs of shrink-wrapped meat. "Summer sausage, AJ?"

"I literally just ate," I said.

Dan sat on the top step of the porch, facing the street. A twenty-something dog-walker passed, led by five large short-haired, nub-tailed dogs. She looked self-satisfied and waved at us. When she was no longer looking our way, Dan shook his head and sighed.

"What are those bird dogs doing in the city with a gal like that, Abe? It's a damn shame."

Abe didn't seem compelled to respond or hadn't paid any attention to the question to begin with. "So, what about you?" he said. "What's your story?"

I gave them a few of the not-very-evocative specifics. Born and raised a few miles south of Evergreen, English Lit degree from DU, former bartender, comedy emcee.

"Were you a gymnast?" Dan asked, his mouth half-full of meat. Very few people have ever asked me this, and exactly no one has asked in the last decade or more. It was a fact of my pre-teen years that rarely even crossed *my* mind anymore.

"How could you tell?" I asked, certain that any physical evidence or mannerisms I'd acquired in my six years of training had completely eroded. It didn't seem Dan had paid more than a few minutes of attention to me up to this point.

"The way you carry yourself," he began. "I notice you approach basic things—that chair you're sitting on, for example—in an unusual way. And your posture and poise is remarkable."

Abe scoffed. "Wow, Dan. You're starting to sound like George again."

"Ah, well," Dan said, turning toward the street, cutting another slice of his meat log.

An ice cream truck turned onto the block, playing its repetitive jack-in-the-box jingle. Both brothers watched the entirety of its 10mph trek from one end of the block to the other. They stood to watch which way the truck was going to turn. They'd apparently never seen an ice cream truck before.

It seemed the perfect time to throw the question out there. "Are you guys interested in doing some more shows around town?"

Both returned to their seats.

"Hadn't even thought about it," Abe said. "That gal running sound the other night doesn't seem to want us back. I figured we were one-and-done."

I laughed. "That bitch don't know shit. And she owes me money."

Dan turned to Abe. "See, I told you so."

"Better pay, bigger stages," I continued. Both seemed at turns surprised and perplexed by the proposition. Not the knee-jerk "yes" I'd been hoping for, but neither was it the opposite.

"No hurry. Talk it over. If it's something you want to do, I can make it happen."

There was a sparkle in their eyes that hadn't been there when I'd arrived, and this was more than enough for me.

"We'll think about it, for sure," Abe said. Dan nodded in agreement.

I stood and checked my phone, to appear important and in-demand. There was nothing.

"I'm going to jump the gun and make some calls," I said, moving toward the stairs. "Most venues book several months out, so I'll let you know what I find."

I asked for an e-mail address, but neither had one. I asked for a phone number and Abe volunteered his, mentioning all he had was a flip phone. That was good enough for a text message, at least.

We did fist bumps and I left, attempting—with all my former-gymnast poise—to appear determined, confident, and focused on showing the Haugenberrys that I was the best of the best.

So proud and self-assured was I, that I almost called my dad.

I DON'T ALWAYS GO for a full-blast comedy routine on Monday nights. Sometimes it's more of a journal entry or confessional-type thing. Sometimes I show up with nothing, and just have to wing it. This was one of those times. The Haugenberry experience had hijacked my weekend, so I explained this and my quixotic plans to the crowd.

"…And four or five years from now I'll own a rocketship company. All my friends and I will be in low-earth orbit. Prince will walk out of the restroom spraying air-freshener hither and thither. I think you know the rest."

No matter what, I always call out an audience member during my intro, so I went for the first face I didn't recognize— an older Hispanic man sitting in a booth with family and friends who'd all just done shots. I walked toward him.

"Hello, Fernando," I began. "What's your name?"

He blushed and shifted his weight.

"How 'bout we go back to my place? Hop on my shoulders. We'll take my tricycle. You look like you're ready for the ride of your life."

He laughed and gave me an enthusiastic double thumbs-up. It occurred to me that maybe his English wasn't *el supremo*.

"There are probably twenty or thirty used mattresses in the alleys between here and there, Fernando," I continued. "I'll bet one of them is less disgusting than the others. What do you say?"

More thumbs-up and blushing.

I returned to the stage and went for the sign-up sheet. Someone named "Clint" was first up. I called for him twice, waiting for him to appear. Nothing.

"Clint, with a silent *N?*" I shouted, loud enough to distort the sound system.

No Clint.

The second person on the list came up and started her act. I walked to the back of the lounge, bumping a few fists on the way, and then ducked through the kitchen, out to the alley for some alone time.

I've been running the Monday night open mic at the Knights Errant Tavern for almost eleven years. This has made me something of a minor local celebrity. The tavern sits a couple blocks from the capitol building, at the edge of Denver's *gay-borhood* and so is weighted in that direction most nights. This suits me fine. I can get as crass as I want. I do, and it's expected of me. At some point early on I decided the night needed a name, so I chose to call it *Lewd & Learned*. On rare occasion a professor or other subject matter expert will come discuss something humor-related, a mini-lecture. That accounts for the "Learned" half.

I met Rikki at the open mic six years ago. He's always been an audience member only. As funny as he can be, he refuses to get up on stage. He's not afraid to heckle, and he's let me call him out on countless jokes and insults too brutal to try on a stranger.

He found me in the alley, and I guess I looked sad because he asked if I was doing okay.

"I'm golden," I said. "Just thinking about all the crap that I don't want to do. You want to do it for me?"

By crap I meant all the social media and other promo stuff

the Haugenberry project would need before anything else could move forward. I hadn't launched any sort of campaign since I'd gotten the open mic night going. That had been a protracted, somewhat casual, learn-as-you-go, fits-and-starts process.

"Take some pics on your cell," he said. "Shoot 'em to me. I'll get you set up. Get that VHS tape. I'll digitize it."

The VHS tape—I definitely needed that, and soon. The only physical copy of *anything* inevitably gets lost or damaged. I mostly just wanted to watch it, but it would probably be useful. Josh at the Lo-Ball still had it, I assumed. I texted him to see if I could get it from him.

He responded, *Yes, stop by the bar tomorrow night.*

There was still much to do, even with Rikki helping with the web stuff. I needed to contact other venues and talent buyers around town, get some merch and posters designed and ordered, reach out to local media people.

Before you get the impression that I'm some independently wealthy, lady-about-town, with nothing but time on my hands, I'll tell you that I'm not even close. I have a day job. I sit at a desk at an insurance office, setting up new policies for whomever walks through the door.

Boring, I know. The only relevant matter about my day job is this: how much of the Haugenberry campaign could be done on company time?

Unfortunately, not much. A few sketches and lists on company stationery, an e-mail here and there. A few phone calls on my breaks. Still, by the time I clocked out Tuesday, I had a game plan. I called Abe on my drive home to see if he and Dan wanted to grab some dinner and go over some ideas.

I drove directly to their house with my sketches and lists. The front door was wide open, and the aroma of fresh-cut lumber was strong. I waited for a break in the noise and announced my presence. No response. One brother was upstairs, the other in the back yard. So, I took a minute to look around the first floor—the main living room, dining room, a small bedroom, a restroom. The kitchen was the only space that hadn't undergone any significant changes. It looked just as I remembered it, minus some clutter—the yellow 1970s top-bottom fridge, Formica counter tops, faux brick back-splash.

I opened the fridge, ya know, just to see. The remainder of the summer sausage, a twelve-pack of Diet Coke, half a loaf of potato bread, a small plastic jar of dollar store peanut butter. Pretty desperate. I could see Abe ascending the back porch stairs, so I shut the fridge and tried to look unobtrusive.

He entered the kitchen, brushing sawdust and other debris from his shirt and jeans. I got straight to the point, suggesting we walk to the Lo-Ball for burgers. "Josh has your VHS tape."

Abe froze and looked mildly alarmed. "Damn, I forgot all about that. It's the only copy."

This seemed to motivate him. "Let me wash the staples and glass shards out of my eyes," he said before walking upstairs and shouting at Dan to get cleaned up. Whichever power tool Dan was using revved each time Abe began speaking. Once the tool quieted down, Abe would get another couple words out before Dan would rev it again. This went on several more rounds until I could hear Dan laughing—a menacing, Vincent Price, horror movie laugh.

Abe eventually descended the stairs wearing a clean white T-shirt, drying his hair with a red shop rag.

"Let's go," he said. "That fool can meet us there."

We began the short walk, and he filled me in on the progress they'd made on the renovation, which he described as not very impressive. They needed to fetch more tools from the "old farm" and spend less time and money at Home Depot. I wanted to know more about the farm, but our conversation was derailed as we entered the Lo-Ball.

The bar stools were full, so we went for a booth. The waitress was new—new to me anyway. I asked for menus and ordered an IPA. Abe ordered a Diet Coke.

"Not a beer drinker?" I asked him.

"Only on the weekends," he said.

I asked the waitress if Josh was around. She said she'd go find him, and within a couple minutes, he walked out from the back room. He grabbed an empty chair from an adjacent table, spun it around and sat on it backwards. "AJ and Abe, Abe and AJ," he said. "I have your tape in the office, don't let me forget. You should get that up on YouTube. Classic."

I almost mentioned Rikki's plan to digitize it, but I still hadn't asked permission. "Dan's on his way down," I said. "We're going to go over some plans. Do you have any open weekend slots in the next month or so?"

He pulled his phone from his back pocket. "A weekend—maybe not. But I can usually move shit around. Someone's always canceling."

Dan walked in right then and spotted us. The booths were tight, even for average-sized folk, so he grabbed an empty chair, moved it near us and sat.

"How tall are you guys exactly?" Josh asked. "It's hard to judge from way down here."

Abe answered with no hesitation. "I'm seven one. Dan's seven two."

The IPA and Diet Coke arrived. Abe took a sip, then nodded toward Dan. "He's hit his head on a lot more door-frames and ceilings, and that's made him about ten or fifteen dumber over the years."

Dan scoffed. "Ten or fifteen *what?*"

Abe looked at me, then Josh, and then nodded toward Dan. "See? The sonofabitch can't even understand what I'm trying to say."

Abe took another sip and continued. "He's lucky he still

has a full head of hair. Once that shit moves south, it's gonna look like a Jackson Pollock up there."

The waitress took our food orders and Josh walked back to the office. I took the folded list out of my purse. "So, here's what I'm thinking," I began. The brothers had their eyes locked on me, anxious. Dan scooted closer.

"We're going to need some photos. Nothing extravagant. Cell phone photos will do just fine. We can do those at your house tonight." I looked up from my list to check their reaction. Slight nodding from both, so I continued, mentioning that my "internet guy" was getting the website stuff together. "He's just waiting on photos, but the basic site should be ready by the end of week."

More nodding. For whatever reason, I was anticipating an objection to the VHS being digitized and uploaded. "We're going to need some video content. Are you guys okay with putting some of the tape on the website?"

They looked at each other briefly. I added that I hadn't seen the video.

"I don't know," Abe said. "What do you think, brother?"

Dan looked as though he were reviewing the content of the tape in his mind. "Nah. I don't think that needs to be on the internet for the whole world to see."

Abe looked at me, seeming to agree. "Yeah, it's...well, it's...let's just say we could do better."

"Okay," I said, looking back at my list. It was a slight setback, if the goal was to launch this campaign for zero dollars. I knew a few self-styled videographers whom I could call, and I mentioned this.

I'd sketched a few mock-up poster and T-shirt designs—on company time and stationery. The one that seemed to work the best depicted two opposing bare-fisted fighters standing behind a poorly-rendered downtown Denver skyline. I was hoping to achieve something evocative of an old circus poster, but I'm

just not there yet as a visual artist. I'd written *The Fightin'*
Haugenberrys in block letters in an arch above the drawing. "It's
just a rough idea," I said, handing it to Abe.

"I like it," he said. "Dan's pretty good with pen and ink.
What can you do with this?"

Dan grabbed the notepad and had a quick look. "Consider
it done," he said.

I brought up the matter of what they should call themselves
—the Fightin' Haugenberrys, the Fightin' Haugenberry Brothers, or just the Haugenberrys. Dan started sketching on a new
page with one of those thick construction worker pencils. "The
Fightin' Haugenberry Brothers," he said. "Brothers abbrevi-
ated b-r-o-s period. Looks more old-school."

Abe didn't object. He asked for a brief review of what all
needed to be done, and so we did that, writing it all down,
including the different graphic elements we'd need for posters,
T-shirts, stickers, and etcetera. I was in charge of the textual
elements—blurbs, bios, elevator pitches, and contacting other
venues around town. The list filled about half a page.

Abe looked over the list. "What do you want *me* to do?"

I didn't have an answer, but I knew a brainstorming session
was inevitable. The brothers could probably get away with
doing the exact same routine one more time at the Lo-Ball, but
they'd have to change it up beyond that. I still didn't know how,
if, or to what degree they planned their routine. I didn't recall
seeing a set list the previous Friday, and it seemed as though
they were just playing whichever song came to mind. The set I
witnessed only ran twenty or twenty-five minutes, tops, and
that could be an issue in either direction. Could they stretch
their act to ninety minutes? Could they squeeze it into a four-
minute television spot?

Television—now I was getting ahead of myself.

"How many songs do you guys know?" I asked.

Abe thought a moment. "I've never counted. A couple hundred probably."

"More than that," Dan said, mildly annoyed. "And we could probably half-ass another hundred or two."

I asked if they wrote any of their own songs, and neither brother spoke up right away. Dan returned to his drawing. Abe mentioned a notebook of ideas. "Nothing I've finished," he added.

I'd just sort of assumed that we would need some original songs, but after further consideration, it occurred to me that maybe it wasn't necessary. Not of immediate importance, anyway.

Josh returned to our booth, VHS tape in hand. It was a relief to see it safe and sound.

"I've got a Saturday open in two weeks," he said. "Probably a nine-to-ten time slot like last time."

The brothers and I looked around at each other. "Let's do it," Abe said. Dan gave a thumbs-up. We left the Lo-Ball full on burgers, with the VHS tape in hand, a plan, and a date booked. Not bad for a Tuesday. I walked with the brothers back to their house and took a couple dozen outdoor photos just before the sun dipped behind the mountains. I asked to borrow the VHS tape as I prepared to leave, and with a bit of hesitation, they agreed.

"Don't get your hopes up with that," Dan said.

WEDNESDAY, after work, I walked to Rikki's with the VHS and a six pack of IPAs. Rikki has a thing for A/V gear from bygone eras, and therefore owns a working VCR. He inserted the tape and did some finagling on his dual-monitor desktop computer setup. A small screen within a screen appeared inside the window of whatever software program he was using. The visual detritus of vintage videotape was immediately clear—erratic tracking lines, randomly-appearing rainbow fragments, ghostly halo-like shadows of—you guessed it—Judge Wapner and Doug Llewelyn of *The People's Court*. I hadn't thought about those ass-crushers in decades. Why on earth would anyone record an episode of *The People's Court*?

"Are you sure you grabbed the right tape?" Rikki said, expanding the image on the computer monitor and tweaking some color settings. I suggested he rewind it, he did, and we were in business.

Soon enough, we were watching what couldn't be mistaken for anything else. There were the brothers wearing burgundy and silver wrestling tights, holding their instruments. An elderly woman introduced them and then exited the frame. A moderate amount of applause ensued, interrupted by the voice of the camera operator—George Haugenberry, I assumed—saying "There's my boys! What could go wrong?"

The brothers started with "Hummingbird" sounding not quite as polished as I knew them to be. It was hard to judge, but they had not yet reached their final heights and were noticeably thinner—lanky and awkward.

A minute or so into the song, a janitor moved into the background of the frame and stopped to watch. George zoomed in, removing the janitor.

Things got blurry for a moment, then cleared up as the song reached its conclusion. Dan approached his microphone as Abe tuned his instrument. "Hey Abe, when you gonna learn to sing?" he asked. "You sound like a llama with its head stuck in a fence."

Some laughter from the crowd.

"And you smell like the back end of the same deal. They make deodorant sticks for that, you know. You'd probably try to take a bite out of it if I handed you one."

More laughter. Abe didn't look offended. He approached his mic. "This next song goes out to my big brother. Our mom yelled at him last night."

Light laughter, then George shouted. "What did she say?"

"She said, 'Show me, young man, where in any of the Star Wars movies does Luke Skywalker pee all over a dang toilet seat?'"

Rikki and I looked at each other, acknowledging the odd coincidence of the *Star Wars* reference. I'd made one only a few days previous, and now this.

"Maybe it's a sign," Rikki said.

"Pretty good jokes for a couple of teenagers," I said. "Maybe George did some coaching, maybe not, I'll have to ask."

I didn't recognize the second song, and it didn't last very long before Dan stopped playing and began detuning the strings on Abe's guitar. As Dan started another song, Abe exited the camera frame, returning with a pitcher of water that he emptied onto Dan's head. Dan then left the frame while Abe started another song. Dan returned with a wet towel that he twisted into a whip. He took a snap at Abe's ass and critical mass was reached. Abe set his guitar down and met Dan in the middle of the frame.

"Bust some chops!" George shouted. "The both of ye!"

And the match began. Abe got the initial upper hand. The audience was now cheering like you might expect at an actual match. Audience members were calling out for specific moves, or specific limbs to be targeted. After a minute or so of various attacks and reversals, Abe flipped Dan on his back. A loud slapping noise echoed and it was done. Abe raised his hand in victory and approached the microphone. "We're the Haugenberrys, but you already knew that. Thanks for watching. Eat your Wheaties."

Dan was upright by then and took a bow.

Then the footage cut to ol' man Wapner again.

"Who wouldn't pay to see that?" Rikki asked.

We watched it a couple more times, looking for details and nuance we may have missed the first go-round. It was just shy of eight minutes in length. Rikki suggested some possible edits and loops that would look good on the website. I told him to try whatever he wanted, but not to upload anything just yet. The VHS content was a minor revelation. While their Lo-Ball set had been without any back-and-forth, cut-downs, or insults, they were both capable, and certainly better at it now with sixty years of life experience between them. This was a whole new element to be developed and expanded. I didn't have any expertise with the musical side of things, but I could contribute insults for days.

I needed to finish their bio, write blurbs, fake reviews, and some elevator pitches to send to local media. Getting a pre-show write-up was unlikely with the gig only ten days away. I considered calling Abe to gather more details about their background, upbringing, and so on. I was curious on a personal level, but for the purposes of a brief artist's bio it wasn't necessary. In fact, it would be a completely avoidable obstruction having to craft a bio around a few mundane facts. The brothers were basically an unknown entity, so why not start from scratch entirely? And by scratch, I mean why not create my own system of ethics and journalistic integrity—or lack thereof?

Behold the Brothers Haugenberry, giant warrior-minstrels descended from the fog-enshrouded peaks of a land that time forgot, as they sing of love, battle, and pastoral splendor in the tradition of the traveling bards and troubadours of bygone epochs...

Step into the big tent ladies and gents and witness the Fightin' Haugenberry Brothers. Watch two giants from the northernmost reaches of the Yukon perform the greatest songs ever devised by the human mind, and then battle to the death!

Floating untethered in the twilight zone of musical entertainment are Abe and Dan Haugenberry—brothers of superhuman physical proportions and uncanny musical abilities. The hypnotic effects of their vocal harmonies defy any attempts of the laboratory and clinical study. The listener must submit to a dream-state—subject to unpredictable and inescapable extremes of magnificence and horror, stellar alignment and total disorder...

It was a start, and I'd need to run it all by the brothers before spending too much time on any of them. If they wanted a more fact-based presentation, well...that would be too bad —*Home-renovators-by-day, and hailing from the small town of Cowchip, Colorado...*

Boring.

One central question came to mind: who came up with this act anyway? Who says *why don't you two boys play a medley of decid-*

edly un-hip early-seventies soft-rock hits, then start physically assaulting one another, and then end up in a Greco-Roman-style wrestling match? I assumed it was their dad's idea, but maybe it was more complicated. Either way, it seemed like the sort of detail you'd want to keep secret, for mystery's sake, at least for the time being.

Abe texted me late-afternoon Thursday: *Stop by the house after work. Dan has posters ready.*

So I did, armed with my first-draft blurbs. My god, did Dan know what he was doing. Three large posters hung on a wire in the front room. One had a superhero-comic vibe, the second looked closer to the circus poster I originally had in mind, and the third consisted of a black and white spiral vortex with paper doll-like figures of the brothers overlaid, one of them topsy-turvy from the other.

The vortex piece was the obvious choice, and it fit perfectly with the "twilight zone" blurb. I drew an imaginary box with my index finger at the bottom of the poster and recited the blurb.

The brothers stood silent, arms folded, contemplating.

"We'll use all of them eventually," I said. "We just need to pick one for now since we're short on time and money."

Dan seemed to like my choice and my blurb. Abe looked uncertain.

"Maybe it's a little too bizarre? False advertising, possibly?"

"Absolutely," I said. "That's what we're going for. Deceptive, snake-oil promo tactics."

Dan mentioned the vortex poster was the most eye-catching of the three. "People will notice that from across the street," he said.

This seemed to make sense to Abe, and he gave in. "That one just creeps me out a little."

Dan laughed and began walking away. "Are you feeling a little light in the loafers, Abe? Sexually disoriented?" He did another Vincent Price laugh as he ascended the stairs.

Abe clapped his hands. "Great then. Let's go make some copies."

The poster wasn't ready to be copied, but it was ready for Rikki to scan and manipulate. It needed the blurb added, and a blank area to write the date, time, venue, and cover charge.

So, I left it at Rikki's and went to my apartment, exhausted. It was too early for a shower, so I went for the balcony with an IPA and a single Nat Sherman cigarette. I reflected on all we'd accomplished in the previous five days.

It had been since *never* that I'd been in any sort of creative collaborative situation that ran so seamless, everyone involved equally enthused, active, and timely. It was perhaps too early in the campaign to be spending much thought on the matter. My muse returned and I began writing down some fake promo quotes for the brothers.

"What an enchanting pair. There's still a little dew on the lily!"

Harriet Davis, 1985-91 Needlepoint Grand Champion, Strattford County Fair

"Splendid entertainers and gentleman. If only I were thirteen and available again!"

Beatrice McCormick, Postmaster, Atwood, KS

"I drove the tour bus for the Village People back in the 1970s, so I've seen some freaks. These two fellas don't stand a chance out in the wild!"

Patty Yankowski, OTR Truck Driver, Knuckle, WY

IT WAS DECIDED that we'd all meet at the Haugenberry house Saturday morning. It was the first official meeting of the core team, but really no different than any previous meeting except for the addition of Rikki. He had crisp posters and two armloads of technology to transport so I offered him a ride. This would be his first time meeting the brothers in person.

We arrived with a dozen bagels and a carton of coffee. I'm going to say for the last time that the front door was open and there was noise from at least one power tool reverberating from somewhere upstairs. Rikki looked around for a clear surface to place his laptop and the posters. There was nothing of the sort, no tables or chairs, and the kitchen looked straight out of modern-day Pripyat, Ukraine. I suggested we move everything out onto the porch.

A strange detail I noticed while in the kitchen, looking out a window at the backyard—camping tents. Is this where the brothers had been sleeping this whole time? Abe was digging around in an enormous dumpster in the back yard. It reminded me of the trash compactor scene in the first *Star Wars* movie. There's that damn movie again. I walked out to the back patio and let him know we were there.

"Dropped my goddamn phone," he shouted. "I can *see* it. I need one of those grabber tools. Fuck it all!"

I offered help, but he refused, grumbling.

When I returned to the front porch, Dan and Rikki were inspecting the poster, with Rikki explaining something specific about it. I immediately got the sense that Rikki was talking himself out of an aesthetic corner, so I moved in. The dispute was over the blank rectangular space that Rikki had added to the bottom of the poster.

"Maybe there's been some miscommunication?" Rikki asked, looking at me for support. I explained the intention to use the same poster for other gigs, and how the blank space allowed for venue and date-specific customization—standard practice for low and mid-budget artists since time immemorial. "It's how the Mafia does it," I added, drawing heavily from Oliver's earlier remark, which I had yet to research.

Dan turned and walked in the house and up the stairs without another word.

Rikki looked worried and desperate. "I'm fired. Hell, they haven't even seen the website—and I re-fucked with that more than the poster!"

Abe appeared a minute later, to my great relief, seemingly not aware what had just transpired. "Well, what do we have?" he asked, rubbing his hands together.

I handed him a poster. His eyes scanned it and he read the blurb aloud. I'd modified the earlier text by a word or two.

"Awesome," he said.

The tension in Rikki's shoulders eased and he turned his attention to his laptop. "Let me know what you think about this," Rikki said, turning his screen to where Abe could see it. "Super simple, bold, effective. Dan's design elements, plus the basic info."

Abe was transfixed, as though he'd never seen his name or likeness on a website. He pointed to the "reviews" button on the page and asked Rikki to click there. I had yet to see this page myself, but immediately recognized the content as the fake quotes I'd written on my balcony a couple nights previous. I felt compelled to make excuses before Abe had the time to read through them. "These are just placeholders for now. We can take 'em or leave 'em."

Abe laughed as he read. "I like Harriet. She sounds like a loose caboose. George would've liked this."

Rikki clicked on the Instagram icon he'd placed at the top right corner of the home page. There wasn't much to see on the Instagram page other than a photo I'd taken on my phone. "I'll add a YouTube link once we have some video," he added. "Maybe a TikTok...whatever the kids are using this week."

Abe thanked us for all the time and effort, mentioning how he had no idea how to go about doing any of it. "What's left?"

"T-shirts and stickers," I said. "I need to contact local media, get a videographer lined up."

Rikki suggested that we do the video ourselves, or that he do it. "I have cameras. It'll look good enough." He reached into his backpack and pulled out the VHS tape and three CD cases that he handed to Abe. "Here's the tape and some digital copies."

Abe thanked him, before asking if there was anything else he and Dan needed to do. "Where is Dan anyway?"

"He just kind of walked away mid-thing before you came out here," I said.

Dan shouted something from upstairs, and Abe stepped inside.

"What?" Abe yelled.

"Can you turn the water back on?" Dan responded.

"I love it when he sounds vulnerable," Abe said. "That, my friends, is the sound of opportunity."

By late afternoon Saturday, we were in prime shape. Rikki had the website live for the world to see, and the vortex design sent to the silk-screeners. We'd fertilized the neighborhood with posters. Stickers weren't going to arrive in time without doubling the price, so that would have to wait.

I'd alerted the few entertainment editors left in Denver to the upcoming show. I knew each one of them, barely, and didn't have much clout with any of them. No one in town knew me as a band manager or booking agent, so I had that hill to climb. Josh knew all of them, and did have clout, so I walked down to the Lo-Ball to talk to him—just in time for happy hour.

One of the bartenders had called in sick, so Josh was helping run the taps. He served me my usual vodka cran but was too busy to be drawn into a conversation. I considered calling the brothers or Rikki to come join me, but I didn't plan on sticking around very long.

My agenda increased to two items as I walked around the room. Seeing the sound booth, I was reminded that we'd have to find someone other than Jill to run the knobs and faders. The Haugenberrys' debut gig had almost killed her, and we didn't need blood all over the place. Rikki knew how to run a sound system, but he'd be busy with the cameras, so I hoped Josh would have some ideas.

When I finally got a moment of Josh's time, I came straight out with the important question. "How do we get a write-up in the *Westword?*" I told him I'd already sent them a link to the website and a brief promo letter. "I assume they get a hundred of those a day."

"At least," Josh said. "Even in these trying, confusing times."

"Is it even possible? In these difficult, disorienting times?"

He winced slightly. "I don't know—especially in these uncertain times. The *Westword* guys come in here Monday nights occasionally. I do know they have a Tuesday deadline for pretty much anything that goes in that week's print issue."

This was good info, but not particularly useful. Monday nights were out for me, so I wouldn't get the chance to sit around the Lo-Ball waiting for some entertainment editors to *maybe* show up. I hoped Josh would offer to make a quick phone call on my behalf, but it wasn't happening, and it seemed a bit of an overreach to ask him the favor.

Josh got busy again. I finished my drink and left disappointed.

I'd been dreading the social media, and now it was next on my to-do list. This was going to be a vodka cranberry night, the perfect occasion to listen through the stack of records Ollie gave me. I set my Fisher Price record player on the balcony, a bucket of ice, bottles, laptop, and the records, ready to hunker down for a night of robotic, repetitive *liking* and *following*.

First up, Seals & Crofts *Greatest Hits*. Wow, those sounds brought me back—at the grocery store, sitting on the red plastic flappy thing in the shopping cart, my legs swinging and occasionally kicking Mom in the stomach. Her boobs, or maybe a necklace, was right there, and I'd reach for those, and she'd swat my hands and shout at me, apologizing to passing shoppers for my behavior. How do I remember this? I couldn't have been more than four years old, and probably hadn't thought about it since. The right music will do that.

Two songs into the stack of vinyl and I was on the verge of weeping. It'd been two years and a month since my mother died. Breast cancer. She and Dad insisted I take the genetic test. I did. This will provide a clue as to why I'm working at an insurance desk.

Things were getting too heavy, too early in the night. My therapist, Rikki, would have suggested I take a walk around the block and make a random phone call. Soon enough, I got a call from Abe.

"You found your phone," I said.

"I bought a new one. A smartphone. We're on our second thirty-pack of Pabst Blue Ribbon," he said. "We're brain-storming."

I could hear Dan strumming and singing in the background. I tried to identify the tune, but failed. Abe asked what I was doing, and I told him.

"Hey Dan, Dan, Dan—she's listening to Seals & Crofts *Greatest Hits*."

Dan howled, then returned to his song.

"We had a whole box of that on 8-track tape—brand new, in the shrink-wrap. Not big sellers at the auto parts store."

"I know most of these songs," I said. "Reminds me of shopping with my mom."

"What is completely off limits?" he asked. It was an abrupt change of topic, so I asked for clarification.

"At these venues," he continued. "On stage. Guns, fire-works—what else?"

"Good question. I'll have to ask Josh." I already knew I wasn't going to ask anything about it. We were going to push every boundary we came to.

"And what are the chances of getting a different sound-man? That Jill is a real downer."

"That bitch is completely out of the picture," I said. "Don't you worry about it!"

I got a Facebook message right then from Charlie, the owner of the Knights Errant.

R.I.P. Marc Weiss, it read.

"Oh, fuck it all to hell," I said. I needed to call Charlie, or maybe drive to the bar. Either way, I needed to end the conversation with Abe. He invited me over, and I gave him a maybe. "Hanging out by myself has not been working so far."

I tried Charlie's phone, but couldn't get through, so I left a message. An inventory of the night's alcohol intake *so far* put me at five drinks, probably six squeezed into five. I wasn't driving anywhere.

Marc Weiss had been a Knights Errant regular for as long as I could remember, pre-dating my decade of bartending there. A retired attorney, public media volunteer, autograph collector, occasional open mic comedy performer, and a thousand other things. He had no kids, and only a few far-flung estranged blood relatives that I was aware of.

As open mic host, I'd sort of acquired the role of head eulogist for deceased regulars. The next Monday's open mic would be a wake. I typed up a brief announcement on the *Lewd & Learned* Facebook page and shut the laptop. "Enough," I said to an empty patio.

The Seals & Crofts record began to skip.

And my dreams did not unfold—skip—and my dreams did not unfold—skip—and my dreams did not unfold—skip

Even as late as ten years ago, I probably would have dwelt on this bit of detail—its metaphorical suggestions, the notion that some ghostly hand was producing the skip in that particular spot as an omen.

But not tonight. Screw it. It was not a porch night. Time to venture out.

Rikki's would've been my first choice, but he was at a concert in Boulder. He'd known Marc. We could talk about it the next morning at breakfast.

So, it was off to the Haugenberrys'. The walk didn't magically improve my mood or distract me, unfortunately. As their house came into view, I slowed my pace and questioned what, if anything, I had to gain or contribute by making an appearance. I'd only known the guys for exactly one week, and it seemed like bad form and a probable slip-up of professionalism to drop my baggage at their threshold. *Too soon.*

I bought a Choco Taco at the 7-Eleven and went home.

THE KNIGHTS ERRANT was at full capacity. All of Marc's close friends were there—his attorney buddies, public radio friends, and drink-stirring colleagues—all in the same room at the same time. The bar was woefully understaffed, so I jumped back to help pour drinks.

Rikki arrived and got the microphone and sound system ready. We hadn't met for breakfast the day before, for reasons we hadn't yet discussed.

Marc's people were all talkers, so all I'd need to do is get the ball rolling. I had a bit of an intro worked up, fairly tame by my standards, but it was a unique atmosphere with some attendees that didn't look in-shape enough to endure the battery of gay attorney jokes I might've thrown at them on a regular roast night.

I thanked everyone for attending, before immediately calling out a few of the public figures in the room. The first two weren't deserving of the disrespect I had to unleash, but I did go straight for one of the most infamous personal injury lawyers in Colorado. He will not be named yet, but you know the kind—their face on every other billboard, bus, bus bench, and TV commercial. I named him over the microphone.

"I take the bus to and from work," I began, repeating and emphasizing his full name and nickname—just as he does. "I sit on your face at least ten times a week. I know it's a lot to take in!"

"I'm available twenty-four seven," he shouted.

"For those of you who don't know me, I'm Marc's adopted daughter," I said. "The problem with a memorial for someone as gay and perverted as Marc is you really have to avoid a lot of the typical compassionate language. You can't just come up here and say shit like, 'Wow, what a great turnout. As I look around the room, I can tell Marc touched a lot of people during his lifetime.'

"You can't say that sort of thing without some turd burglar in the back corner laughing, breaking all decorum, destroying the solemnity and seriousness of the occasion."

So it began. I returned to the back of the bar and let Marc's friends take over. Lawyers, radio people, the aging gay community—a self-propelled, perfect talking machine. There was some group discussion of Marc's autograph collection and his "Walls of Shame" located in his first-floor restroom. I'd been in there several times. There were dozens of autographs —each one framed, with an engraved description of signor and year acquired. A few photos.

The aforementioned personal injury lawyer was on the mic. "You'd go in to do what you do, and get completely lost in contemplation," he began. "Until somebody knocked on the door, reminding you of your place in the world. Trump, Jim Baker...who else?"

Anyone who'd been in there shouted out a name they remembered. Quite the random list—Phil Spector, the Reverend Jim Jones, Milli *and* Vanilli, and several names I didn't recognize. Rival attorneys, I assumed.

It went on for a solid two hours before everyone started paying tabs and leaving. I was too busy at the bar to do any sort of outro. Rikki had left the microphone on the stool on the empty stage, and the sight of it had a certain closure to it.

An elderly woman I didn't recognize attempted to pay her tab. Two club sodas.

"I didn't know he was *gay*," she said. "Always learning, always learning."

I handed her credit card back to her without charging anything to it. She reached into her purse and pulled out a crumpled-up twenty that she placed on the bar and began to flatten. She thanked me for hosting the event. "I have to give you *something*," she said.

I slid the twenty back toward her. "Marc wouldn't have this," I said. "Just look at this thing. It's wrinkled."

"I'm going to remember you," she said, wagging her index finger toward me, before walking away.

The room emptied. Rikki'd left. A couple booths of riff-raff remained, enough for one bartender to handle. Without doing an official count, I knew we'd cleared at least a thousand dollars in tips. I'd been stressing over how I was going to cough up three hundred bucks for T-shirts and another two hundred for posters in time for the gig, but now that was taken care of.

WEDNESDAY MORNING ROLLED AROUND. I was at the insurance office, setting up a home/auto bundle with some newlyweds when an e-mail arrived from Rikki.

Nice, it read, followed by a link to a *Westword* article. I clicked on it immediately.

> *Every few years a burning circus train arrives on the local music scene— an act so bizarre, unexpected, and awe-inspiring that you can't tear your eyes away. Enter Abe and Dan Haugenberry: brothers of ginormous physical proportions, with voices to match, and what appears to be a decades-long ambition to destroy one another. Lo-Ball, Saturday 9pm*

I found it impossible to contain my excitement as the young

couple signed their forms and disclosures. The husband asked if something was the matter. "No, no. I just got some good news."

When the couple was out the door, I went straight for the break room and called Abe. He was at Sally's Beauty Supply. I read the blurb to him.

"That's it?" he said.

"Yes, that's it. It's their weekly recommended gig blurb."

"Oh, that's good, I guess."

"It's awesome, Abe. That's what it is. They only do one a week, and this week we won the lottery."

I wasn't effectively communicating the significance of this. Maybe if Abe saw the article online, he'd be appropriately aroused. But, for now, moderate indifference.

"Now, what I need from you is an explanation of why you're at Sally's Beauty Supply."

"Just getting a few things for the show," he said.

"Like what?"

"Oh, you'll see," he said. "I'm going to up my game. Dan is *going down*."

We scored the parking spot directly in front of the Lo-Ball, right under the marquee. This was win number one for the night. I had Rikki take some photos of me standing under the marquee in various *Charlie's Angels* poses. "Fighting Haugenberrys" was spelled out completely, with no missing letters. The headliner act was missing an X, and the L was an upside-down seven. They were sound-checking as we emptied my hatchback onto the sidewalk—one giant box of T-shirts, two army surplus duffel bags and three small suitcases of camera equipment, and a thin box of archival quality posters.

Foot traffic on the sidewalk was heavy, so I kept an eye on the gear as Rikki moved it inside. A group of eight or nine non-hipster dudes entered the venue looking to buy tickets. I have Platinum Plus facial recognition and had never seen these people before. Something about them bothered me. Maybe it was the fog of Axe body spray. They were there solely due to the *Westword* write-up, I assumed, and they probably thought it was some type of UFC match.

The headliner's soundcheck wrapped up as I began setting up our woefully underpopulated merch table. I'd found a black and white tablecloth at Goodwill the previous night that helped pretty things up a little, but it was still pathetic. *Quality, not quantity,* I kept telling myself.

Rikki was on a ladder setting up a camera near the sound booth. Josh was behind the soundboard, writing notes on a stretch of masking tape. I offered my assistance to both, with no immediate response from either.

"How about that write-up?" Josh said, looking up from his notes. "That was a surprise."

I made a comment about pants-wetting.

"Actually, it was not a surprise," he added. "I knew Monday night. I thought about telling you," he raised an eyebrow, "*...or did I?*"

Josh confirmed that he, not Jill, would be running sound for the night. "And I told the other band that they might not want to have their instruments on the stage while the brothers do their thing."

There were three expensive-looking electric guitars sitting up there waiting to get wet, knocked over, lit on fire, stepped on, or worse. I looked around the room hoping to spot one of the band members, and I even checked the basement, but they'd all left.

Rikki was now setting up a camera behind the drum set—a rear-view perspective. He asked for help handing him things, so I climbed on the stage. I'd never actually been on the stage before, just seen about a thousand bands play on it.

"My," Rikki said, struggling to find a spot to place all three legs of a fully-extended tripod. "How much crap does one band need?"

The stage was considerably more congested than it had been at the previous show. Small metal boxes, cables and shit everywhere, with only a few small areas to stand near the microphones. This was not going to do. Abe pointed this out when he arrived carrying a guitar case and a large canvas bag.

"All of this crap has a one-way ticket to as-is, parts-only status," Abe said, setting his things on the floor and climbing onto the stage. "My feet don't even fit up here. Maybe one here, and another here," he said, contorting as though playing a game of Twister.

Problem number one of the night was established. I asked Josh if he knew where I might find the other band. "Probably across the street," he said.

So, off I went. There are three bars on that block, one of them a borderline dilapidated hold-out from the pre-gentrification era that I assumed would be their hangout, based on the bands' Vietnam-Vet-chic fashion sense. My ability to stereotype, judge, and profile proved to be a great time-saver once again.

They turned toward me as I entered the excessively dark barroom. It took a moment for my eyes to adjust. I saw their one female bandmember sitting on the far end, so I sat a couple stools down from her and introduced myself, mentioning that I'm *with* the opening act. I asked if Josh had mentioned anything about moving their gear.

"Not to me," she said.

"Well...my boys usually make quite the mess."

"Oh?"

"And, let's just say things get physical."

"Ok."

"I guess I'm suggesting that you might want to strike the stage as much as possible."

"Ok."

She wasn't helping. "At least move anything you don't want to get wet or damaged to the back wall."

"Ok."

"That's all."

"Ok. I'll tell the guys."

I walked back to the Lo-Ball, unsure that I'd gotten my message across. They'd been warned.

Seven-thirty came around and some familiar faces began to filter in. Rikki and I were standing around the merch table.

He'd spent a considerable amount of time explaining his strategy for capturing video of the night, and then explained all that he planned to do with it. It all sounded wonderful, but quickly exceeded my capacity to understand videography jargon. To my great relief, Oliver approached, handing me a fresh vodka cran, my first of the night.

"Congratulations, AJ. This is all coming together very quickly," he said, inspecting the shirts and posters. He mentioned the *Westword* write-up, and how the first Haugenberry show was a mere fifteen days previous. I deferred all the credit to Rikki and the brothers. He complimented me about the artwork.

"I'm just air-traffic control," I said. "I'm no artist. Even my best stick figure clearly has special needs."

He asked what the night's set list had in store.

"They don't tell me anything. They're just gonna do what they do."

A group of folks from Marc's wake walked through the door. I recognized them but couldn't name any of them. All men in their early sixties, in suits, looking fabulous but completely out of place. How did they know to come? Had I used Marc's wake as an opportunity to promote the show? Yes ma'am. Had that been in poor taste?

When the last of them had paid their cover charge, the wakers approached me. They resembled federal agents more so than they did hipsters. Every eye in the room followed them.

"Ms. Washburn?" the lead federal agent said, extending his hand. He introduced himself and his four colleagues. "From Marc's wake."

"Did you see the *Westword* write-up?" I asked.

"You told us about it Monday. Sounded like a perfect geezer's night out."

We made some small talk about the wake. As that conversation waned, the least talkative of the bunch handed me a business card, asking me to shoot him an e-mail in the next week or so. This was weird. The name on the card looked familiar, and it soon dawned on me that this was Donald R. Hirsh Esq., the Knights Errant attorney. I remembered the name from mail we'd get at the bar back in the day.

"May I ask what this is regarding?" I said. He sensed my unease.

"Just a few things about Marc. At your convenience."

Well, this was enough to distract me from everything else I needed to focus on. Rikki had been standing there the whole time, and once the men were out of earshot, I turned to him. "What the hell do you suppose that's about?" I asked. He shrugged.

"C'mon. Speculate."

Abe and Dan made a quick stop at the merch table, clearly pissed that the stage still hadn't been cleared and asked me who needed a talking to. We had an hour til showtime and the room was already half-full. Josh was nowhere to be found, so I led the charge to the green room.

We got to the top of the stairs and looked down. The aroma of marijuana was strong and I could sense the brothers were hesitant to go any further. I hadn't been around them long enough to know what their feelings were regarding the weed. I hoped they'd follow me and that their physical enormity would help expedite things. I took several steps down and looked back at them. They weren't moving "Well, are you coming?" I asked.

"I don't do crawlspaces," Dan said.

I looked up and around. There were a few steps of lower-than-usual head room. It's nothing I'd ever had to adapt to at five-seven, but now I noticed it. I could hear voices in the green room. "Hold on."

I descended the stairs, turned the corner, and stood in the doorway. A couple of the band members and assorted hangers-on were sitting on the array of disgusting, vermin-infested couches. I thought to turn around and try to coax the brothers downstairs for backup, but decided to handle it myself. And in a lightning-strike of self-empowerment. I approached the guitar player who was scrolling.

"Hi," I said, hoping that would get his attention. "You're with the second band?" I continued. He eventually looked at me, glassy-eyed, like everyone else in the room.

"Yes."

"We need to get the stage cleared a little. A lot, actually. Did anyone mention that earlier?"

He didn't respond right away, and things began to get awkward. I could sense the matter had annoyed him earlier, and was now returning to encroach on his personal comfort. "It's just an acoustic duo, yeah?" he asked.

Abe and Dan couldn't have picked a better time to enter the room, ducking their heads around old light fixtures, cobwebs, and other obstacles normal-sized folk never have to contend with. They bumped fists with a few of the couch-sitters, exuding affability in ways I was not. I felt as though I'd made a shift to bitchy manager status right then and there.

"Smells like Uncle Virgil's barn down here," Dan exclaimed.

"And his house, pickup truck, grain bin, camper...always happy places," Abe added.

Dan shot straight at the guitar player. "We're going to need some room up there on the stage—if you don't mind."

This got a very different reaction from what I'd gotten.

"Anything you don't want destroyed probably oughtta move to the back. Shit gets crazy. My brother gets clumsy."

The guitar player didn't look happy about it, but he stood from the couch, gathered another bandmember, and was off.

"I'm going to put you in charge of physical intimidation and mafia tactics," I said to Dan. "It's not in my wheelhouse."

"Uncle Virgil's *wheelhouse*," Abe said. "Another happy, silly place."

We emerged from the basement, and it occurred to me that no plan had been discussed for the show introduction. At the previous show the brothers simply got up on stage, lights up, and started playing. No showbiz about it. I stopped them as we approached the sound booth. Josh was sitting there, scrolling. I asserted myself and made sure the brothers were listening.

"I'm thinking let's drop the lights right at nine o'clock, you guys get on stage, I'll introduce you, and as soon as the lights come up, go for it."

Nods all around. I felt mildly in-charge.

At nine, Josh cut the stage lights and faded out whatever music he'd been playing. He handed me a microphone. The brothers climbed on the stage and plugged in their instruments. Abe had brought an electric guitar this time.

"Ladies, and wannabe ladies," I began, attempting to sound like a WWE announcer. There was a light surge of applause. I thought about freestyling, but I could see that the brothers were ready to rock.

"*These* motherfuckers," I shouted.

Josh hit the lights. Dan strummed something uptempo and began singing, Abe harmonizing immediately. A perfect launch.

They did a full three songs without any shtick or banter. Beautiful pop songs I couldn't identify. Then Dan spoke up, thanking the crowd.

"The next band—they left a list up here. That makes things easier. We don't have to do no thinkin'."

They played a Byrds song—"You Ain't Goin' Nowhere"— that I knew to be the usual opener of the headliner's show. It was a mildly transgressive act. I assumed the high-strung members of the second band might get upset about it, but what of it?

Abe began the next song with an electric guitar riff that most people in the front rows seemed to recognize. After the first chorus, Dan's attention waned. He stopped playing and took a drink of water, looking behind a couple of the other band's amplifiers for a moment, then very impulsively stepped toward Abe, detuned a couple of Abe's guitar strings, and then grabbed Abe's microphone stand. "That's enough of that one," Dan said, moving the stand next to the one he'd been using. "Two microphones. Two too many, if you ask me."

He walked to the center of the stage and began singing "Hummingbird" without a microphone. Abe finished re-tuning his guitar and joined on harmonies. Their guitars were a bit too loud in the PA system for a verse or two, until Josh turned them down. The crowd noise faded, and the brothers made it through most of the song. Abe dropped out after a couple of choruses and reached into his back jeans pocket. Wire cutters. He walked behind Dan and snipped the low E string of Dan's guitar. The loose end of the string hit Dan in the face before he had his eyes open. He said a series of expletives under his breath, looking annoyed. "Dude, we're not even half done up here."

Abe approached the pair of microphones, inspecting each one. He leaned in closer to sniff them, wincing after getting a whiff of Dan's microphone.

"Warm latex," Abe said, moving the mic to the side of the stage furthest from Dan. "Warm, agitated latex with some guilt on the back end."

Dan removed the loose string from his guitar with a small plastic device. Abe started another song that I could identify immediately, having done my research with Oliver's stack of LPs—"He Ain't Heavy (He's My Brother)" by the Hollies. Abe made it through most of the song before Dan's string was replaced and tuned. Dan watched without singing or playing along. He went for a full pitcher of beer sitting at the edge of the stage. He took a two-gulp drink from it and then in an underhand motion, splashed Abe with the rest of it. Abe stopped for only a beat or two and then finished the song.

The individual whose pitcher Dan had just emptied was upset, and started to make a scene, trying to get Dan's attention through some chest-beating and other rap and hip-hop-influenced gesticulations. The individual was clearly of the white "Bro" subclass, with thick, solid black wavy tattoos on each arm displaying his allegiance with Polynesian tribes. He'd spent much time lifting heavy weights in front of mirrors. This was not the typical Lo-Ball patron, but you expected a few anytime the *Westword* recommended a show.

Both brothers were amused by the bro's tantrum. Dan pulled out his wallet and began filing through it. "How 'bout you don't put your beer on our stage, fool," Dan said, tossing a bill of unknown denomination at the bro. "What are you doing here anyway? You look like you oughtta be at a strip joint with one hand down your pants."

One peculiarity about the Lo-Ball is its lack of a security staff. There are bartenders, a soundperson, and a typically waifish doorperson. Altercations were usually moved out onto the sidewalk via a herd of patrons, rather than a bouncer. Members of the crowd began taunting the bro, shouting at him to go home, get out, etcetera. Abe and Dan stood, arms crossed, as the crowd began to chant "go home, go home." The bro turned toward the door, both arms and middle fingers raised.

Life is cruel. The poor bro had done nothing more than place his pitcher of beer at the edge of the stage. There are no rules against this. Everybody does it. Next thing he knows the pitcher is stolen from him, spilled out, he's the target of an insult from the performer, and then a hundred strangers are yelling at him to go home. It would've taken me awhile to recover. I'd probably find a sushi restaurant and dunk my head in their aquarium.

Dan grabbed a microphone stand and got situated. "Poor guy," he said. "I feel bad, really. If anyone here happens to know where he lives, please let me know. I'll do him a singing telegram. Maybe bring him a hairless kitten in a box full of that green plastic Easter hay."

Abe gave Dan the side-eye. "Well. That was a fuckin' weird thing to say. Maybe you'd better start another song before you feel the need to explain yourself."

Dan started singing "The Air That I Breathe." I'd made it to the front row by this point. Abe got my attention and knelt down at the edge of the stage to say something to me.

"Too many people," he said. "No room for wrestling."

It was a problem. The crowd was shoulder-to-shoulder as far back as I could see. There wasn't enough room on stage to do much of anything. I didn't have a solution. "Make it work," I said.

Abe looked amused as he shuffled to the back of the stage. He began rummaging through the canvas bag he'd brought. A familiar item from my youth emerged—a can of Aqua Net. Abe kept his back turned to Dan as he prepped his Zippo lighter and removed the white cap from the hairspray can.

He began spraying Dan with short spurts of flame. Dan attempted to move away, but there wasn't anywhere to go, so he removed his guitar and began swinging and jabbing it through Abe's continued spurts. It sent Abe moving backward a few steps at a time, but the flames continued, some aimed high, some low. Abe eventually ran out of room and began looking for a way off the stage. He ditched the Aqua Net and Zippo atop the PA speakers and made the four-foot drop off the stage and onto the dance floor. The crowd began to clear around him, as though enough people knew what was coming next.

Dan set his guitar down and began descending the stairs. Abe took me aside for a moment and handed me a coaches' whistle. "Blow this after about a minute," he said.

So it began, the brothers facing each other, moving clockwise, then reversing course. The area that had cleared wasn't large enough yet. You could sense it in the brothers' faces and movements. A bulge of cleared space opened suddenly and Dan went for Abe's knees. He got a solid grasp of one of Abe's legs, but Abe managed to sprawl on top of Dan and break the grip. Abe paused a moment, taking in the area around him as though he were considering the safety of the crowd. Dan took advantage of this and went for Abe's legs again. This time, he flipped him over and on his back. Pinned under his brother, Abe looked around with desperation as though he were searching for someone in particular. It was me, I figured. I blew the whistle.

The brothers stood up and moved away from each other, dusting themselves off and adjusting their clothing, their crotches most obviously. It occurred to me that wrestling in jeans might not be something that goes on the top of a resume.

After a moment of breath-catching, Abe got down on his hands and knees. Dan knelt next to him in what I'd later learn is called the "referee's position." Abe gestured for me to blow the whistle. I did, and Abe exploded out of his hands-and-knees position into a crabwalk position, and then was back on his feet. The brothers were once again moving in a circle opposite one another. They looked fatigued, shirts torn, their hairdos going every which way. Abe made a time-out gesture with his hands and said something to Dan. Dan nodded, and Abe made a time-in gesture. Dan then went for Abe's legs and in only a matter of two or three maneuvers, had him on his back. Abe struggled for a few seconds, but it was clear that he was pinned. Dan slapped the floor and released his brother. I blew the whistle, and the crowd cheered. Neither brother stood up quickly, but they eventually were upright, adjusting themselves. I approached Abe.

"Do one more song," I said. "Something real hippy-dippy."

"You've got to be kidding," Abe said.

I requested "Summer Side of Life" by Gordon Lightfoot. They'd played it at their first show. Abe didn't respond but returned to the stage and put his guitar back on. Dan remained on the dance floor, several feet away. He looked over at me confused, sweat-drenched, in some degree of pain. He mouthed the words "what the?"

Abe began the song to great applause. Dan eventually returned to the stage, grabbed his guitar and joined in. His guitar was obviously out of tune. This added a bit of charm to their encore.

"We're the Haugenberrys," Abe said, as the last chord rang out. "Thanks for your patience. We're gonna go jump in the South Platte River. You're all welcome to join. We can fit ten or fifteen in the back of our pickup."

I didn't assume anyone in the crowd took the idea seriously, but it was an endearing way to end the show. The brothers descended the staircase onto the dance floor and approached me. "You're coming with," Abe said, before turning his attention to the rest of the crowd. "You coming? You coming?"

Let's just say that the females seemed more receptive to the idea than the males.

They continued asking people as they made their way to the front door. I followed, after some hesitation, and without checking in with Rikki. He was busy at the merch table. I'd text him when I got the chance.

The brothers had managed to score the other of the two parking spots in front of the Lo-Ball. Dan already had the engine running, lights on, and Slayer playing on the stereo at an insanely reasonable volume. Abe opened the tailgate and shouted for everyone to hop up. I was the first to make the move. "You can ride in front," Abe said. I considered it, but I'd never ridden in the back of a pickup in the middle of Denver, or any city for that matter. I mentioned this, and Abe shrugged it off. "Suit yourself."

Within moments, the bed of the pickup was full, plus a couple dudes stuffed into the front bench seat—a cop magnet if there ever was one. I couldn't be sure that Dan fully appreciated this, so I mentioned it before we departed. "Poorly-lit sidestreets, alleyways, you know the deal," I said.

It was a nerve-racking drive, even though Dan seemed to have everything under control. I felt compelled to get the other twelve folks riding in the back to use their inside voices, but I didn't want to spoil the revelry. It was about a mile of dark side streets and stop signs before we'd have to cross the main roads. We crossed the first without much worry and then Dan turned into an alley behind a 7-Eleven and parked. Abe hopped out and in a word announced the reason for the stop. Beer.

The rest of the way was alleyways and dark streets. Years before, I'd delivered pizzas in the neighborhood, and thought I knew every street, but not so. We parked at the end of a cul-de-sac and hopped out. The peaty aromas of the riverfront and the relative silence of the off-hours warehouse district was spiritually cleansing, as though we'd found a wormhole out of the city.

"This is my favorite spot," Dan announced. "Tree swing, some good deep areas, slabs of concrete for sitting and contemplation." He started across a small patch of weeds toward an opening in a chain link fence. We followed with much hesitation, half-expecting to step on a hypodermic needle, or stub a toe on a human skull. Dan sensed our hesitancy. "Don't worry," he said. "I've got it pretty well cleaned up out here. Aside from the bodies."

"So, there *are* bodies," I said.

"Mostly dead ones," he said, removing his shirt. "But that's not very clear." He began removing his jeans. "Most of the bodies you'll encounter will be dead. That's what I mean to say."

With no hesitation, he performed a cannonball and began swimming toward a rope swing hanging from a cottonwood branch that extended ten or fifteen feet from shore. Abe took a seat on a slab of concrete and began tossing beers around. It was safe to say that no one on premise had anticipated a swim in the river that night. Two decades of parties and gatherings of all varieties in that neighborhood, and I never once swum the South Platte. Seeking out some good ol' fashioned country-style fun in the middle of the city just didn't occur to people.

I sat next to Abe and he handed me a beer. I wasn't disrobing like everyone else. He mentioned this, and I struggled to put forth a simple answer. "Too dark," I said. "I like to be able to see what I'm doing." This was a small sampling of the truth, but it was my somewhat-complicated bra-padding arrangement that was the real deterrent. Neither of the brothers were aware of my surgery, and it seemed an absurd time to raise that topic.

"I'm not really a water person," Abe volunteered. "Since I was about six. Dan and a couple of his buddies threw me into an irrigation canal."

"That's awful."

"And just when I was convinced that I was dead, one of his friends managed to get me to the bank. And Dan stayed dry the whole time! What a prick!"

He made it sound funny in the telling, but it wasn't.

He took a drink of beer. "And then, a couple years later, that same buddy that saved my life accidentally killed himself cleaning a gun. Dan was right there for all of it. Came running home with blood all over him."

Dan was waist deep in the water, handing the rope to someone.

"I'd say he was twenty-five, maybe thirty percent less of a prick after that day," Abe added. "I think he could've done better, personally."

I tried to evacuate certain images from my mind. We seemed to have come to an understanding that the current conversation was at odds with the celebratory nature of the gathering. We were only *maybe* thirty minutes removed from the end of the show. But there we were, sharing a slab of contemplation. I asked him how he thought the show had gone.

"I'm gonna be hurting for a week, probably two."

I'd already been thinking about what to do next—other venues, people to contact—but it seemed a bit pushy and premature to bring this up before the night's bruises even had a chance to appear.

"Do you want a Midol?" I asked.

"Never tried one."

I got excited and began digging in my purse, feeling for the bottle. There were two pills left and I handed them to him. He tossed them in his mouth and washed them back with a swig of Pabst.

"At this point, anything will do," he said.

Dan remained in the river, handing the rope swing to any of the four or five people who were taking turns. I couldn't get the image out of my mind of him running down a country road as a kid, in blood-spattered shock. Had Abe really needed to tell me that story? I assumed it was just one of many gruesome details I'd be subjected to. The arm up the cow's uterus came to mind, which then got the Bee Gees song playing on an imaginary phonograph.

"Come on, AJ," Dan shouted, much louder than was necessary—as though I were making the whole crew late for something. "Your turn."

"Go for it," Abe said. "Or live to regret it."

Without much thought, I undid my bra under my T-shirt,

and jammed the bra and filler into my purse as far as it would go. Shirt still on, skirt on, and Chuck Taylors.

Dan handed me the rope and I swung out without hesitation, and let go.

"Welcome to the club," Dan shouted.

I woke Sunday to the hiss and gurgle of the coffee percolator. I no longer allow myself to lay idle in the morning, letting my thoughts have their way. On the rare occasion that I wake from a vivid and perplexing dream, I may stare at the ceiling and try to recount what happened. But aside from that, things get dark when I'm left undistracted.

I filled a mug of coffee and went out to the patio. Most of my body from the waist up was sore from holding onto the rope swing. This physical cue led me to consider the events of the night before, and all that'd happened in the previous two weeks. An elusive sense of accomplishment remained elusive, but some facts were established that would prove useful in maintaining our momentum.

I'd been able to settle with Josh shortly after 1AM, after we returned from the river outing. It had been one-in, one-out at the door for most of the night, which is to say it had been a sell-out. Josh noted it had probably been three years—pandemic included—since they'd had such a big night. Rikki and I'd left with two envelopes of cash and just a few remaining posters and T-shirts.

I stood at the railing, looking out over the neighborhood. It was shortly after 6AM, and I heard a jackhammer in the distance, in the general direction of the Haugenberry house. I decided to pay the brothers a visit.

Had my personal safety not been an issue, I could've walked the entire way blindfolded with only the sound of the jackhammer beckoning. By the time I reached their block, the noise had been replaced by the back-and-forth shouting of Dan and his next-door neighbor to the north. One needn't mention the topic of their dispute. By the time I reached their gate, Dan and the neighbor had either reached an impasse, or Dan had agreed to stop using obscenely loud power tools until a more-reasonable time of day. My arrival seemed to be just what was needed to send the disheveled neighbor back into his house.

Dan stretched and massaged his right shoulder as I approached. I sat on the top step facing the street. "Ouch is all I can say."

"What a drag it is getting old," Dan sang.

"I have some money for you guys," I said, standing briefly and handing him the envelope of cash. "This is what you made at the door."

Dan sat on the ledge, removed the cash and began counting. I'd already sorted, counted, and flattened the bills myself. "No way," he said. "Did you take your cut?"

"It's all yours."

We hadn't yet discussed what my percentage would be moving forward. Rikki and I would split the T-shirt and poster money for the time being.

"We did twenty-four shirts and nineteen posters," I said. "I'll have to order a new batch."

"Almost five hundred dollars here," Dan said, amused. "For a half hour of jackassery. Who woulda thunk?"

We sat silent awhile, taking in the birdsong and squirrel chatter.

"Look at the size of this thing," he said, standing and lifting his shirt, exposing a bruise on his left-side rib cage, just below the armpit. A ray of sunlight broke through a cloud, fully illuminating the entire porch and the bruise.

I've been accused on countless occasions, usually amid heated arguments with males, of having an *imagination*. I've learned to own this, but it didn't take any longer than the speed of light to recognize the bruise for what it was—an uncanny representation of the bust of the Blessed Virgin Mary. Dan had a large mole in the center of the bruise, so a cyclops Virgin Mary.

"I have to take a picture of this," I said. Dan let his shirt down. I got my phone camera in position to snap a photo and gestured for Dan to lift his shirt. "Have you looked at this in the mirror?"

"No. I've been more focused on the pain."

I took several shots from as many angles, then moved into the shade to look at them. They were clear enough for my purposes. I showed Dan the best of them. "Do you see what I see?" I sang.

"Well, sweet Jesus," he said, laughing. "It's Christmas in July."

He went inside to brew some coffee and check on Abe as I worked up a social media post. The pages I'd made for the brothers had maybe three hundred followers after only a few days, which seemed okay. I posted the clearest, but not necessarily least-awkward of the photos, accompanied by the following message:

Blessed Sunday morning, Haugenberry fans. Let us behold this apparition—the Virgin de Guadalupe arrives in the form of a bruise on Dan's rib cage. Glory be!

Rikki was the first to respond, adding a meme of Dan Aykroyd as Elwood Blues that read WE'RE ON A MISSION FROM GOD. It was the obvious conclusion, and I thought the pre-fab meme to be below Rikki's level of sophistication. However, it did serve to clarify the intended subtext of my original post. I caught myself over-thinking the whole matter, so put down my phone and turned my attention back to the birds and squirrels.

Abe walked out onto the porch, holding a pair of coffee mugs. He handed one to me, and then sat on the ledge, swinging his legs over to face the street. Dan returned seconds later and sat on a folding chair that creaked and buckled enough to cause him to stand back up and go for the other street-facing ledge.

"We need to get you fellas some furniture," I said. The brothers were receptive to the idea. "You've got the truck. I'll bet we can find the basics for close to zero dollars. Probably by the end of the day."

Abe groaned. "I'm not lifting anything today, or tomorrow."

Dan had demonstrated some degree of physical capacity that morning in his use of the jackhammer. I mentioned this, causing Abe to tear into him about breaking up concrete at six o'clock on a Sunday morning. During their back-and-forth, it occurred to me that my dad had half a two-car garage full of aesthetically dated, but pet and smoke-free furniture that needed a new home. I'd call him about it later in the day.

Talk turned briefly to the events of the previous night, the physical consequences in particular, each brother cataloging their various aches and pains. I'd hoped we might, *might*, discuss some plans, and that one of the brothers, not I, would be the one to bring up the subject.

It was not to be. Dan announced his need to get back to

work on the house. Abe had some errands to run. I made my exit, checking my phone as I turned onto the sidewalk. Rikki's earlier post meant that he was at least conscious. Our usual breakfast routine didn't appeal to me, as I felt there were greater things to accomplish that morning. I didn't know yet what those were, but they lurked around every corner on my walk back to my apartment.

It had been almost three weeks since I'd successfully contacted my father, and it seemed a good time to do so. I had something new to brag about, and an offer to help clear some space in his garage. I phoned him only to confirm that he'd be home and to let him know I'd be dropping by later in the morning.

A visit to my father's place requires a multi-tier exit strategy, so I called Rikki to see if he'd make the drive with me. The asking was a mere formality, as he found my father highly entertaining, and it'd been several months since they'd had a chance to catch up. Within an hour we were on the highway, takeout bagel sandwiches and coffees in hand.

Traffic was perfect, so I maintained a solid ten-over-the-limit clip. Rikki cycled through the FM radio stations, then the AM, stopping only on the church-oriented programming, and only momentarily.

"What exactly are you looking for?" I asked.

"Joel Osteen," he said. "I need to get in the right head space."

"Headspace for what?"

"Talking to your dad."

I'd never been one for televangelism, or any evangelism, but I suspected something perverse and theatrical was afoot, so decided to go with it. I got Rikki set up on my phone's streaming app and for the remainder of the forty-minute drive we listened to Mr. Osteen.

We let ourselves in through the side door that opens to the

kitchen. Dad sat in the living room, in his deluxe therapeutic recliner—a chair that cost roughly the same as my car. He was dressed for the occasion—a Rocky Flats T-shirt from the eighties and tighty whities. Rikki shut the door behind us, and the noise of it alerted Dad to our presence. He turned away from the documentary he'd been watching.

"I brought Rikki," I said. "And a breakfast sandwich."

And, without further ado, Mr. Roger T. Washburn.

"Bosons, neutrinos, dark matter—*who cares,*" he began, the recliner beginning its slow transition to a more-upright position. "Eggheads of the first order. It's like what your grandpa used to say about welfare—sometimes you just have to pay people to stay out of the way. Some bucktooth, cross-eyed sonofabitch points at a convergence of squiggles on a computer monitor—*we're optimistic that we'll be able to detect such-n-such by 2030,* he says. Then what? What's the goal? Are we still trying to prove the existence of God? Give me a break. Good to see you, Rikki."

The recliner was now in full upright position.

"Instead of investing in any of the near-infinite other things that would help make life better for most of humanity, let's funnel multiple billions of dollars into building particle accelerators for a cadre of dweebs to fuss over."

He was now standing and facing us, cane in hand, ready to tackle the short walk to the kitchen table where I had his sandwich prepared.

"I know these people," he continued. "I went to school with, worked with, fished with thousands of these nerds. They have no other place in society. Put them in an underground bunker. Let them interpret—and I use that term very loosely—their blips and squiggles."

He inspected his sandwich. "Oooh, bacon," he said. "What do you think, Rikki? You're an educated, thoughtful man. Say in 2030 dark matter is detected—you've been at the edge of your seat for years now, waiting for this very moment, right? Will that relieve you of even one of life's burdens?"

"Can I take those green metal chairs that are in the garage?" I asked.

"Have at 'em," he said.

Rikki cleared his throat. "Today is the day the Lord has designed for you," he began, a quote lifted verbatim from Osteen. I was only a few steps from the door to the garage, and was able to hold my laughter. I kept the door open so I could hear what would unfold as I looked for the chairs.

I don't know a world without my father's rants. They've always been there, not having become more or less vitriolic with age, though the breadth of subject matter had narrowed somewhat. I remember the quoting of Homer, Virgil, Aristotle and other antiquarian literary figures being more prominent in my high school days when boys would pick me up for dates.

The chairs were hidden under a moving blanket. I removed the blanket and began separating them. Behind them, on the floor, was a dust-covered hardback copy of Bill O'Reilly's *Culture Warrior*. I was awash with memories and sadness. The house had been cleared of all right-wing conservative media after my mother's passing. My father and I spent a good couple hours on the task the day after her funeral, aided by liberal amounts of wine and bourbon. It proved to be very therapeutic for both of us.

I raised the garage door and began loading the chairs into the back of my car. There was still room for more, so I looked through the rest of the garage for other things Abe and Dan could use. I found my old drafting table for Dan, and a small coffee table that just barely fit.

Dad and Rikki were now deep in Osteenian waters, Dad's face red with amusement. I'd carried the O'Reilly book with me into the kitchen and began rinsing the dust off under the faucet—the main faucet at first, then with the sprayer. Dad noticed what I was doing and cut Rikki off.

"What in the world?"

"We missed one," I said. "Looks like Mom was hiding her bottles." I tossed the book onto the table. "Lord have mercy on the tree that gave its life in the making of that book."

"Lord have mercy," Rikki said.

"Christ have mercy," Dad added. "Now go toss that in the chiminea."

It seemed as good a time as any to tell Dad about the Haugenberrys. I described them and their act, just to get the information out there. My enthusiasm for the project remained fervent, but I felt the need to downplay it. In doing so, I hoped to circumnavigate his propensity for unsolicited warnings and emotional prophylactics. My dad had seen me weather several disappointments, and I knew they'd affected him deeply.

"Are these fellas reliable?" he asked.

"Yes."

"Married, divorced, kids, no kids. What."

"Not married. Not divorced—no kids that I'm aware of."

"Mid-forties?"

"Yes—a year or two apart."

Having Rikki there to nod in agreement was comforting.

"Handsome guys?" Dad asked.

"Yes," I said. "Above average, I'd say. Just awkward, out of place."

Dad turned to Rikki. "Would you say they are handsome men?"

Rikki pushed himself back in his chair, looking as though he'd really been put on the spot. "I'd say yes—*but*," he extended his index finger upward. "*But*, only in the way a judge at a county fair looks at a sheep or rooster."

Dad and I stared at him.

"They seem to me to be a different species," Rikki continued. "I don't feel compelled to decide whether or not I'm phys-ically attracted to them." He pointed toward the window. "For instance, look at that magpie dicking around by your trash cans. We can all probably agree that it's an attractive, hand-some bird. Right?"

Dad and I nodded.

"I can only speak for myself here, of course," he contin-ued. "But I don't feel any need to go beyond that. I don't feel the need to ask myself whether or not I'd like to *get it on* with the bird."

Dad and I laughed. Rikki looked back and forth at us with flat affect.

"What I will say is that they are not *unattractive.* Any further inquiry seems to me to be a flirtation with the event horizon of zoophilia."

Dad dabbed the corners of his mouth with a napkin. "Well, let's see. A couple of handsome country boys their age, neither one married, neither one divorced—highly improbable."

Rikki chimed in. "The laws of probability don't really apply to these guys."

Dad began massaging the bridge of his nose, as he does when confronted with a difficult proposition. Rikki mentioned the VHS tape and the previous night's footage. "Watching that will eliminate as many questions as it raises. I'll send you a link."

I left the two of them to converse as I did my routine house inspection. Despite his many ailments, Dad had been able to maintain a high level of self-sufficiency. Laundry and dishes got done, but not necessarily put away. I'd need to send over a house cleaner soon. Dust accumulation was notable on any surfaces that he didn't regularly use. All the appliances seemed to be in working order. No sign of leaks or other damage. I gave him a B+ overall.

Small talk had taken hold when I returned to the kitchen. Rikki looked a bit fatigued, and I'd accomplished what I'd set out to accomplish. Dad sensed that we were preparing to leave and looked a bit sad about it.

"Rikki has to work tonight," I lied.

Dad suggested that I bring the Haugenberrys over for a visit some not-too-distant weekend, and I promised to look into it.

The Osteen program blasted from the car stereo suddenly as we turned onto the highway. I turned it down, but not off. "Were we really listening that loud?" I said. "What a couple of nerds."

Rikki reached into his leather man-purse and removed the envelope of merch money.

"Some of your lawyer buddies overpaid," he said. "There's an extra forty or fifty in here."

I'd forgotten all about the lawyers until that moment, and I asked myself how long it would be before I made the call to Hirsh Esq. Where did I put that business card? Was it floating down the South Platte, halfway to Nebraska by now?

"Eight hundred and ten dollars," Rikki said. He asked what expenses were, and I gave him rounded numbers for both the posters and shirts that he wrote on the envelope. In a matter of seconds, he determined that we'd made three hundred and fifty dollars, and without much ado we decided to split it fifty-fifty.

We discussed the as-yet-unwatched Lo-Ball video footage and what to do with it. A twenty-to-thirty-second highlight reel focused on the slapstick gags and wrestling, and an edit of the entire show was enough for the time being. If we could somehow include the movement of river-goers toward the front door, that would be a plus.

The Haugenberrys weren't home. I'd call them later, or maybe they'd call me. Maybe several days would pass. We couldn't do much else until we had the promo video. I hoped

Rikki would provide a self-imposed deadline for getting the edits done, but this wasn't to be. As I let him off at his house, I mentioned my plans to reach out to a few other venues in the coming days. I hoped this might wring a promise out of Rikki.

No.

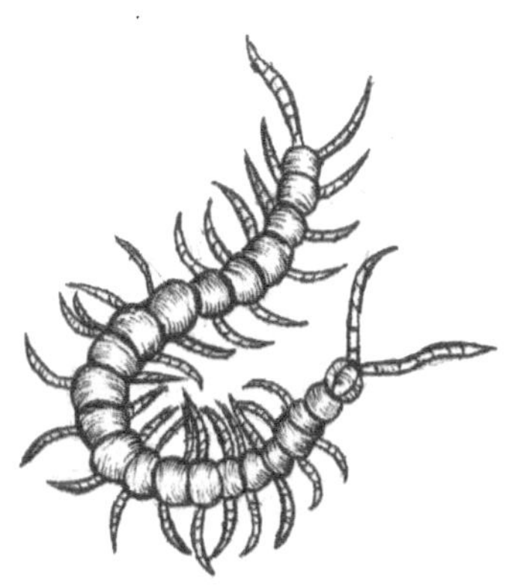

I'M NOT MUCH of a relaxer. When anyone suggests I relax, a newsreel of canonical Vietnam war footage plays in my head: the burned little girl running down the middle of the road, the guy in the street getting shot in the temple. "Take time for yourself" they say. "Just sit with yourself" they say.

Um, no.

What better time than a breezy, not-too-hot Sunday afternoon to sit on the patio and relax, maybe a hit of grass, perhaps indulge in a little self-reflection.

Nah. I was out of pot, and my period was due any minute now. A visit to the dispensary was imminent. The nearest shop stands in the direct path of Panopticon Records, and I had some questions for Oliver, so away I went.

I entered the record store just before closing time, packing a hundred bucks worth of buds and gummies—a year supply at my current dosage rate. Oliver stood at the cash register, obviously frustrated with it. I offered to assist. He described the problem, the solution, and that the solution was "within the domain of a two-armed individual."

The drawer was stuck. As instructed, I pushed the right side in with my thumb while simultaneously slapping the left side of the register. After three attempts, the drawer slid open, and then onto the floor like a projectile, sending bills, coins, keys, and credit card receipts every which way. We stood silent, waiting for the final rolling coin to topple.

"Well, shit," I said.

"That's another unique feature of this particular machine," Oliver said, amused. "Sort of an over-active prostate situation."

He walked to the front door, turned the OPEN sign around, and pulled down the blind. "To hell with it. Anyone wanting to have a staring contest with Judy Collins at the bargain bins is out of luck."

I sat on the floor with the drawer in my lap, sorting the bills and receipts. Oliver opened a small refrigerator, pulled out a couple of cans, and offered one to me. Canned wine, pinot grigio. I thanked him.

"I'd say your boys have pretty much conquered that room," he said about the previous night's show. He mentioned that most of the crowd had emptied out after the Haugenberry's set, something I would've noticed had I not been whisked away to the South Platte. "What's next?"

"I'm glad you asked," I said. "I was hoping you might have some ideas."

He sat on a swivel chair and took a sip. "I've been thinking about it. Quite a bit, actually. Sustainability issues come to mind."

I thought I probably knew what he meant, but it was vague, so I asked for more.

"I'd plan on the wrestling portion phasing itself out, unfortunately."

I'd repressed that thought a number of times already.

"Wrestling on concrete floors, wrestling *at all* at their age—not something you can do night after night. Once or twice a month, *maybe*."

The thought of eventually booking a short tour had crossed

my mind. Expecting the brothers to do their full act on consecutive nights was masochistic and preposterous.

"What are their ambitions? How much do they want to scale things up?"

"I wish I knew," I said. "I've got all sorts of plans, but I don't want to be too pushy. I can get pushy. That'll ruin a good thing."

"But you have to be, to some degree. You've got to keep momentum going. Don't snooze and lose."

I showed him a photo of Dan's bruise. He suggested using it for a poster.

"I'll let that bruise heal before I go at them with any more plans."

He picked up a few coins that had strayed farthest from the central catastrophe. "You've probably realized this," he said. "Only about five, maybe ten percent of ideas, plans and whatnot actually happen—I'm talking about the independent arts and music world here."

"Oooh, Oliver. That might be a bit optimistic."

"Okay. Four percent, let's say."

"I'll go with that."

"Take a shotgun approach to booking, media queries, everything. Don't mention any of it to the guys until something comes through."

That seemed reasonable, and considerably less work than getting approval from the brothers on every detail, which had been my approach up to that point.

"The hipsters already know what you're doing," he continued. "I'd say go after the jam band crowd next. You can't conquer this city without them."

This gave me a slight shiver. "The hippies. *Really?*"

"They aren't *all* crusties. You can't tell by looking at most of them. Remember, I get to see exactly who's buying what."

The cash and receipts were back in the drawer. I started

sorting the coins. I asked Oliver if he thought we needed to do an album, as it seemed to be on the immediate to-do list.

"They'll need some original material first," he said, setting a handful of coins on the counter.

"That may be a problem."

"They don't write songs?"

"There's been some loose mention of some 'ideas'."

"Hmm."

"Hmm."

Oliver began stacking coins according to denomination. "What about you? You write comedy. You could surely write a song."

"I know a couple chords on guitar, but that's it. I *knew* a couple chords. I don't even own a guitar."

"Take mine," he said. "Study up. I've got some books around here somewhere."

This seemed completely absurd—charging me with writing original songs for a pair of singing male giants. He brought a guitar case and an instructional book out of a back room. "Take these."

"Don't get your hopes up," I said, picking a nickel off the floor.

"Don't think too hard about it. You might be surprised what comes..." A thought of some sort interrupted him. "I know a guy that'd be perfect for this sort of thing. *If* I can get in touch with him."

He asked if I'd read Joseph Conrad's *Heart of Darkness*. Yes, I had, as an undergraduate.

"He's sort of like Colonel Kurtz," Oliver said. "Brilliant, eccentric, lives in the middle of nowhere. Who knows what he's got the locals doing. He likes meat."

That final odd detail needed clarification. I reminded him of my years at a mostly-gay bar.

"Pork, beef, chicken," he said. "A post-reformed Jew, you might say."

The cash drawer was back in order. Oliver had me place it in a safe in the back room. A new cash register was his first thing to do the next morning. He turned off the eyeball and the lights and we moved toward the front door.

"I think you're all set, AJ. Aim at the jam band scene next, try writing a song or two. Things will fall into place."

"You make it sound so easy."

"Things unfold that way if you let them," he said, locking the door behind us. "Remember this: you're driving the chariot. The horses don't know the destination, but they'll get you there. Zeus permitting."

At the sidewalk, we parted ways, his house being in the opposite direction of mine. He made it a dozen or so steps then turned back.

"Oh, and watch out for a guy named Gil Barbieri. Jam band guy. Owns the Purgatory Ballroom."

The name sounded familiar. I'd probably heard it at a party, but I really had no idea. I asked why I should avoid the guy.

"Remember what I told you about mob hierarchies," Ollie said. "I can't say for sure, but the dude never seems to have a problem fundraising, and he's originally from Jersey."

Ollie started off again. I stood in front of the store for a moment, guitar case in one hand, and a half-full can of wine in the other. I hesitated to move, something to do with my raising. Do I walk a busy street carrying an open container of alcohol in broad daylight? I asked myself.

Yes, myself said.

And then, in the elevator to my apartment, *splgooosh*—my period dropped. I went straight for the gummies, and bit off half of one as the elevator door opened. One of my neighbors was waiting outside the door, prepared to attend a yoga session.

She'd obviously been crying in the previous five to ten minutes. I offered her the other half of the gummy and she accepted with zero hesitation.

I figured I had a while before the gummy kicked in. Oliver's advice was still fresh on my mind, and it seemed like a good time to revise my priority list before things got mildly freaky.

A simple list, really: edit and post video, contact Josh and steal any venue and/or press contacts he had, e-mail said contacts, wait, research jam band scene.

Jam bands. What did I know about jam bands. I had a clunky list of preconceptions, stereotypes, and probable misconceptions, so that was a start. I'd have to ask Josh about this, maybe check back in with Oliver as well. Would we have to modify the act to accommodate the jam band crowd? I didn't even want to think about it, so headed to the bathroom for a shower.

I caught myself looking at the mirror longer than usual, nude, examining my breastless, almost boyish physique. The scars were still noticeable from most angles, but their pigment had finally blended. I was told at my last doctor's appointment a couple months previous that I *could start thinking about implant options soon.*

Start thinking? That's a male doctor for you.

My final thought before stepping into the tub: there has to be—the world being as it is—a group of internet pervs who have a thing for mastectomy patients. I wouldn't be surprised to discover there are a few lurking on the outskirts of my social circles.

The THC made for a relaxing shower, and many unexpected turns of thought. The guitar didn't seem so intimidating, and so, after drying off and wrapping myself in my favorite purple towel, I sat on the couch and made my first attempts at remembering the little I'd learned years before.

There were four basic chords tucked away in my brain that made a reappearance without having to consult the book—the open *G, C, D*, and *E*.

Another weedy thought—something from undergrad philosophy class about a centipede who's asked *how do you coordinate all those legs? How do you make them all work so seamlessly?* Now that it's being made to think about what it's doing instead of just doing it, the centipede suddenly can't move.

I was clearly not a gifted coordinator in terms of playing the guitar, but the strange attention I found myself giving to every detail, move, and decision I made began to spring forth short little phrases, like a children's song:

> *Here are the frets and here are my fingers*
> *Six strings, a pick, and self-doubt that lingers*
> *Why must this all be so difficult for me?*
> *Leave all this shit for the Haugenberrys*

THERE WERE zero names on the sign-up sheet when I arrived at Knights Errant. This wasn't unheard of, just unusual. A combination of cramps, fatigue, and apathy kept me from obsessing about the probable causes. Most-likely a big-name touring comic was performing elsewhere in town.

Fifteen minutes before start time and there were no performers lined up, so I called it off.

On my way home, I drove past the office of Donald R. Hirsh Esq. and saw that most of the lights were on. It was just after eight o'clock and there was a parking space available, so I stopped.

The entrance was locked, so I rang the doorbell-cam, prepared to ask if it was an appropriate time to do so. He answered, and invited me in, but didn't immediately offer me a seat, though there were several chairs and a pair of couches right there. This suited me fine, suggesting that the message he had for me wasn't too serious or complicated.

"What do you know about estate sales, Ms. Washburn?" he asked, walking to his receptionist's desk and opening a drawer. I always feel compelled to elevate my diction in the presence of gray-haired attorneys.

"I frequent them," I said, waiting for him to focus his question. I found the open-endedness to be inadequate.

He lifted a large, densely-packed manila envelope from the drawer and set it atop the desk. "Internet auctions? What do you know about those?"

"A fair amount," I said, seating myself on a couch.

"Marc wanted to give you the option—the opportunity, really—to be in charge of selling his stuff. I'm assuming you've been inside his home?"

"Several times."

"So, you have an idea of what you'd be getting into."

I had yet to agree to anything, but the momentum seemed to be in the direction of me having already agreed to something. He handed me the envelope. It was sealed by that little bendy metal clip that such envelopes have. By feel and weight, I could tell it contained about the equivalent of a typical three-subject spiral notebook, and what sounded like a set of keys.

"I haven't been in *every* room, but..."

"If you've seen one room, you've seen them all," he laughed. "More a museum than a livable space, in my opinion. There's an attic as well, packed to the gills."

He began listing the contents of the envelope as I opened it. "Spreadsheets of his autograph collection, music collection, library, furniture, odds-and-ends."

There was a sealed letter-sized envelope addressed to me.

"The first question is: are you interested, and if so, do you have time?"

"Interested, possibly. Time? Not so much."

He looked at his watch and mentioned having to leave for a meeting. I sealed the envelope and stood.

"I have to go," he said. "Take a few days to review the materials and let me know what you decide."

I walked out to the small porch. He locked the door with a remote control. "There's a realtor involved, and she wants this all done yesterday, but we'll take our time."

He grumbled something about vultures as he got into his car.

The questions proliferated as I raced to my apartment, anxious to read the letter. *Why me?* was the obvious one, followed by *why not an estate sale company or auction house?* The whole endeavor presented itself as a full-time job for two people, at least, if it was to be done in a reasonable amount of time. I already had a full-time job, and Marc had been well aware of this.

As I waited for the parking garage gate to open, I received a text from Josh. It read simply: *Denver Post wants to do write-up. Email forwarded.*

The forwarded e-mail was from Kyle Nosodosteros, one of the *Denver Post*'s entertainment editors, addressed to the Lo-Ball's generic info@e-mail address:

I witnessed the majesty of the Haugenberry Brothers this past Saturday and would like to do a feature article for the Post in the near future. Can you get me in touch with them?

A feature article is a good thing, but it doesn't reap maximum return unless there's a show date attached to it. I had yet to send any queries to the larger venues or jam bands. The fact that Nosodosteros wanted to do a write-up would add a good deal of weight to these queries when I did send them, so my lack of initiative wasn't entirely a bad thing. This is how I justify my occasional bouts of dragassery.

The nice thing to do—the most appreciative-of-Josh thing to do—would be booking a headliner slot at the Lo-Ball. However, we'd already filled that room without the help of a *Denver Post* feature. With only two gigs, we'd already outgrown the dive-bar scene. Time to matriculate into the old theaters and ballrooms, but how to do this? I didn't have any promo video to send, sound files, or anything of the sort. It was just going to have to wait.

I moved my crampy self to the couch and turned my attention to Marc's affairs. The sealed letter-sized envelope had my handwritten name on it only. For some reason, I pinched and shook the thing. Something life-changing was contained within, and the moment begged for some type of ritual, a candle-lighting or monastic chant perhaps.

Marc was a jazz fan, so I fired up my streaming music service and did a search for someone whom I suspect many novices do a search for: Miles Davis. I tapped on the first thumbnail album art that looked weirder than the others. *Bitches Brew.*

I lit a scentless candle with a paper match. A pitiful attempt at ritual, but that's all I had. I opened the envelope.

AJ,

Greetings from the afterlife! I struggle to describe how it is here using the five senses. It's more of a concept than a sensory experience. Similar to what St. Augustine thought it would be: a climax that won't stop, pure energy that seems to be moving in a forward direction.

I'm adjusting to this relentless, heightened state of affairs.

I want to thank you for hosting my wake. I was able to attend in spirit. Hank Ajax had a difficult time not dominating the whole affair. That old slut.

Anyhow, many laughs were had, and great memories shared.

I made it to 65. All but a handful of my best friends and lovers did not. I wish they could've been in attendance.

You made that bar a safe place. Charlie never gave a damn. He'll never know what he's doing.

We have joked on many occasions about you being my adopted daughter. For whatever it's worth, this was a notion that eventually seeped into my sense of being. I have no heirs, or relatives close enough to matter. Even if I did, chances are they would look at this undertaking as an inconvenience and burden, rather than an opportunity.

This seems like something you're cut out for, and I don't wish to see thirty-to-forty percent of the proceeds go to the coffers of strangers.

You've been waiting for a chance to re-evaluate your life. Here it is. What I'm really offering you is time. I estimate it will take six months to properly liquidate my collections and ephemera—give or take a month or two. There will be work involved, of course, and you will be compensated (see attached documents). I've prepared several lists of contacts and resources to help you get started.

You are also welcome to stay at the house at any time during the process (keys and security codes enclosed).

You'll find more messages from the afterlife as you comb through the house. They're hidden in record sleeves, behind picture frames, under cushions. These will be an aid in helping you determine value, with an occasional historical note or anecdote related to the associated item or items.

You know me well, and vice-versa, so you won't be surprised to learn I've already convinced myself that you will agree to do this. Either way, let Don know when you've made your decision and he'll get you going.

Posthumously,

Marc

Dammit, Marc.

Somewhere between laughter and tears, I looked at the ceiling. That's where dead people hang out, among the dust atop ceiling fan blades in rental apartments. I couldn't think of any reason *not* to take the offer. I'd be uninsured for some amount of time, probably. I found myself trying to prevent myself from thinking of reasons not to go for it.

I read through the attached documents. They laid out where the proceeds were to be allocated, the vast majority split among various not-for-profits. The local jazz station was to receive the largest percentage, followed by a variety of LGBTQ+ organizations. My cut was to be twenty percent of the final tally, not including the house and property.

I had no idea the value of autographs, but ten percent of Abe Lincoln's, FDR's, MLK Jr.'s, and thousands of others probably wasn't too modest a sum. Oliver could help me with the vinyl records and novels. I knew a little about Mid-Century Modern furniture.

The gist of the flow chart was this: start with the rare expensive stuff via online auction, then sale-by-appointment of the high-end furniture and larger items, eventually wrapping up the whole affair with a public sale to get rid of the leftover, less-collectible fare—dishes, clothing, appliances, decor and whatnot. It would be a lot of screen time, picture-taking, phone calls, and research, but nothing I couldn't handle.

I'd call Hirsh first thing in the morning. I fell asleep on the couch skimming through the spreadsheet of autographs: Oppenheimer, Stravinsky, Henry VIII. People like that.

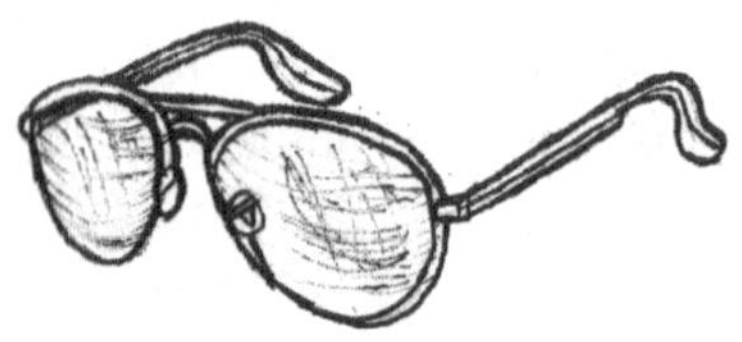

Next morning, I called the boss at eight o'clock sharp to report Covid-like symptoms. I felt fine, of course, ecstatic actually. Current company policy would keep me out of the office for a minimum of five calendar days.

I'd need to submit Covid test results to HR in order to get paid for my sick days. The nearest drive-thru test site was a half mile away, so I rode my bike, using the time to think about the content of my two-week notice. I'd submit it the following Monday, I decided, and the only information I would divulge is my end date and that I had another opportunity to pursue. Why say more?

There were no cars ahead of me when I got to the site. I handed my information to the technician. He seemed highly amused by my presence.

"You know this is a Covid test site, right?"

It was an odd question, as there was clear signage in every direction.

"You ain't got no mask, you're on a bike. Who rides a bike to a Covid drive-thru?" he laughed, before calling out to the other technician. "Seriously, you ever seen anybody come through here on a bike?"

The other tech shook her head. "Hell no."

The tech did a couple rotations of the swab in each of my nostrils. "You even got any symptoms?"

"No, not really. Not at all, actually."

"What you doin' here then?"

I had to make something up. "Pre-employment screening."

"Right, right," he said, waving me on.

I pedaled back to my apartment, stopping only to grab the manila envelope of documents and a backpack to carry it in. I was ready to commit to Marc's offer, so why not pay a visit to Hirsh and get the ball rolling.

After the hazardous ride across the south end of downtown, I learned Hirsh was out of the office. I introduced myself to his secretary/receptionist/assistant-lady, assuming I might be a minor fixture around there in the months to come. We made some small talk, and she really didn't have much to say, or any idea when Hirsh might return. Awkward silence ensued, and the only thing to do was leave.

Another five-block ride north and east put me at Marc's house. A teenage boy was mowing Marc's lawn. I carried my bike up the steps to the front porch and caught my breath. The house faces the southern border of City Park, with a mostly unobstructed view of the lake and pavilion. I sat on an uncomfortable cast-iron bench and took in the sights; joggers, bicyclists, dog-walkers, Canada geese, paddle-boaters on the lake.

I entered the house and disarmed the security system without incident, and then went straight for the kitchen and set my bag on the island. I faced my first great task of this endeavor —Marc's coffee-making systems. He had both a cappuccino/espresso machine and a rather complicated-looking bean grinder/coffee maker combo. Fortunately, the user manuals were in the pantry, next to what I estimated to be a two-week supply of various whole-bean coffees. Within a couple minutes, the percolator was running, and I was ready to get my hands dirty.

But where to start? I reviewed the flow chart and other documents looking for a definitive answer. There wasn't one so I decided to start with the autographs. Most were in file cabinets in the den.

The den, as with almost every other room in the house, was new to me. A set of five matching four-drawer wood file cabinets lined the south wall. I opened a random drawer in the "M" section and flipped through the hanging folders. I stopped at *Mondale, Walter*. It contained a letter from Mr. Mondale to a senator whose name wasn't familiar to me enclosed in a clear, rigid mylar sleeve. I looked through a few more folders, each one including at least an autographed document and a mylar sleeve, with some accompanied by a Certificate of Authenticity or other supporting documents.

The coffee maker beeped, so I closed the drawer and returned to the kitchen, bringing with me another manila envelope that'd been placed atop one of the file cabinets, containing a jump drive and some lists of names and phone numbers, websites, forums, and other online resources. The only pointed instruction was to contact a guy named Walt Flickinger first thing, and he would help get me started. I didn't have my laptop, so the jump drive would have to wait.

It probably all needed to wait until I talked with Hirsh and signed whatever contracts or other documents needed signed. I took a quick look around the rest of the house, basement, second floor, and a quick peek into the attic. While it was true that Marc's list of possessions exceeded those of any reasonable person, none of it appeared to be junk. I could possibly get by without the roll-away dumpster common to most estate sales. After a quick glance at the back yard, I realized there wasn't a good place to put one if I did need one.

The paralyzed, overly self-aware centipede started whispering to me. I sat at the island, at a loss of what to do. I'd made a full pot of coffee, anticipating a few hours of progress.

Progress would have to wait. I locked the house and got on my bike headed for my apartment.

I wouldn't hear from Hirsh until late that afternoon. I called both my father and Rikki with the news of my career change. Dad sounded mildly excited. Rikki asked if Marc had any random audio-visual accessories, more specifically some type of adapter that he needed.

"I call to inform you of a huge transformation in my life, and you ask about an adapter," I said. He then went on to describe the dimensions of the adapter, and the ways in which I could confuse it with another, similar adapter.

"I give up," I said.

"You're wondering about the Haugenberry footage."

This was true, and if not my second reason for calling him, then tied for first.

"I do need something, and quickly," I said, before listing the venues I hoped to contact, and the *Denver Post* write-up. I asked if he could have anything ready by the end of the week. He hesitated, and it almost seemed as though he'd put his phone down to attend to an unrelated matter.

"End of the weekend. Sunday night at the latest," he said. And, before we hung up. "Let me know if you run across one of those adapters."

Hirsh called just before five o'clock as I prepared to open a bottle of wine and begin drafting some e-mail queries. He asked if I could make it over to his office before six. It was rush hour, but I'd make it in time.

And I did, with twenty minutes to spare. I followed him into his office and had a seat in front of his queen-sized antique desk. He handed me a stack of five manila envelopes, and then laid out a spread of other documents. I set the stack on an adjacent table and picked up the first of the documents: a list of Wells Fargo, PayPal, eBay, and other accounts and their associated usernames and passwords, including a description of what each account was to be used for.

He asked about my current monthly income, and I wrote it down in a blank space on one of the documents. I'd be paid on a weekly basis via direct deposit to my existing bank account. Any expenses related to the sale—office supplies, trash services, advertising, signage—was to be paid from such and such account. The details and instructions went on and on, stretching the limits of my attention span. Only three signatures were required of me, and I signed without hesitation, trusting Hirsh's earlier description of the proceedings as "just the usual routine." He gathered the loose documents and stuffed them into yet another manila envelope and put it in a file cabinet at the far end of the room.

"We're all set," he said, his mood noticeably elevated. He handed me another business card with a handwritten phone number on the back side. "This is my personal phone. Feel free to call with any pressing questions. Text messages preferred."

I drove away from Hirsh's office in a celebratory mood, debating between my porch and the Lo-Ball as a location for some modest revelry. Neither was to be. I passed the Haugenberry house, where Abe was sitting on the porch. I honked the car horn for a split second as I parked. The chairs and tables were still in the back of my car. Abe approached as I lifted the hatchback.

"I've got some furniture," I said, lifting the coffee table onto the asphalt. "Some chairs for the porch, a drawing table for Dan."

Abe thanked me and asked where it all came from. I told him. "Good quality stuff. Dated perhaps."

We moved the four pieces up to the porch. Abe inspected the design and construction of one of the chairs before sitting on it, adjusting his weight this way and that, eventually giving it his verbal stamp of approval. "You never know with a chair."

I asked how he was feeling, and he looked at me with a raised brow. "I feel okay. Do I not seem well?"

"Fully recovered from the weekend?"

"Oh yeah," he said, sitting back in the chair. "Dan got the worst of it. I'm back to ninety-five percent, which is my upper limit anyway."

"You're on a sliding scale."

"Aren't you?" he asked.

I pondered it for a moment, before briefly describing my new employment arrangement. "I feel like I'm at ninety-nine percent for once. It'll be fleeting. That much I know."

"That last one percent is for assholes. The kind of people who are always telling other people to smile."

"Live, laugh, love."

"Yes. You know the type."

Dan made his appearance, again with the summer sausage and a pocketknife. I asked about his bruise, and he lifted his shirt. The discoloration had spread and faded into a yellowish green color.

"Looks like one of your dudes puked on you while you slept," Abe said.

"One of my *dudes?*"

"Yes, one of your dudes."

Dan looked at me, puzzled, before turning his attention to the new furniture. I pointed to the still-collapsed drafting table. "That's for you," I said, mentioning I'd gotten it as a Christmas gift as a teenager. "I never flourished as a visual artist."

Dan brought the table inside the house and began assembling it. "I've never actually owned one of these," he said, clearly excited.

I hadn't yet informed them about the pending *Denver Post* article, or even suggested any future ambitions. The brothers seemed physically and mentally fit for it, so I told Abe about the forwarded e-mail from Kyle Nosodosteros. He seemed slightly less excited about it than any other local musician would be upon receiving such news.

"They don't typically pay attention to local acts," I said. "Maybe a handful of articles a year."

"Hmm. When do they want to do this?"

"Not sure. I'm hoping to book another gig beforehand."

He seemed a bit put-off by the suggestion, so I attempted to sweeten the pot with some vague promises of better pay and bigger stages. I had nothing to support any of it, just the momentum of odds that had been working overwhelmingly in our favor. He shouted for Dan to come out to the porch.

"Some guy from the *Post* wants to interview us," Abe said. Dan stopped in the doorjamb holding a rag and a squirt bottle, looking impatient.

"We need to do another show," Abe said. "Are you up for it?" Abe asked.

"When?"

"When what?" Abe said, annoyed.

"When's the show?"

"It's not booked yet."

Dan thought a second. "I can't commit, sorry."

"No one's asking you to commit, just are you up for it?"

"Sure," Dan said, turning and walking back toward his new table. "No more Lo-Ball. Can't do a damn thing in there."

Oliver's advice about not sharing information too early rose to the top of my mind. I hadn't extracted a hard "yes" out of the brothers about either the article or a future gig, but I wasn't really in need of one. Not until I had an offer from a venue.

Our first offer arrived just after noon the next day, via e-mail, from a talent buyer for Purgatory Ballroom, offering August thirteenth, opening for a national act. The e-mail was signed "Che" with no other title, contact information, or links of any sort appended. I perused the Purgatory website and calendar, which led me to the website of who I assumed was the act referred to in the e-mail—a "jamgrass" band with a Sony contract and a calendar of gigs that stretched into next spring.

This was promising, but I'd need to do more detective work before replying. I texted Josh: *Do you know Che from Purgatory Ballroom?*

I'd spent the better part of that morning studying the opening chapters of the *Sanders Price Guide to Autographs 5th Edition*, familiarizing myself with the jargon and the finer points. The edition was over two decades old, so the values weren't current, but the concepts, terminology, and anecdotes were probably still relevant. Walt Flickinger, Marc's autograph expert buddy, had agreed via phone to come over Saturday morning for a meeting. I mentioned that none of the local bookstores had a more-current edition of the guide in stock. He told me not to bother with the price guides.

Josh called as I was sitting at the kitchen island lunching on a peanut butter-smeared rice cake.

"I don't know a 'Che', but I do know a 'Gil'," he began. "Entirely possible that 'Che' is 'Gil'. He's got a hundred nicknames."

I told him about the query e-mail, and that the show looked legitimate. I also mentioned Oliver's warning about dealing with Gil. "A Harvey Weinstein wanna-be, from what I've heard."

We briefly discussed how "Che" might've acquired my contact info, or how he knew I was associated with the Haugenberrys but came up with nothing definitive.

"Maybe I should pay this dude a visit."

Josh laughed before recommending I bring a recording device and bear spray. We hung up, and I went directly to the query e-mail and clicked **REPLY**.

Good afternoon Che,

Thank you for the offer. We are potentially interested. Will you be in the office this afternoon?

And, before I had a chance to do a search on Mr. Barbieri, I received a reply:

Gil will be at Purgatory from 3-4pm. There's a doorbell hidden under the box office window ledge. Ring that and someone will let you in.

The microwave clock read twelve-thirty, which meant I had a couple hours to prepare. I made a quick assessment of my current ensemble: T-shirt, shorts, no bra or padding, flip-flops. I had hat-hair.

It wasn't going to do, so I drove back to my apartment for a shower, some light makeup, and my only season-appropriate pantsuit.

In an hour flat I was looking crisp and intimidating, my agenda rehearsed, backup plans aplenty, ready to go brow-to-brow with any Harvey Weinstein knock-off.

The parking garage door lifted, and sunlight crept over the hood of my 2005 Ford Focus, revealing dimples from a long-ago hailstorm, color fading from UV damage, general filth, apathy, and neglect. All that, plus the persistent low-level hum of owning the homeliest car in the complex. I'd have to do something about that.

I arrived at the Purgatory Ballroom a few minutes before three. The building takes up most of a city block, and the surrounding businesses don't attract any foot traffic, so I was able to park directly in front of the box office. I found the doorbell, pushed it, then walked to the Mercedes, leaned against the passenger door, and waited, looking cool in a pair of Marc's aviator shades.

Within a minute, one of the glass double-doors opened and part of a male human head emerged, eyes squinting.

"Are you AJ?" the head asked.

I removed the sunglasses and confirmed my identity, still leaning against the car.

The head said: "Gil will be out in a minute."

The door closed and I could hear it being locked, which sounded more complicated than unlocking it. The temptation was to scroll on my phone as I waited, but I opted to check out the dozens of show bills and fliers posted on the double doors and box office glass. None of them displayed any tendencies toward uniqueness. Four long-haired, bearded white guys on this poster, five of the same on the next, some holding instruments, some not, a nice mountain backdrop here, a dilapidated grain silo or farmhouse there.

The door unlocked, and out stepped Gil. I met him halfway on the sidewalk. He looked either like an aging surfer or glam metal musician: cargo shorts, hair down to his lower back, running shoes, a few bracelets, rings, and a thick gold necklace. I hadn't gotten a good look at the first guy that opened the door, but I suspected he and Gil were the same person.

We fist-bumped and he introduced himself, apologizing for the wait. He stepped to the side and approached the Mercedes. "Nice wheels," he said. "Is this a '68? '69?"

I picked one.

"Let's go to my office," he said, and I followed him into the dark ballroom, pitch-black except for a couple of red EXIT signs on opposite ends of the room. We took a hard left and climbed a long staircase lined with giant framed photographs of various performers—Taj Mahal, Ziggy Marley, Vanilla Ice.

The aroma of marijuana was fresh as we reached the top of the stairs. I followed him around a few more corners, eventually entering his office. There were no windows with a view of nature, just a large one overlooking the ballroom and stage. The walls of the office were covered floor to ceiling with more framed posters and large photos, most of them autographed. He offered me a seat, and then took his behind the desk.

"It's nice to see a non-employee sitting in that chair," he said. "I don't do a lot of in-person meetings these days. Even before the apocalypse."

I shifted my weight, eventually settling with my legs crossed and hands folded at my knees. "I was in the neighborhood. Thought I'd come have a look at the place."

"You've never been? You must be new to town."

"Never been," I lied. I'd been to at least a dozen shows there in as many years.

"Well, welcome to the Purgatory Ballroom." He mentioned a little about the history of the place—built in the twenties, closed for a few years in the thirties, and then reopened in time for the big band swing era. He dropped some names—Louis Armstrong, Duke Ellington, Count Basie, Ella Fitzgerald. "And that's just before 1950," he added. "I could go on and on, but I'm guessing neither of us has all day."

The small talk was eating into the no-nonsense persona I wished to exude, so I cut to the chase:

"We're working with the *Denver Post* on a feature article," I began. "If we could sync the August thirteenth show with that, that would be ideal."

He was now sitting at the edge of his chair, elbows on the desk. "Well, well. That *would* be ideal."

"We sold out the Lo-Ball last weekend, but it just isn't large enough for a pair of singing, wrestling giants," I said. "They need more room. Some wrestling mats would be nice."

The part about the mats wasn't planned, just kinda flopped out.

Gil looked at the ceiling. "Where would you even find wrestling mats? Craigslist?"

All I remembered about mats was that it took an entire high school wrestling team to roll them up and move them. Not an item that you can just stuff in the back of a van and move from city to city.

"I'll have one of my assistants look into it," he said. "I'm just curious for my own sake."

I asked him to tell me more about the August thirteenth headliner, mentioning that I'd only had a chance to check their website on my phone.

"*The Dangle State Stompers*. Up-and-coming jamgrass band from Florida, booked solid everywhere for the next six or seven months, huge Sony money behind them, have a song on a movie soundtrack that'll be coming out in a couple weeks," he said. "They'll be in the amphitheaters and arenas this time next year, without a doubt."

"This gig will sell out, then?"

"Within hours. I'm not even worried about it."

I spun my chair around to face the window overlooking the still-dark ballroom. "Do you have a ticket price settled?"

"Not set in stone. Fifty bucks, ballpark."

I asked how long a set the Haugenberrys would be expected to perform, should they agree to do the show. "They can play all night if need be."

"Forty-five is the usual, give or take."

I paused again, then swung my chair back to face him. "Fifteen hundred dollars for forty-five minutes seems fair to me."

He leaned back in his chair, and it rolled a few inches. "Hmm."

I grabbed my purse and stood, checking my phone. "Ooh, I need to be at the courthouse."

And, as hoped, he stood from his chair and began following me as I retraced my way to the staircase. "Think it over. E-mail is as good as anything. Let me know about the wrestling mats."

I descended the stairs rather quickly, at the frontier of my ability while wearing pumps unrehearsed.

"I will," he said. "Give me a couple days to move some numbers around."

And with that, I sped away in Marc's Mercedes, headed not to any courthouse, but a Dairy Queen. The meeting had gone well, and I didn't leave it with any glaring red flags of creepiness from Gil. Maybe the people in my circles didn't really understand the guy, but who knew. I figured the car, my outfit, and a few lies had been enough to throw him off his usual game. Had the real AJ Washburn showed up at three o'clock, she probably wouldn't have made it past the front door.

Within the hour, I was sitting on Marc's porch, finishing the last of a large Strawberry CheeseQuake Blizzard. Although a pay guarantee had yet to be agreed upon, it was safe to say the Purgatory gig was on. I was fairly certain the brothers would do it for half of what I asked, as even that would be a two hundred and fifty dollar improvement over the Lo-Ball.

It was time to get the plate spinning on the *Denver Post* article, so I dug up the Kyle Nosodosteros e-mail and replied, mentioning the Purgatory gig details and adding a few stretchers about recording an album and an upcoming tour. I hadn't put together a press kit, and that was worrisome. Kyle probably wanted some juicy backstory, but extracting that was his job, not mine.

It occurred to me then just how little I knew of the brothers' backstory. All our interactions had been fairly brief. We hadn't spent hours in a car or even pulled an all-nighter together. Forced boredom in each other's presence had evaded us thus far.

They'd mentioned driving back east to fetch tools and take care of other errands. Maybe I could tag along sometime. In the case that their backstory wasn't all that exciting, a road trip would give us a chance to finesse the lies.

By mid-morning Thursday, I'd photographed and cataloged fifty grand worth of furniture: all Mid-Century Modern pieces from Eames-Herman Miller, Heywood-Wakefield, and the like. Lots of molded plywood and fiberglass; a cast aluminum lounge chair and ottoman set worth more than my entire estate. Hutches, bookcases, side tables; a sofa-and-chairs set I suspect could fetch another twenty thousand. That was all just in the main living room.

There's a lack of natural light in the house, being surrounded by several old trees, and in the shadow of high-rise apartments for long portions of the day. This had become a source of frustration while taking photos. I'd need to buy some flood lights and a decent camera, so I turned to craigslist.

I received an e-mail from Gil while hunting for photo gear: *We can do $1500. Call to confirm.*

"Goddamn right you can!" I shouted to no one. I stood and took what might be called a victory lap around the room in order to release some energy. This continued out onto the porch, down the sidewalk, and all the way around the block.

I thought to call Abe right then, but decided I'd pay the brothers a visit on my way home. I wanted to see the look on their faces when I mentioned the fifteen hundred dollar guarantee. That kind of money wasn't unheard of for a popular local band as a headliner, but it usually took a few years, not weeks, to build up to it. Fifteen hundred for a duo with just two short opening gigs under their belt—that was unheard of.

I didn't call Gil, but I did respond to his e-mail: *Excellent. $1500 for 45-mins. I'm in a meeting, will call later.*

Might call eventually, is what I really wanted to reply. I was still suspicious of the dude. Why did he want me to call when an e-mail would do just fine? He probably wanted to offer to take me out to lunch, or to a Rockies game, maybe a little hacky sack at the park.

The rest of the afternoon consisted of crisscrossing Denver

buying used photography gear from talkative, shut-in weirdos in their wood-paneled basements. I returned to Marc's woozy from the odor of mothballs and cat spray. By six o'clock I had the main living room looking like a small television studio. That was enough work for one day. I could start fresh first thing in the morning with plenty of light.

I brought a twelve-pack of beer to the Haugenberry house on my way home, excited to share the news. The expected sound of power tools could be heard as I approached. I let myself in and went for the kitchen where Abe was standing flat-footed, drilling a hole into the ceiling—a task that most humans would need a ladder to perform. I set the twelve-pack down on the kitchen counter with enough force to get Abe's attention. He stopped with the drill and lifted the safety glasses from his face.

"I've got some news," I said, tearing open the twelve-pack. "Let's get Dan down here."

Abe shouted for Dan, and Dan descended the stairs.

"Do you guys ever take a break?" I asked, handing Abe a can of beer, and then one to Dan as he entered the kitchen. "Seems like twelve-hour shifts every day around here."

No answer. Dan stuck his head under the faucet and let the water run. I opened my beer, took a sip, and asked them if they'd ever heard of the Purgatory Ballroom. They hadn't, so I gave them an abridged version of what Gil had told me.

"Anyway, *huge* place. They want you guys to play August thirteenth. You interested?"

Maybe they were just tired, but neither one looked the least bit interested.

"How much they paying?" Dan asked, drying his hair with the front of his shirt.

"Well, that's the thing," I began. "You'd be opening for a national act, to a sell-out crowd. It's a thousand-person room."

Dan looked slightly annoyed. "And they don't want to pay us anything. Is that what you're getting at?"

"It's a legendary venue. Duke Ellington, Count Basie, Seals & Crofts. Very hard to get in there as a local act."

Abe seemed to have an idea that I was up to something. "I love a good exposure gig," he said, slapping his hand on the counter. "Let's do it."

"*I love a good exposure gig, let's do it,*" Dan repeated in a slack-jawed, whiny voice. "No thanks."

I took another sip, looking somber, and let a few moments of silence pass. "I tried to get more out of them, but the most they'd offer was fifteen hundred." I shrugged.

Dan looked at me sideways. "One thousand and five hundred?"

"Yes. I'm afraid," I said, avoiding eye contact.

Dan looked over at Abe, then back at me, then back at Abe who was now looking at me, smirking. "Why must you two always be fucking with me?"

"Well, Dan. You wanna do it, or not?" Abe asked, in more of a shout than I was expecting. "Let's not waste this young lady's time. Stay focused, brother. *Focus.*"

Dan looked both frustrated and confused, then disgusted. "To hell with the both of you," he said, leaving the kitchen, headed for the front porch, pausing briefly to look at his latest drawing on the drafting table.

I assumed the eventual answer would be yes, and so mentioned the *Denver Post* interview, as it was the next thing to worry about. We'd need to arrange a time, but I still hadn't heard back from the writer. I suggested we do some prep work beforehand; a mock-interview of sorts.

"We need to be several moves ahead of this guy," I began. "And ready to hijack the entire thing."

"We do, huh," Abe said, looking fatigued.

"When it's over, he needs to leave wondering what just happened to him."

This notion seemed to amuse Abe.

"Sounds like you've done this before."

"No," I said. "But I've read hundreds of these write-ups. Unmemorable, every one. It's a shame we can't just write it ourselves. Your future is on the line."

He flicked the pop-top of his can a few times. "Well, I ain't too worried about it."

I proposed the three of us get together Saturday night at Marc's and work up a strategy. I'd order dinner and we'd sit on obscenely expensive vintage furniture, drink beers, and work up some backstory and press kit material; another chance for each of us to get out of our routines. Abe agreed to it, and shouted the details to Dan, who was facing away from us, doing some detailed erasing on his drawing.

He raised his fist and extended his middle finger.

Most of the major furniture pieces in the basement, second story, and attic were photographed and cataloged by late-afternoon Friday; five to ten photos of each item, along with a 100-150 word description of manufacturer/model, condition, and any other relevant information I could find. I'd need help moving some of the items away from the walls, so I prepared a chore list for when Abe and Dan came over.

I posted one of the fiberglass chairs on craigslist at an admittedly delusional asking price. I had three responses within an hour, two of them from out-of-state.

Rikki called as I was responding to a collector from Santa Fe.

"You need to come over and watch these on the big screen," he said.

"These what?"

"These Haugenberry edits. Can you make it over tonight?"

I'd planned on staying in, exhausted from the day, but Rikki's excitement was infectious, and usually warranted, so I told him seven o'clock.

That didn't buy me a lot of time, and certainly not enough to dig around for an adapter. However, I don't like to go anywhere empty-handed, so I picked up a bottle of pinot gris, and arrived a few minutes early, still over-caffeinated, chewing two sticks of gum. Rikki's big-screen was ready to play the edits. I sat on his couch. A cat I didn't recognize crept toward me from his kitchen.

"*Another* one," I said.

"I got her yesterday from the shelter," he said. "Super curious, super friendly, occasionally violent."

"It walks like Robin Williams doing an impression of John Wayne."

It hopped onto my lap and pawed at my thigh—a healthy-looking black cat with no otherwise distinguishing features.

"I think we'll name you...*Kleethith,*" I said.

Rikki looked at me from his computer desk as though I'd just slapped him in the face and was waiting for a reaction. "What?"

"Yes," I said, massaging the cat behind the ears. "A mash-up of the surname *Klebold,* and the word *fleethith.*"

"No, and no" he said. "What is *fleethith?*"

"I don't remember. You'd have to look it up."

"No. You don't come over here smacking gum like Ted Nugent, imposing a hideous name on my new cat."

"It's the times we live in, Rikki. You know it. I know it."

"No."

I continued petting the cat. She looked blissful.

"That's the most heinous name I've ever heard," Rikki said.

"It'll give her something to struggle against, something to overcome."

"A school shooter and a word you just made up."

"I didn't make it up," I said. "It's been around."

He reminded me of his two-year reign as runner-up spelling bee champion for the state of New Mexico as a youth. "You're not going to fool me with vocab."

"Do a search."

He did, and spent way too much time scrolling, while I relaxed with the cat.

"Kleethith," I said. "Pretty sure that's gonna stick."

"No."

"Going, going..."

"I'm going to kill you."

"Can I see these edits first?"

He started with the "TV commercial" edit we'd discussed. It began with about five seconds of Abe singing, the microphone steal, Dan singing, the string cutting, and then a gradually sped-up back and forth of the remaining antics, until the final ten seconds cut to a jerky cell phone video of the wrestling match. It was weird, lo-fi, anarchic, and perfect.

"Once more," I said, and we watched it five more times, Rikki pointing out minor details each run-through.

Then he showed me a version that could be customized to suit whatever show needed promoting. The same footage as the first edit, but with seizure-inducing flashes of retro digital text against a fluorescent green or pink background.

He prefaced the full set edit as not being finalized.

"I haven't put much time into this," he said. "I'm not sure you really want to post a video of the whole thing."

I thought about this as we watched the first few minutes and began to agree with him. It would give away too much, spoil the magic. Rikki suggested the camera angles, distances, and inconsistent sound quality weren't up to par.

"Only a few minutes in and I'm getting fidgety," he said. "You'll probably want to spend some money on a pro if you want the whole set to look and sound good."

I didn't find myself feeling fidgety, but a more-professional production was probably something to look into. The thirty-second promo edits were all I needed right then. I drank wine and watched Rikki add the Purgatory Ballroom info into his video editing software. I hadn't previously mentioned anything about the gig to Rikki.

"That's a Gil Barbieri venue, right?"

"Yes."

Rikki laughed. "Have you been dealing with Gil himself, or one of his assistants?"

"Gil himself."

"Just through e-mail, I'm assuming?"

"No, I met with him in person yesterday."

"And you walked away from this meeting without feeling exploited or sexually harassed in some way?"

"I think he was thrown off by the pantsuit and Mercedes convertible."

Rikki demanded further explanation, so I provided it.

"For all he knows, I'm a real mover and shaker in this Queen City."

Rikki uploaded the Purgatory-impregnated video file to the Haugenberry website and to YouTube. I immediately sent the links to Kyle at the *Post*, asking him when and where he'd like to conduct the interview, assuming it would be sometime during the upcoming week. He responded within minutes, requesting that I name a time and place and that he'd make it work.

I texted Abe: *Denver Post interview, your place, Monday night 7pm?*

And in no time at all, he replied: *Works for us.*

Then an e-mail back to Kyle and that was done.

Rikki shut his computer down and began looking through a crate of records, eventually picking one and putting it on the turntable. He filled a glass to the brim with wine and sat on the opposite end of the couch. Kleethith sat between us. I complimented Rikki on the videos and thanked him.

"I think we're on the edge of actually making some money from this," I said, mentioning the guarantee that I'd squeezed out of Gil. "How much do I owe you for your time?"

He waved it off, insisting that it had only taken him a couple hours. I doubted this, as I knew the way he usually did things while in his manic phases. I had some leftover cash from my photo gear binge that I handed to him, amounting to roughly seventy dollars.

"There. Buy yourself some gummies," I said.

"If you insist."

We sat back, fully sunk into the couch, feet up on the coffee table, taking in the music. It sounded like early Joni Mitchell, but not entirely, so I asked about it. Rikki handed me the album sleeve.

"Judee Sill," he said. "If you're a sucker for backstory, she's your gal. Armed robbery, prostitution, scam artistry, forgery." He took a sip of wine and continued. "Reform schools, church organist, drugs of course, and—*gasp* – bisexuality."

"Oh my. What it must be like to be so talented!"

"Blacklisted, obscurity, death from overdose, the end."

I mentioned the impending *Denver Post* interview, and that it'd been causing me mild anxiety.

"Why, if you're not the one being interviewed?"

"These articles usually suck, as you know," I said. "And nothing's changed since I stopped reading them years ago. When was the last time you read a feature article on a band?"

"Years ago."

"Always a description of the bar where the interview takes place, then how the band got together, with a few quirky details and inside jokes thrown in; then some recounting of the awkward first gigs, personnel changes, the usual minor setbacks not even worth mentioning, then some future plans. Then, when you least expect it, here comes a reference to that earlier quirky detail to add a twist to the ending. Boring, boring, boring."

"That about sums it up."

"I'm trying to figure out a way to avoid that."

"Hm."

"Going off the very realistic assumption that this is the only *Denver Post* write-up we're ever going to get."

"Yes, I'd say that's realistic."

I scooted to the edge of the couch. "If we could somehow make the experience traumatic for the interviewer, maybe we could increase our chances of a worthwhile article."

Rikki laughed.

"And maybe," I added. "Maybe—with the right set of extreme circumstances—we could make it onto the real news pages," I added. It all felt like a true revelation to me.

"A crossover."

"Yes! A crossover."

"And how are you going to pull that off?"

"I'll think of something."

We sat silent awhile, listening to the record. "*If we could somehow make the experience traumatic,*" Rikki said, in a contemplative tone. "My god. I think you might've just secured your own concentric circle in hell."

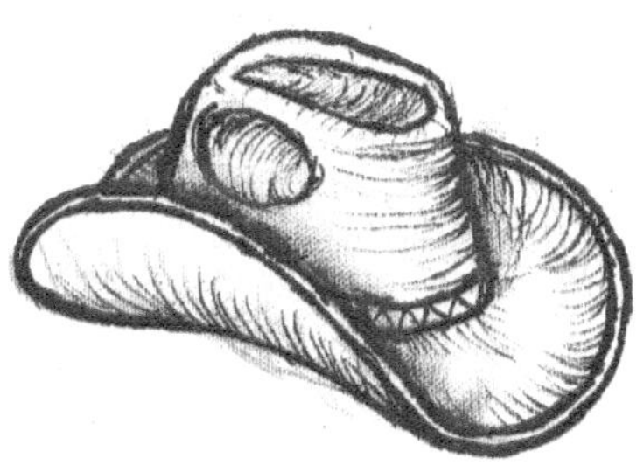

WALT FLICKINGER: autograph expert. He arrived at Marc's front door in well-pressed western wear and a cowboy hat. I don't know where the lines are drawn between formal western wear and regular-ass western wear, but Walt looked a bit over-dressed for the occasion. I invited him in, and he hung his hat on a hook adjacent to the door, taking a moment to assess the layout of the room, the portable lighting in particular.

"You planning on conducting a TV interview this morning?" he asked.

"No, just taking photos of the furniture."

"It looks like 1963 in here. Like the Beatles could invade any minute."

I turned off the brightest lights, calming the room a bit. "What were you doing in 1963, Mr. Flickinger?"

"I was three years from being shipped to Vietnam is what I was doing."

I feared he might expand on that, but no. I offered him a cup of coffee, which he refused, asking for a glass of water. He walked the room inspecting the various furniture as I poured his glass, and then set it on the kitchen island. I asked him how he got into the autograph business.

"I worked for the USO for a few years after my tour of

duty," he said. "Lots of photo ops and celeb exposure with that job. It all just started to accumulate after a while."

I asked if he knew how Marc got involved with collecting.

"Let me tell *you*," he said, approaching the glass of water and pulling out a stool. "Let me sit down right here and tell you all about it."

Marc had received most of the collection from Earl Noso-dosteros, a seventies-era Denver radio and TV broadcaster, and, turns out, father of Kyle Nosodosteros of *Denver Post* fame. Small world. The elder Mr. Nosodosteros had become embroiled in a scandal and had hired Marc as his attorney. When the scandal and lawsuits passed, Nosodosteros wasn't able to pay Marc in full, so they negotiated a trade that included the autograph collection.

"He acquired a lot of things that way," Walt added. "Some fantastic under-the-table deals, back when all of it was at a fraction of today's value."

He asked if I had a general idea of Marc's organizational scheme. I handed him the stack of spreadsheets, and he flipped through them briefly, as though they were generally irrelevant. He stood from the chair.

"Let me show you. Follow me," he said.

We went to the den first, and he mentioned having spent a couple days looking through everything a few years previous. He pointed to a refrigerator-sized safe on the wall opposite from the file cabinets. "All of the US presidents are in there. European royalty, chancellors, prime ministers. Certain books, a couple old albums, a few sports items."

He opened the doors of a cabinet adjacent to the safe. "All books, as you can see. Signed firsts—most of them. Novelists, poets, philosophers, anything in book form."

The file cabinets were next. He happened to open the same drawer I'd opened a few days before. He sighed and bowed his head. "This is your big challenge. Alphabetized, no segregation."

It seemed perfectly rational to do things this way, so I asked.

"Nobody does it like this," he said. "Keep your politicians separate from your celebs, keep your athletes separate from criminals and assassins."

The *Mondale, Walter* folder was sticking up a smidge higher than the others—my fault—and he went straight for it, before fingering through adjacent folders.

"Mondale and Ricardo Montelban back-to-back?" He patted both folders down. "I just don't know."

He closed the drawer, placed his fists on his hips, and looked around the den. "Any movie posters or show bills that aren't hanging on the walls are up in the attic in cardboard tubes. The records are downstairs in the lounge. You'll probably find a random box in a closet or under a bed."

I followed him back to the kitchen island and we both sat. My laptop was open, and Marc's eBay page was up. Walt looked at it briefly, noting Marc's twenty-year seller history. He scrolled through Marc's feedback, nodding, his brow lifting every so often. "He's sold to most of the major autograph dealers in the past, so you're starting with a decent amount of credibility. That's a big deal.

"Once they catch wind that the whole collection is being sold, watch out. You'll be getting bulk offers from every corner of the world."

I asked him if he had a ballpark value to put on the entire collection, or if Marc had ever mentioned one.

"No idea. It's too diverse, too large, too many unique pieces."

"If someone came over with a check for a million dollars, should I take it?"

"You could ask more."

I asked if he'd help me put together a priority list, as I had no idea where to start. I removed a spiral notebook and pen from my bag, intending to jot down notes myself, but he reached for them. "This is what I would do."

And he began writing. I sat and watched, until he paused and looked up from the page. "I'll be awhile if you have other things you need to do."

I needed to pee, so excused myself from the kitchen and went for the restroom at the back of the house; the one with the "Wall of Shame" that had been joked about at Marc's wake. Signed photos, framed letters, postcards, voided checks, and one restaurant tab signed by the first orange US president. I removed the frame from the wall and turned it around. There was a small handwritten note taped to the back with a date, name and location of the restaurant, and a brief description, part of which read: note the *0% gratuity*.

I brought it to Walt, and he inspected it. "This is a nice conversation piece, but not worth much, unfortunately."

He wrote in the notebook for another few minutes, before standing and stretching. "Hell, I could spend all day," he said. "That'll get you started."

I glanced at the three pages of lists and other notes. First item of business:

US presidents—all in gun safe, post on eBay in reverse order (Biden first, Washington last) Include photos of ALL supporting documents. ten-day auction...

He began walking toward the front door, announcing his shopping itinerary for the morning. I'd anticipated a longer visit, and more instruction on what to do, but the thirty minutes was all I was going to get. I followed him out to the porch, and he told me to phone him with any questions. He hadn't mentioned being interested in acquiring any of the autographs for himself, which seemed odd. I asked if I should put any aside for him.

"No. Well, maybe. Yes, actually. I'll get back to you."

AROUND FOUR O'CLOCK, I called it a day and went for Marc's porch chaise for a cat nap. A duel of some sort was underway between two homeless women across the street. One had a short length of PVC pipe, the other a branch. They were distant enough that I couldn't make out what they were shouting at each other. It seemed as though the PVC-wielder was attempting to capture the branch-wielder's shopping cart, or some of its contents.

Something about the scene seemed to trigger a sense of information-overload within me, and a confirmation that I had too much on my plate. The reality of tackling the autograph project was starting to sink in, while the craigslist furniture e-mails multiplied. The realization that I'd double-booked the *Denver Post* interview at the same time as comedy night had finally hit me not an hour earlier. I couldn't cancel another comedy night, but maybe I could find a fill-in. Or, maybe I *could* cancel comedy night. Maybe it had run its course. Maybe it was time to pass the torch.

Shit was getting to be too much. I know this about myself: when circumstances get overwhelming, my controlling tendencies begin to kick in, requiring a public execution.

My mother was a savant of control and manipulation. At some point in her early life, she'd acquired an almost aristocratic "Southern charm" completely inconsistent with her suburban Philadelphia raising. There was always a lot of touching and winking, and the *blessing of hearts*. It was her catchphrase, and a platitude so burned into my psyche that every time I encounter a situation that threatens to evoke or extract pity or smugness, my mother's voice pops up: *Bless your heart.*

A passing fire truck and ambulance startled me out of my all-too-brief nap. The homeless duel was still underway. I watched the duel for a moment under some brain fog. The PVC warrior had her opponent on her knees, and then kicked her onto her back.

And here it comes, here it comes: *bless her heart*, echoed in my mind. I hadn't intended to think it, say it, or have anything to do with it whatsoever. But, what can you do?

The brothers were due in less than an hour, so I went in the house, made a shot of espresso, and did some cleaning and rearranging. The kitchen island had become Command Central, strewn with notebooks and spreadsheets, the rest of the main room a mess of portable lighting and power cords.

To hell with it. Who am I trying to impress?

I returned to the porch with a jar of wine and a notebook and began jotting down a skeletal agenda for the evening: backstory—real or fiction? interview manipulation, controlling the narrative, deflection/diversion, among other things.

The brothers arrived earlier than expected. They approached the house and were immediately distracted by separate aspects of it, Abe walking around the east side of the house, Dan the west. They'd both encounter a fence and locked gates, so would have to reverse course and return to the porch.

Abe was first. "Needs some brick work, maybe some new gutters."

"Repairs aren't in my mandate," I said. "I'm just selling stuff."

Dan climbed the steps moments later. "The spigot is dripping. I attached a hose to divert the water away from the foundation. I would get that fixed asap."

"Thank you, Dan. I'll let somebody know." I didn't know who to contact, so made a note to e-mail Hirsh about it.

The brothers did their typical patio furniture inspections before sitting down, commenting on the high quality of Marc's chairs.

"You should see what's inside," I said. "It's a furniture lover's wet dream. More like a carwash. A carwash of ejaculate."

They wasted no time entering the house and marveling. I soon followed, asking what they wanted on their pizza. They'd already eaten, so that was that. I refilled my wine jar. By then, both brothers were either sitting on the floor or on their back inspecting the undercarriage of this or that sofa, chair or table, commenting on construction techniques and materials from the bygone era. Neither seemed especially concerned with brand names or manufacturers.

It was time to set the mood, and so I approached Marc's stereo system, one of the few elements of the room that wasn't mid-century. The turntable had two arms and looked more like a piece of high-precision laboratory equipment than the record players I was used to. I didn't dare touch it. I pushed the clearly marked power button on the stereo, and after a few seconds of boot-up time, a familiar voice from the jazz station filled the room, one of the many DJs that had spoken at the wake. After having spent a few days in Marc's house alone, it felt as though his spirit had finally returned.

Mood set.

Several minutes passed and the brothers were still scooting around on the floor. Their size and limited flexibility added an element of physical comedy to the situation. I felt the need to get the meeting agenda started, but decided to let them do their thing, for a few more minutes anyway.

My patience is finite, however. "So, this interview," I began, both brothers on their backs at separate ends of the room. "Do you guys want me to be there?"

I expected at least one of them to sit up, but no.

"Up to you," Abe said. No response from Dan.

"I was planning on it, but I just realized I have comedy night."

Abe sat up, then rose to a standing-with-an-aching-back position. "Do you have prices for all of these?" he asked.

"Just a general idea," I said. He crossed the room, focused on a pair of Eames lounge chairs and ottomans that I'd done quite a bit of research on. A single chair/ottoman set had recently sold for eleven thousand, and I mentioned it to Abe who was now sitting on one. He stood when he heard the dollar amount. "So, where can a poor boy safely sit around here?"

"You can sit wherever you'd like. Just don't go carving your names into things and sticking gum under shit."

Abe decided to join me at the island, and after fetching a thirty-pack of PBR from the bed of their pickup truck, Dan did the same. We small-talked awhile about their renovation project, ongoing struggles with their neighbor over noise and the trauma it was forcing upon their neighbor's pets. I gave a heavily-embellished account of the duel I'd witnessed that afternoon.

A specialty show called "The R&B Jukebox" played on the radio; the DJ spinning songs from the pre-Beatles, pre-surf music era, before the electric guitar had fully pushed the saxophone out of the way.

"Ah," Dan said. "Those were simpler times."

Abe laughed. "*Simpler times.* You *are* simpler times, Dan. In fact, any part of the space-time fabric you just happen to be at is—almost by definition—made simpler by your mere presence."

I bit my lip.

Dan looked at him as though he'd crossed a rhetorical line usually reserved for the intoxicated and emotionally over-extended. He looked at me and shrugged.

"I do my best."

Abe wasn't finished, however. He took a sip of beer and looked at the ceiling.

"A young Geraldo Rivera walks out of Willowbrook State Hospital. He's about to collapse after all the filth and neglect he's just seen. His camera crew are all popping cyanide pills. Up walks little Danny Haugenberry, inspecting a booger he's just picked. He shows the booger to Mr. Rivera, and Mr. Rivera yells at his convulsing, frothing-at-the-mouth camera crew. 'Let's roll tape! I think we've got something special here. Show your booger to the camera, Danny…"

I was no longer keeping a straight face, nor was Dan.

After another quick sip, Abe continued: "It's okay, little Dan-Dan. Don't be shy. They aren't going to take it from you. That's *your* booger, Dan-Dan."

Dan looked at me, the repressive squirminess and tension around his mouth clear for all to see.

"I'd say I handled that pretty well," he said, reaching for his beer. "I didn't cry, I didn't shit myself."

Abe scoffed. "When? Just now, or back at Willowbrook?"

With a slap on the granite top of the island, Dan began a slow wander around the room. Abe had clearly won this round, and Dan was moving on. Any sense of awkwardness or tension disappeared, as though the previous discourse hadn't happened, or was immaterial and irrelevant.

A slow doo-wop song began playing, and Abe caught me staring blankly out a side window.

"You're worrying about the interview," he said. "Stop it."

"Sort of."

"Why?"

"Oh, I've just been over-thinking things again," I said, half joking.

"Are you worried we're going to mess it up? Is that it?"

"No, not at all," I said. "You guys can hold your own against any so-called journalist Denver has to toss at you."

"Well then, what?"

"Worried is the wrong word. I'm scheming, strategizing."

"Okay."

"It's the backstory. Kyle's going to ask. These writers usually have a press release or one-sheet to steal from. This guy has nothing. There's nothing out there about you guys."

"Is that a bad thing?"

"No, it's a huge advantage. A tremendous opportunity."

"We could make it all up, if we wanted," Abe said.

"Exactly! That's what I'm hoping you want to do."

The prospect excited Abe. He shouted to Dan, who was across the room scanning a bookshelf. "Hey, are you paying attention here?"

"No," Dan said.

Abe looked at me and shook his head, before shouting to Dan again. "We need to rewrite our entire personal history before Monday night. You up for it?"

"Why? The real one isn't fucked up enough as it is?"

This gave Abe some pause. He turned to me. "He does have a point."

"Well, maybe we don't need to rewrite the *whole* thing," I said. "Just the stuff that's most likely to come up in the interview."

I got my notebook and a pen and started jotting some things down. "Let's start with the most basic stuff."

And so it began, a solid twenty minutes of Journalism 101.

We tweaked or eliminated some of the least-compelling details as they presented themselves. Many previously unknown locations, events, and personalities of Eastern Colorado history moved from the fictional to the non-fictional realm.

Their father's auto parts store had been a hub of their childhood and adolescence, more important in many ways than the family home and ranch. Most of their spare time after school and weekends had been spent there, and music filled most of that time via an AM radio, 8-track tapes, and a shared guitar. Their first public performances as a duo happened on the sidewalk in front of the store.

"Every Saturday afternoon during the summers," Dan said. "Two, sometimes three hours depending on the tip jar."

Their brief high school athletic careers were described as "win by forfeiture in a land that high school athletic programs forgot."

The reality was, most of what they told me was perfectly interesting and unique, sharing nothing with the typical privileged-white-kid-claims-victory-over-some-inflated-odds narrative.

"This is all pretty fascinating," I said, reviewing the pages I'd filled. "I'm still thinking we—or you guys, rather—need to take a more aggressive approach."

Both brothers were standing with their arms crossed, looking straight at me. I felt like I was watching an atomic energy propaganda film and the fourth wall had just melted down.

"How so?" Abe asked.

"What do you mean?" Dan asked.

I felt thoroughly intimidated. "What am I trying to say here, exactly," I said, under my breath. Everything began organizing itself in my mind, and I began explaining my strategy:

"All of this," I said, holding up the notebook. "Everything we've just talked about, is just for backup, just for emergency use. Let's assume you're going to get an hour with this dude. The less time you spend passively answering questions, the better. If you spent no time passively answering questions, that would be ideal."

This seemed to get through to the brothers, but I wasn't finished. I pointed to the notebook again.

"If none of this information is relayed, fine. If you can sustain an hour of riffs and insults like the Geraldo-booger story, that would be awesome. Try not to give him much chance to talk. Maybe one of you could fake a heart attack and force the writer into a mad rush to the hospital, that would be awesome. Am I making sense?"

"You're suggesting we make a total clusterfuck out of this thing?" Dan asked.

"That's one possibility."

"Seems like a waste of everyone's time," Dan added.

"And that's another possibility, yes!"

Dan looked puzzled, or skeptical, so I continued:

"The most important thing is that you guys run the show. Keep the interviewer on edge, disoriented even. You want him walking away from the experience asking himself, *How did I let that get so far out of control?* Visualize Kyle Nosodosteros cowered in a fetal position in his shower an hour after the interview. That might be a good place to start, from a motivational perspective."

Both brothers were laughing at this point. "You are out of your mind," Dan said.

Abe looked at Dan. "This sounds just like something Dad would've told us."

Dan nodded. "Just like Dad," he said, before leaning toward me with a jarring, creepy, possessed stare. He waved his hand in front of my face, as though he were trying to snap me out of a hypnotic trance. "Dad? Are you in there?"

"I think we get the gist," Abe said. "I don't know about

Puddin' Head over here, but I think I understand the strategy. Fortunately, both of us have a good deal of experience with this sort of thing."

"Great!" I went for some more wine, a celebratory glass at the end of a successful business meeting. "When all is said and done, I think we'll have an article worth reading."

Both brothers seemed energized behind the concept and had become fidgety. I offered to lead them through the rest of the house. They stalled in the den, looking through drawer after drawer of autographs. I let them be, and went to the porch, bathing in the milk of self-satisfaction. The ball was in their hands now. I wouldn't attend the interview, but missing it was no longer a concern.

WILDFIRE SEASON BEGAN the next morning, thicker to the north, but guaranteed to blanket the city with haze and camp-fire aromas within days. I took advantage of the remaining moments of clarity and went for the porch of my apartment to rid my mind of burnt ends.

Once an insurance agent, always an insurance agent.

Now, there's something that's never been said.

I couldn't face two more weeks of the day job; the chronic coworker references to *Office Space* or *The Office*, the festering right-wing news misery of the break room, and the past-due obsolescence of the job itself—one that only continues to exist due to the insurance industry's ontological fear of change and risk. It was time for me to *become* that change.

The Covid bit needed resolution, so I checked the website.

Positive.

Huh, was my response, barely a blip on an EKG. At the time of the test, I was positive for mild menstrual cramps, but that's it. No symptoms whatsoever. I imagine everyone at the Lo-Ball the previous Saturday had been exposed, including Hirsh, Rikki, Josh, Abe & Dan and a hundred others. No one I'd encountered since had mentioned feeling sick, or off in any way. Was the whole matter over with?

I attached the required medical documents to an e-mail

with a short message stating my symptoms had improved, but that I wasn't able to provide a two week notice and would need to resign immediately. After a few moments of now-or-later deliberation, I chose to send it to my manager right away.

This sigh of relief was worth texting Rikki about, and so I did, asking if he wanted to join me for a celebratory breakfast. A half-hour passed, then another. I called. No answer, but no cause for alarm, just concern. He may have just gone to sleep after an all-night binge of reading and note-taking. No way to tell with that guy. I'd give him a few more hours.

My various intuitions about Rikki and his cycles had become highly refined and generally reliable. When it takes eight or more hours for him to respond to a text message or e-mail, then I can almost be sure he's made the turn. It's usually preceded by long stretches of intense focus on one project or another, inevitably ending in total burnout. For example, he chose to read the entirety of *Moby Dick* over a long weekend, and the question remains, *Why?* You've got to give that stuff time to sink in!

He maintains better when he's been given a project to work on, something to help him feel useful. He'd finished the brilliant promo edits, but we hadn't yet discussed a next thing. It would need to be something even more awkward and lo-fi if I was to keep his attention and hold off the abyss. Some kind of sketch comedy thing maybe, fake interviews, insult wars. Either way, I'd have to come up with it.

It was also possible, but highly unlikely, that he'd found himself a new piece of ass. For this reason, I opted not to drop by his house to check on him. I did that once, and I'll just say that the fog of embarrassment was noxious enough to evacuate an entire apartment complex in the dead of a Stalingrad winter. The freeze-frame of that moment remains in my mind, with the words SOME THINGS CAN'T BE UNSEEN flashing in garish block letters like a vintage cable TV infomercial.

Dear reader, I have a pretty good idea of where your mind is going at this moment. Hold those thoughts. The scene I'm not describing may be the only sex scene this story has to offer. Only time will tell!

Ten o'clock rolled around and still no response. In the meantime, I'd cleaned the kitchen, producing a handful of insults related to cookware and appliances. A chance encounter between my big toe and the acoustic guitar case got me thinking about Oliver. It'd been a week since we'd spoken, and I assumed my encounter with Gil would be of interest to him, so I walked to Panopticon.

His new cash register was the first item of discussion. It wasn't new at all. In fact, it was older than the previous one by a few decades.

"It's vintage," he said. "She's a brick house. The same model as my dad's old machine. The drawer works at least. How's your guitar playing going?"

"Zero progress. But I do remember the few things I remember."

"How about the songwriting?"

"Is it possible to write a song that cancels itself out?"

"I don't know, but I do know someone who probably does. I got in touch with that guy I mentioned."

I didn't recall any guy being mentioned, aside from Gil. Oliver saw the blank look on my face.

"Colonel Kurtz, the meat-lover," he said. "Remember?"

"Oh, yes."

"Do you remember a band called the Mayflies? Maybe before your time. Early-mid nineties. Anyway—and hardly a band in the traditional sense. More of an art project."

And Oliver went on about the guy, describing a mysterious hermit-like character who lives somewhere on the wastes of

Southeastern Colorado. A mad genius of sorts, capable of writing entire albums of convincing, cohesive songs in any genre in a matter of days or weeks.

He inserted a record into a shiny new automated cleaning apparatus and pushed the ON button. "Anyway, I described the Haugenberrys to him. He sounds very interested. Motivated even."

"Okay." I wasn't sure exactly what this guy's role would be, so I asked for some clarification.

"You need to do an album," Ollie said.

"Yes, we do. I'm not entirely sure how to go about it."

"This would be the quickest way to get it done. Hell, he's probably got a few hundred songs to choose from that the boys can sing with some minor adjustments."

He made it sound like a simple, no-brainer solution, but life is always more complicated than that. I asked how much cash we'd have to cough up, and he seemed mildly offended.

"You'd have to take that up with him."

I watched the record spin slowly in the cleaning machine, while several large dollar amounts shifted between various accounts in my mind. Getting a third party involved didn't really appeal to me. I knew making a record would be time-consuming and expensive, even under ideal conditions. The idea of working with some strange dude in a faraway land didn't exactly moisten my lily.

"He's got a full recording studio out there," Oliver continued. "But he's basically off the information grid. His only phone plugs into the wall. Very spotty internet."

"I don't know, Ollie. Everything you've told me about this dude sounds sketchy. Not sure I'm sold on this guy."

He removed the record from the cleaner and set it on the display case between us. "Why don't the four of us take a drive out there and check things out. He's a magician. The right guy for the job, I can almost guarantee it."

"Hmm."

"Worth a shot, anyway. A road trip."

The idea of a road trip sold me. Here was an opportunity to get the brothers into an enclosed space for hours at a time.

"How far away is this place?"

Oliver turned to his laptop and brought up a map application. "Burg, Colorado. The Dust Bowl," he said, typing in an address. He turned the laptop around so that I could see. I clicked around and zoomed in and out. A four-hour drive east and south, then some.

"I'm going to ignore all of my instincts," I said, already imagining the drive across the plains, the mountains disappearing in the mirrors, the skeletons of old homesteads, wells, and other farm infrastructure. "Let's do it."

A line of customers had developed in the meantime, and I was in their way. Oliver and I agreed to make our various phone calls and scheduling maneuvers, with a tentative plan to make the trip happen the next weekend or the following.

"I'll check with the fellas," I said, exiting the store, and after a stop at a coffee shop, that's what I did.

I'd somehow failed to learn this hermit's name and had nothing more than a name of a pre-internet art rock band with which to do any web research. I continued to the Haugenberrys' with a whole lot of nothing to work with.

Dan sat at the drafting table working on a large drawing of a public lynching. Someone involved had screwed up, and the lynchee was hanging by one leg, and not his neck. An oldies station played quietly out of a pocket-sized transistor radio.

"Hey, Dan. Have you ever heard of Burg, Colorado?"

He removed the undersized reading glasses and swiveled around to face me.

"Yes. Burg. One of God's afterthoughts."

Abe ascended the back porch staircase and noticed me.

"Hey Abe, have you been to Burg, Colorado?" I shouted.

He approached, wiping his hands with a rag. "That's about ninety miles due south of our folks' place."

"Nobody goes to Burg," Dan added. "People drive past it. Maybe stop to take a leak behind an old shed. Nothing there that wasn't abandoned fifty years ago."

Abe walked past me to the front porch. "If you're driving through Burg, it means you're being detoured around a highway closure, you're lost, or running from the law."

A confused, offended look came to Dan's face. "Why are we talking about Burg? This can't be good."

"Oliver knows a guy who can help us make a record," I said. "He lives about twenty miles south of Burg."

"Twenty miles *south* of Burg? Dear God," Dan said, placing his glasses back on his face and turning back to his drawing.

"He has a few million acres all to himself, it sounds to me," Abe said. "The buffalo don't want anything to do with it, grasshoppers don't want any part of it."

"The Native Americans didn't want it in the first place, and definitely don't *want it back*," Dan added.

"Oliver claims this guy is some kind of musical genius," I said. "And he doesn't toss that word around every day."

Dan laughed. "Musical genius, perhaps. His geographical whereabouts disqualify him from being any other kind."

"If you guys want to make a record, this sounds like a one-stop shop. He's got the songs, the studio."

"The songs?" Dan asked.

I had to improvise a bit here. "Hundreds and hundreds," I began. "Sounds like you guys could pick ten or twelve you like, tweak them however you want, record them, and *voila*—you have a record."

"Hmm," Dan said. "The Milli Vanilli approach."

I had to correct him on this. "You'd be singing on the record."

"I'd prefer if we wrote the songs," Dan said. "Just my two cents."

"*We?*" Abe laughed. "What you're actually saying is you prefer *I* write the songs." He affected a slouched posture, and the voice of a stock geezer character from an old hillbilly sitcom. "'Let ol' Abe do the writin' and me, heck, I'll just a-hop in on the singin'.'" He followed that with a bar or two of a jig-like dance.

Dan had no response, so I improvised a bit more.

"The songs might not be one hundred percent yours," I said. "But you can make them yours. Change some words, rework a verse here and there if need be, rework the whole thing if you want. Sounds kinda fun. You won't have to start from scratch."

Again, no response from Dan. Abe seemed to be on board, as he'd proven himself to be up for whatever, whenever, and with whomever, generally speaking.

"In Burg, Colorado," Dan said, almost under his breath.

"We should go check it out at least," I said. "If it isn't going to work, then so be it. Are you guys game?"

"I'm in," Abe said.

Dan removed his eyeglasses again and swung around to face us, arms crossed. "Ok. But I'm not driving."

We quickly determined that all three of us could make any day work aside from the Purgatory weekend, which was three weeks away. This led to further discussion about the nature and experience of time in the area of the state to which we'd be traveling.

"Out there, a Monday is just as good as a Friday or Saturday night," Dan said. "There's nothing worth going to, or getting excited about any day of the year, or decade for that matter. A tornado maybe, if you're awake for it."

I called Oliver immediately after leaving, informing him of our availability and interest. As is typical, I added an unnecessary ASAP feel to the proceedings, suggesting we do weekdays, if possible.

"I'd plan on two days," Oliver said. "At least an overnighter, and drive home first thing the next morning, or however it plays out."

This was acceptable to me, but I'd have to confirm with the brothers. Oliver said he'd get back to me with some dates, hopefully within a day or two. I could hear that he was busy with customers, so we left it at that.

I returned to my patio, realizing I still hadn't learned the name of this mystical, ascetic musical genius of the wastelands. A web search of "the Mayflies" brought up a few musical items that were obviously not from the early nineties. A search of Burg, Colorado brought up nothing but government data. I called Oliver again, apologizing for interrupting.

"Just one quick question," I said. "What is this guy's name?"

"Herb Bernfeld."

I asked him to spell the surname for me.

"I know what you're thinking," Oliver said. "Good luck. He's nowhere to be found online. I've been looking. Nothing at all. But he's for real. I swear!"

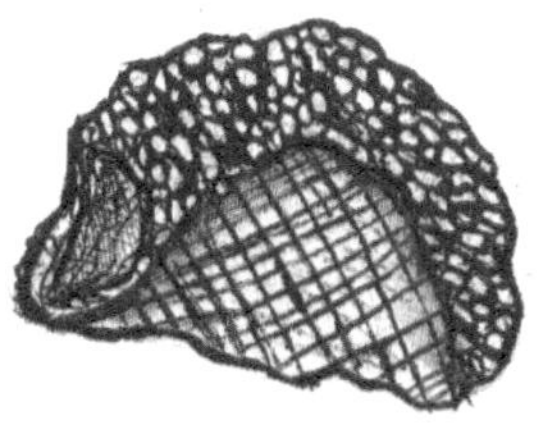

I KICKED off comedy night with one of my recurring charac-
ters and situations:

> *Great to see so many Dan Fogelberg fans here*
> > *tonight*
> *I didn't see your asses here last week, did I?*
> *And you weren't at no Dan Fogelberg concert*
> > *neither, so don't go a sayin'*

Someone familiar with my shtick shouted from the back.
"Who'd you meet at the grocery store?"

> *Oh, y'all know me too well—especially all you*
> > *white-haired nancy-boys in the back booth*

> *I've got your party-line number*

> *Anyway, yes, it was another old lover*
> *This one identified as a sculptor*

> *I stole behind him in the frozen foods, touched*
> > *him on the sleeve, the whole bit*

He didn't recognize me at first
Went at me for a hug, spilled his man purse
Prescription bottles rolling every which way

Next thing ya know we're drinking beers in
    his car
And he starts crying
A car wash of tears

He sez, You ghosted me. Why did you ghost me?
You didn't have to ghost me.

I didn't want to touch him, but I did, on the
    upper arm

And I sez, Old lover, I didn't know what else
    to do!
You were just sitting there at your spinny thing,
    bawling your eyes out
Making one of your stupid bowls, or pots or
    whatever the fuck

I snuck up behind you, did the ol' reacharound,
    and tried to help you out!
Shit, you didn't even look like you knew what
    you were trying to do
A fool oughtta know when it's time to take some
    lessons!

I got out the car and walked away
Now, which one of you pube-scapers is going to
    criticize me?

I made it through the Swayze/Moore/Fogelberg bit just

before a particular distraction appeared in the form of Gil Barbieri. I froze, and quickly went for the sign-up sheet and got the first comic on her way to the stage. I handed her the mic and she whispered what must've been a quote from *Ghost* that didn't register with me.

There stood Gil, grinning, arms crossed, looking full of himself as though he'd just outed me in some way. I approached him with this assumption, said a quick hello, and then excused myself to use the restroom. He didn't seem offended by this. In fact, he was very cordial and nonchalant.

"I found some wrestling mats," he shouted as I walked away, as though he expected me to walk out the back door and never return. The ambient noise of the room was loud enough that I could avoid responding and continue forward, stalwart, with two fists of plausible deniability stuffed in my bra.

I shut and locked the stall door, dropped my skirt and undies, and sat on the toilet. Only a brief squirt hit the water— a perv's ring-tone worth, at most. Why, at my age, I find myself faking a bathroom urgency in order to gather myself and put together a defense against anything I've ever done in my life to a pot-bellied, hair-fixated, male accessorizer—well, that occurred to me.

I left the bathroom, prepared to control the conversation until he backed himself onto the sidewalk with his hands up.

The first comedienne was deep into a confessional story that hadn't yet snapped. The room was too quiet for a conversation, so I gestured for Gil to follow me out to the alley. As emcee, I had to keep an eye on the stage and be ready to facilitate transitions between comedians. This was a perfect excuse to remain somewhat aloof. I mentioned the *Denver Post* interview that was happening that very minute.

"Good for you," Gil said. "I can never get them to write anything about my shows."

What did he want me to say to that? I needed a change of

subject, so mentioned the album we were about to start working on. I asked him if he remembered Herb Bernfeld and he looked uncertain.

"Early nineties, the Mayflies," I said.

Gil lit up. "Oh yes, I never knew his last name. They played at my first bar. The Beatles' *White Album* in reverse—literally. They learned all the songs backwards and played them backwards."

"We're going to be working with him, and doing some sketch videos."

"I found some wrestling mats," he said.

"You did."

"Free, you just need a box truck or a flatbed and a bunch of dudes to move them."

"Where?"

"Green River, Utah. They've got some water damage."

This sounded like a nonstarter in every way.

"What do you think?" he said.

A roar of laughter and applause came from inside the bar, signaling the end of the first performer's set. I rushed inside and got the second performer up. Gil followed me and stood at the edge of the stage. "I picked a bad time," he said. "Are you up for a drink some night this week?"

I hesitated but had to say something. "Possibly, do you have a card or something?"

He pulled his wallet from his cargo shorts. It was attached to a short length of chain. He removed a card and handed it to me. "I've got a couple other ideas I want to run by you."

We said our goodbyes and he left. I'm ashamed to say it, but my first thought was: *am I going to have to buy another pantsuit now?* I'd set myself up to live a fashion lie. My casual dress at comedy night was excusable, but any other contact with him was now going to be complicated by my ensemble. How stupid. My thoughts can't be trusted.

I walked around to the back of the bar and served myself a vodka cranberry. Heather, the bartender, was pouring a beer from the tap. "Isn't that the dude from Purgatory?"

I confirmed.

"I don't know that I'm comfortable with him being in here," Heather said.

"You and me both."

Abe called not long after the last performer wrapped up, and the bar was emptying. I went for the back patio.

"How'd it go?" I asked.

"Oh, *man,*" Abe said, sounding relieved.

"Uh oh. Not good?"

"It was perfect."

"How so?"

"I did most of the talking. Dan answered a few questions, then spent the rest of the time puking."

"What?"

"I basically answered all the questions while Dan puked and moaned—off the porch, the front yard, back yard, bathroom. I just acted like nothing was going on."

"Food poisoning or something?"

Abe laughed. "Ipecac."

"What?"

"Dan's idea, believe it or not. He'll have a good one now and then. He's pretty wiped out right now. Looking pretty spent. I'm walking to 7-Eleven to get him some Gatorade."

"See if they have any Choco Tacos," I said. "Buy all of them. They're being discontinued."

"Okay."

I asked about the interview.

"Just the usual stuff. I was mostly trying not to laugh. I left the room a few times."

I dug a bit more, asking if he'd mentioned the Purgatory show and the upcoming record at least.

"All of that got talked about. Some backstory," Abe said. "We'll just see what turns up in the article. Dan looks like a baby bird that just fell out of its nest."

"Is he okay?"

"Of course he is," Abe said. "I think he may have overdone the whole thing a little. Some over-acting."

"I've never heard anyone criticize someone else's puking performance before."

I heard the familiar ding of the 7-Eleven door being opened. I didn't have any new information to share about the trip to Bernfeld's, or anything else really. Abe told me to keep him posted, and we hung up.

I drove home, imagining the interview, the staging of it all, wondering how much of it would make it to the final printed article. To my surprise, I received an e-mail from Nosodosteros just after I entered my apartment: *Well, that was an experience! I failed to get any contact info before I left. I'd like to offer them a do-over.*

I replied with a thank you, and Abe's cell number, with a couple digits transposed. There was zero chance of a do-over, I'd make sure of that.

A FEW HOURS of text and phone tag Tuesday and the trip to Bernfeld's was inked. We'd meet and leave from the Haugenberry house at six o'clock Saturday morning and return whenever Sunday. This was sooner than expected, but there wasn't any reason to wait. We didn't have any prep work to do, Oliver had someone to cover the store, and Mr. Bernfeld was ready for us.

Everything went as planned Saturday morning, and we were on the east edge of the city by six-thirty. The white tents of Denver International Airport to the north, the giant golf balls of Buckley Air Force Base to the south.

"Well, I'll be," Abe said, backhanding Dan on the thigh in an unexpected outburst of energy. We drove under the E470 overpass, at the frontier of Denver's urban sprawl. "We've got homefield advantage again."

Dan shuffled through a stack of mail that had accumulated on the dash. Oliver and I were sitting not very comfortably in the back. Conversation had been sparse since we'd departed. Coffee hadn't quite kicked in, the sun was in everyone's eyes. We maintained some general silence, listening to NPR.

"Are you planning on using this?" Dan asked, holding a P.F. Chang's coupon mailer out for Abe to see.

"No," Abe said, annoyed by the interruption. "I don't even know where one is."

Dan tore the postcard-sized coupon in half, then quarters, then eighths. "Have you ever wondered what the P and F stand for?" he asked.

"No," Abe said. "Everybody knows already, and if you don't, who cares anyway?"

Abe started cycling through radio stations, eventually turning the radio off. I hoped we might start discussing a game plan for the recording.

"Everybody knows, huh?" Dan turned to consult Oliver and me. Neither of us could muster an answer.

"Peter Frampton," Abe said.

Dan started singing a Frampton song with the Ls and Rs jumbled up, like white dudes do when making fun of Asians who weren't raised speaking English.

Ooh baby I ruv your way, evley day

Frivolous, perhaps, but it was a tone-setter and icebreaker.

It got Oliver engaged, and the Frampton reference led to a conversation about groupie memoirs, the Ogallala aquifer, fracking, back to Frampton, and then a discussion between the brothers about alternative routes to Burg, and Bernfeld's place.

Abe exited at a town called Byers. The off-ramp took us over a dry river lined with dead cottonwood trees and decay of all sorts. Someone had set up shop at the crossroads ahead, selling right-wing flags and T-shirts from the back of his truck and camper. Abe turned to Oliver and me and asked if we wanted to stop and stretch a bit. It'd been an hour, and there wasn't ample room in the back seat, so it was time.

"What do you think, Dan. Should we go fuck with this guy?" Abe said, having already made up his mind, jerking the steering wheel to the left, skidding to a stop in front of the peddler's display, kicking up a thick cloud of dust.

Dan went for his door handle, and Abe stopped him. "New black truck, tinted windows. He probably thinks we're the feds. Try to look like a fed. Stone sober."

The dust cloud settled. The peddler was on his feet, cradling a lap dog, looking prepared to go for a firearm. Abe and Dan exited the truck, both in sunglasses, tucking in their shirts before approaching the peddler's tables. Oliver and I got out and stretched but kept close to the truck.

Good mornings were exchanged, and the peddler sat down on a lawn chair that the brothers eyed warily.

"Where you folks from?" the peddler asked.

Abe popped his knuckles before looking at the shrink-wrapped wares. "From Iowa, originally. Went to school there."

Dan grabbed the corner of the familiar yellow *Don't Tread on Me* flag that was hanging from a pole supporting the peddler's awning. He held it out and inspected it.

"Hawkeyes?" the peddler asked. "You must've been ball players."

Dan got Abe's attention. "This is one foolish-looking rattlesnake. I don't reckon you could come up with a dumber looking rattlesnake. Do you?"

Abe turned and looked for a moment, then turned his attention back to the spread of shrink-wrapped flags. "A *Far Side* reject."

"If I were a rattlesnake, and looked like this, I'd hope you'd stomp the shit out of me," Dan said, letting the flag drop. "Put me out of my misery."

"I'd be first in line," Abe said.

The peddler looked at Oliver and me for a moment, then back at Abe. "I'm gonna guess you two were on the Hawkeye basketball team."

No immediate response from either brother. Abe picked a

book out of a box. I could see that he was holding it upside down.

"No," Abe said. "The Iowa School for the Blind."

Dan jumped in immediately. "Kay through twelve. You ever watch *Little House on The Prairie*? The TV show?"

"I remember it," the peddler said. "My kids watched it."

Dan turned to Abe. "You know who was a hot piece of ass on that show?"

"Merlin Olsen," Abe said.

"Mary—or whoever that actress was," Dan said. "The blinder she got, the hotter she got. All the fumbling around and blank looks. That's when she really came into her own as an objectified woman."

Abe explained to the peddler the connection between the TV show and the Iowa School for the Blind.

"Oh yes, I remember," the peddler said, petting his dog.

"Lots of crying on that show," Dan continued. "But they got one very important detail wrong."

The peddler's patience was nearing its limit.

"Blind people don't cry," Dan said. "That's how you knew for sure that actress wasn't blind in real life."

The peddler set his dog on the ground and stood, pulling a cigarette from a pack in his breast pocket. "You fellas don't look blind to me."

Both brothers stopped and stared at the man. Abe crossed his arms.

"We graduated, obviously," Abe said. "But it's intermittent. You have to keep on top of it."

"Top of our class, as a matter of fact," Dan said. "I'm gonna guess you're from China. All these flags and shirts—made in China. You're a long way from home!"

The peddler lit his cigarette. "One hundred percent American, born and bred."

Dan held out the *Don't Tread* flag again, inspecting the edges of it. "I'm trying to find the tag on this thing."

Abe picked up a Trump 2024 shirt, unfolded it, folded it backwards and placed it on the table. The peddler grabbed the shirt and began re-folding it. "Do you fellas plan on buying anything?"

Dan held out a corner of the flag, drawing attention to where a tag used to be. "Did you cut the tag off this?" he asked the peddler.

"Yes I did. So what?"

"If I buy this, how am I supposed to know how to wash it?" He pulled his Zippo from his back pocket and lit the corner of the flag.

"I hope you're planning on paying for that!" the peddler shouted. "If not, I'll gladly call the sheriff."

The flag burned quicker than Dan expected. He jerked it away from the pole and tossed it onto the ground away from everything else. It continued to burn, thick black smoke.

"There's no sheriff," Dan said.

Abe walked to the burning flag and began stomping on it. "Clapton shot him."

Dan tore another flag from the pole, lit it, and tossed it toward the other half-burnt flag. The peddler had his cell phone out, presumably to call the cops.

Abe looked at his wrist as though there were a watch wrapped around it. "Shit, Dan. We gotta be at P.F. Chang's in ten minutes."

Abe gestured for Oliver and me to get in the truck. Dan approached the peddler's table, removing his wallet from his jeans pocket. "Do you take cards?"

The peddler put his phone down. "You owe me twenty dollars."

Dan closed his wallet and put it back in his pocket. "I'll have to hit an ATM. We'll be back. You didn't tell us you were going to be here this morning. I'd have brought cash if you would've said something."

Abe drove over the still smoldering flags and onto the highway headed south. Oliver and I were still processing.

"Well, we've performed our civic duty for the day," Abe said. "I'm feeling better. Did you pay the man?"

Dan placed his hand on Abe's shoulder and squeezed. "We paid him in memories."

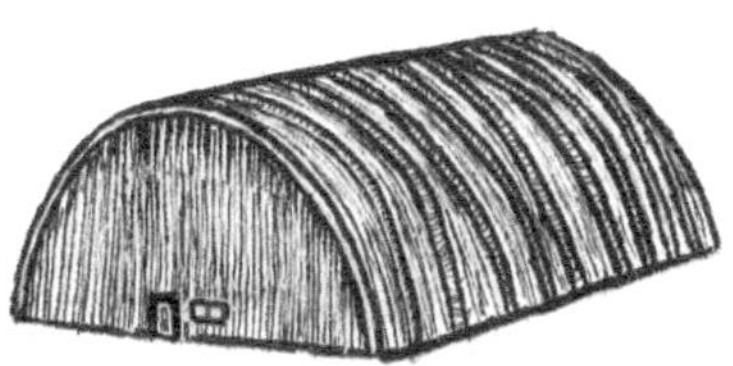

THE TOWN of Burg was almost as I'd imagined it. Boarded up stores, vacant mobile homes, and a few dilapidated garage-type buildings scattered along a quarter-mile of highway. No town limit sign, and the 65mph speed limit maintains all the way through with no slowdown. There appeared to be one occupied mobile home, judging by a barking dog tethered to a stake in its front yard.

We turned onto a southbound highway for the final twenty-mile stretch, having only stopped once since the flag peddler episode to stock up on beer, wine, and food. Aside from the power poles, occasional fencing, and the road itself, there were no man-made structures ahead of us.

"Ain't no one seven degrees from Kevin Bacon out here, I'll tell you that right now," Dan said. It was a morsel of rural American vernacular I was sure to steal and repurpose.

I'd tried and failed to sustain a discussion about a plan for the recording project. Oliver assured us that Bernfeld was likely to "tear any plans we had to shreds" anyway. Oliver did give us some history on the guy. They'd met in graduate school at the University of Denver in the mid-eighties. Bernfeld had been a regular customer at the record store and had led about a dozen different bands before moving east in the mid-nineties. I asked why.

"You'd assume it was some sort of mental breakdown," Oliver said. "But I don't think so. Not that I'm aware of. He's a bit eccentric, but who am I to talk?"

We topped a small hill and a gray dot appeared in the distance. As we got closer, the dot became a Quonset hut. The foundation of a long-since burned house stood between the hut and the road. A half dozen trees in various stages of life were scattered about the property, a large propane tank, a well, and a gathering of ancient farm equipment.

I'd seen many Quonset huts that morning, but this one seemed unusually large, maybe due to the lack of surroundings. A small Toyota pickup and a Subaru Outback were parked in front of the hut, which led me to speculate about Bernfeld's relationship status.

"One person wanting to live out here, that's doable," I said. "Two people? That's a stretch."

"He's not married," Oliver said. "He might have a ladyfriend, but I don't know."

Abe parked in line with the other two vehicles, and we got out and stretched. My spine was not looking forward to the return trip.

Bernfeld emerged from the hut, wearing what I guessed to be an Adidas track suit, purple with white stripes up the side. He very much resembled a certain director of Hollywood blockbusters whose career had spanned my entire lifetime plus five or six years. Sharks, archaeologists, Nazis.

"Welcome to my humble affair!" he said, wasting no time approaching Oliver and extending his left hand. He introduced himself to the rest of us, then stood back and took a measure of all four of us; two giants, a one-armed shopkeep, and me— doing my part to represent the inevitable victory of reality.

"This is what Hit Parader magazine would call a motley crew," he said. "C'mon and let me show you around."

We followed him through the front door into a large living

room area, with couches, chairs, a big-screen, and several pairs of enormous stereo speakers to the right, and a modest kitchen area to the left. The kitchen table was covered in stacks of recording tape and notebooks. Bernfeld noticed my interest in the tapes. "There's no way we're going to get through all that today, but I've got a few things picked out."

We followed him down a hallway, and he pointed out the bathroom, a bedroom, and another bedroom. An old-school ON AIR light hung above the door at the end of the hallway. We walked under it into the studio control room. I don't know what does what, but the guys seemed to, each of them drawn to this or that piece of audio gear.

"You're looking at almost fifty years of accumulation with almost zero liquidation," Bernfeld said. "As with almost every other recording studio known to man, only about five percent of this gets regular use. Hell, some of this crap—a whole hell of a lot of it, in fact—hasn't been powered up in twenty years."

Bernfeld opened another door to the rest of the Quonset hut interior. "Let's keep going," he said. "We'll be spending plenty of time in here."

We followed him out to the rear section of the hut and began wandering. I stopped and turned to look at the house-within-a-hut, and asked Bernfeld if he built it himself.

"How could you tell?" he laughed, as though I might be judging his skills. "Yes, in fits and starts. If you can imagine a chimpanzee trying to solve a Rubik's cube, that would be a suitable visual representation of the process."

The garage door opened on the north-facing side and a warm breeze blew through, kicking up a few swirls of dust. "Soil management continues to be an issue out here, as you can see."

Dan walked outside and did a panoramic spin, then asked about the burned house. Lightning had hit it in 1997, but the house had been abandoned in the early eighties. "I've often thought to scrape the whole mess, but I just can't get started. It's something to look at and ponder, so why not just leave it?"

"I'll get lunch started," he said, lifting the lid of a barbecue grill and lighting it. "I've got pork chops, brats, burgers, bacon —you name it. I'm not a gastronomical Jew, so you're in luck if you appreciate the full spectrum of animal-based protein."

He dusted off a quartet of metal folding chairs and offered them up. I passed, mentioning my need to re-calibrate my spine after the cramped drive. Dan took a seat, and Abe wandered outside.

"So, Oliver has told me a bit about you guys," Bernfeld said, sitting on one of the chairs. "I didn't believe him at first. I still don't."

I offered to show him the video footage I had on my laptop.

"And you want to make a record," he said. "So, I guess my first question is why?"

This is why I hoped we'd discussed this in depth at some point during our drive. Neither brother had an answer at the ready, so I made an attempt.

"Credibility," I said. "Street cred."

"Credibility?" Bernfeld said.

"Maybe that's the wrong word."

Bernfeld stood and went for a refrigerator. "If the Beatles were to walk in here in 1962 and I asked them why they wanted to make a record, I don't think 'credibility' would be the first word out of their mouths—maybe Ringo's."

Oliver chimed in. "Lennon would've called you out, Herb," he said, before shifting into a Liverpool accent. "That's bullocks, Herb. You make a record because you *shouldn't not* make a record."

"A perfectly good answer," Bernfeld said, carrying a tray of meat to the grill. "The next question, then, is what kind of record do you want to make?"

No one had an immediate answer here either, but it seemed a far more manageable question.

"Oliver described your set list," Bernfeld said. "Twice, in fact, because I didn't believe it the first time."

"Not a fan of mellow gold?" Abe asked.

"Absolutely a fan," Bernfeld said with blustery confidence. "I didn't always feel that way. That stuff was my soundtrack of minor childhood trauma. Waiting for my sisters to get their braces on, listening to my mom negotiate prices for fabric. What a waste of perfectly good adolescent frontal-lobe-forming time."

Before the conversation got tangential, each of us contributed a song and artist that reminded us of a childhood trauma. Mine was "My Baby Takes the Morning Train" by Sheena Easton, a song that'd been playing when I witnessed my first car accident and dead bodies.

Bernfeld got us back on track. "A ten-song mellow gold album. That's very doable."

"Heavy on the vocal harmonies," Oliver said. "That's these guys' ace-in-the-hole. Think Everly Brothers, Louvin Brothers."

Bernfeld placed some burgers and brats on the grill. "If you want it to sound contemporary, we can do that. If you want it to sound like 1973, I've got the gear to do that. We'll have to do without the obligatory string section."

"I assumed you could fake that with software," Oliver asked.

"It still sounds like software."

Conversation wandered again, continuing through lunch. Bernfeld and Oliver caught up on the well-being of old friends, acquaintances, professors, businesses. I soaked up every bit of history I could from them while Abe and Dan wandered the property.

The brothers returned to the hut and Bernfeld herded us

into the studio. Everyone found a couch or lounge chair to sit on. Bernfeld sat in his rolling office chair and spun around to face us.

"I'm going to cue up a few songs that I think would work well together," he began. "A few caveats: almost all this material was recorded between 1985 and '95, on tape machines of varying fidelity. Some of the digital reverbs on this stuff dates it, unfortunately. Try to ignore it the best you can. I can cut some of it, but not all."

He pushed the PLAY button on a large tape machine and the reels began their hypnotic spin. "This is the first song that came to mind."

Oliver commented on the opening guitar chord. "The major seventh. Perfect. The very foundation of the genre."

Bernfeld smiled and nodded. "A very polarizing chord in the rock world. It goes straight for the ballsack with hedge trimmers."

The song played through, full of lush harmonies, and unexpected turns of phrase. I was sold on it. When it was over, Bernfeld pushed the STOP button, and swung around to face us.

"I never once claimed to be a great vocalist," he said. "But that's the gist. What do you think?"

"Play it again," Abe said, and so we listened again, and then one more time, Bernfeld mentioning a sonic detail here and there, suggesting a potential tempo change.

"I called it 'Dew Drop', but you can do what you will."

"Dew on the lily," I said, for no particular reason.

Dan spoke up. "That's a keeper."

"We could overdub vocals on that today if you guys are up to it," Bernfeld said.

The brothers looked at each other and agreed to do it. "Let's hear a few more," Abe said.

Bernfeld sorted through a drawer of tape reels and pulled

one out, loading it onto the tape machine. "Have you ever been drawn toward something you have no chance of achieving?" he asked. "I definitely went through a phase of this, trying to write lyrics like Marc Bolan."

Oliver laughed. "T. Rex? I would never have guessed."

"The man was able to disconnect from all logic, convention, and things of this world. I nearly drove myself to a mental breakdown in the attempt. You'll hear it on this next one."

He cued up the tape, apologizing again for the vocals we were about to hear. "This has an obvious padded-cell quality to it. I think if you sing it straight with harmonies it would work. Might even be good *a capella*."

The singing was indeed strange, intentionally bad like the most tone-deaf singer in a choir trying to sing louder than the rest.

"You can hear a beautiful melody fighting to get out," Oliver said. Abe and Dan laughed at the lyrics: *I'm looking for a needle in a haystack that broke the camel's back.*

Bernfeld played another couple songs before we agreed to take a short break. The brothers went for the truck. I used the restroom, then followed them. They'd both cracked a beer.

"Well, what do you guys think?" I asked, whispery, as though there were a chance anyone could hear us, and anything unfavorable might be uttered.

"He's intense," Dan said. "I like the first three."

Abe and I agreed, expressing a mutual desire to hear some uptempo rockers. Abe looked again at his non-existent wristwatch, noting that it was only 1PM. Bernfeld emerged from the front door and clapped his hands.

"Whatta you say we try recording some vocals over that first song?" he said. "Once I actually hear you guys sing, I'll have a better idea of what else to dig out of the vault."

We all agreed to the plan. He requested ten minutes to get

the master tape cued up and a lyric sheet written out, before walking back inside.

The brothers started singing and harmonizing on what they remembered of the lyrics and melody, discussing who should take the lead or harmony. They bickered awhile over this, as they agreed the harmony vocal on the song would be more fun to sing. They eventually hit an impasse over the matter.

I'd witnessed the life cycle of a couple recording sessions, having dated a few musicians in my day, and could spot the tendency to overthink what'd be ultimately out of everyone's control.

"Just go in there and see what happens," I said.

Dan dug his fists into his lower back, looked upward, and shouted: "Why are you always right, AJ?"

Within an hour, they'd sung over Bernfeld's original vocal tracks, each singing on both lead and harmony. The fact that they'd never worked in a recording studio before came up a few times, with Bernfeld marveling over it after each finished take. We listened through both versions, the consensus being that neither one was obviously better than the other.

"How about we try a little studio magic," Bernfeld said, pushing a few buttons and twisting some knobs. "Let's go listen through the big speakers."

We followed him to the front room, and he pointed to a small circular rug that I'd noticed when we first arrived. I'd noticed it because it seemed randomly placed, and randomly selected from a clearing house for hideous, ill-conceived rug designs.

"That's the sweet spot," Bernfeld said. "You can take turns."

He walked back to the studio, and within a few seconds the song began to play through the speakers; the major seventh guitar chord, then Dan's lead vocal hard left, Abe's hard right, with both harmonies at center, swirling, slightly menacing, soft psychedelia. One or the other harmony tracks pushed forward slightly, then receded. It evoked the yellow wallpaper of Charlotte Perkins Gilman's story, minus the impending mental health crisis.

The brothers took turns on the rug, eventually sharing it, one foot on, one off. Bernfeld was now standing behind us, looking through the stacks of recording tape on the kitchen table. The song concluded, and we all stood silent for a moment.

"I'd applaud," Oliver said. "But, well, need I say more?"

"What do you think?" Bernfeld asked the brothers. "We can get weirder if you want. The Twilight Zone knob is only at about ten o'clock currently."

The brothers remained facing the speakers. "Can we hear that again?" Abe asked. "Maybe a touch louder?"

And so it went. I took a turn at the sweet spot, closed my eyes, and made a feeble attempt at meditation. Transcending the material world was not to be, however, and my thoughts scattered toward what to do with the song now it was more or less finished. A video maybe? How soon could I get the thing uploaded?

"Holy shit," Abe said, as the final chord faded. "That's awesome." He backhanded Dan on his forearm. "And don't you piss on the fire."

They looked at each other for a moment, wide-eyed, as though a great discovery had just been made.

"Let's do another," Abe said. "Can we do another?"

I'D TAKEN charge of the grill, and had dinner prepared when Bernfeld and the brothers emerged from the studio a few hours later. They'd completed two more songs, and we listened to them as we ate from the exact same menu as lunch. Neither of the other songs had quite the same impact as the first, but that was to be expected with fatigue and hunger factored in. Bernfeld suggested they wrap up the recording portion of the day.

"I've got the rest of an album laid out in my mind," he said, sorting through tapes on the kitchen table. "Assuming you're going to like these others. Time for some rockers, nonetheless."

"More gold, less mellow," Abe said.

"I'm a bit tired of listening to myself," Bernfeld said. "I'd like to clear the air, if I may."

After a minute or so, someone else's music began playing through the massive speakers. I didn't recognize it, but I correctly guessed it was from the seventies.

"Dave Edmunds," Oliver said. "*Trax on Wax Four*. 1978."

I'd seen the album in a dozen different used bins but had never heard it. The brothers seemed unfamiliar with it.

Bernfeld returned to the kitchen. "Now, I want you all to listen closely to the next song," he said. "And when it's over, I'd like to hear any attempt to explain why it wasn't a hit."

We listened to the song, entitled "Never Been in Love"—an up-tempo power pop song reminiscent of the Everly Brothers. I liked it, the brothers seemed to like it.

"Any guesses?" Bernfeld asked.

"The Bee Gees is why," Oliver said. "Disco. The *Mirror-Ball Ceiling*."

"It wasn't even released as a single," Bernfeld said, looking exasperated. "I think you guys should take a swing at it."

"You won't have to fight the Brothers Gibb for chart space," Oliver said.

"Dan has a Bee Gees story for you," Abe said. "*And* it's beef-related."

My phone decided to join the conversation right then with its robotic beeps. I'd lost service long before we'd driven through Burg, and had given up any hope, or care. I pulled it from my purse. Twenty new e-mails, including one from Gil.

I opened it, and it was brief, offering the brothers two Purgatory gigs in September. *Give me a call*, it read. A quick message from Hirsh followed, wondering how things were going with Marc's sale. By the time I was done reading that, my brief window of internet access was over, as was Dan's Bee Gees story. I asked the brothers if they wanted to do the gig, assuming pay was the same or better.

"I would wait for this first gig to pass before getting in any deeper with Mr. Barbieri," Oliver said.

"Gil Barbieri?" Bernfeld laughed. "*The* Gil Barbieri, from Inferno's?"

"Inferno's?" I asked. "With an ess? Is he from Chicago?"

Oliver explained that Inferno's was Gil's first venue back in the early nineties. "Now a T-Mobile store."

"I played many a gig there," Bernfeld said. "An aptly named venue."

Oliver had something serious to say. "So, you two know Gil better than I," he began, addressing both Bernfeld and me.

"We can assume that he hasn't actually read *The Divine Comedy*. So, my question is—this is a two-part question—to whom does he claim to have read it, and to whom does he reveal the truth?"

"That's probably the least of his secrets," Bernfeld said.

"Do people call him out on it, and how often?" Oliver said.

"Who does he let get close enough to him to reveal the truth?" Bernfeld said.

"And, once the truth is revealed, is that person then in danger of extermination by being a bearer of the truth?" Oliver asked.

They pondered this for a moment. Oliver looked at me as though he were up to something.

"Don't even think about asking me," I said.

"AJ, we're gonna need you to put on your Angela Merkel pantsuit and take the Mercedes over to Purgatory to do some recon."

"Not a chance," I said. "This might be a job for the Haugenberry brothers."

"What are we even talking about here?" Dan asked.

"We'll get you studied up," I said. "It'll be a breeze."

We spent the next couple hours listening to more of Bernfeld's old songs. All but a couple of the twenty or so were up-tempo rock songs. We selected seven additional songs, with a couple of backups, and Bernfeld called it a day.

"Not a bad day's work, people," he said, standing from his office chair and stretching.

"I didn't think Jews were supposed to work on the *Shabbat*," Oliver said.

"Let's agree to disagree" Bernfeld said.

Oliver looked puzzled. "Did we just skip a step somewhere in there?"

Bernfeld and Oliver settled in the front room, drinking wine, listening to Hawaiian music, and catching up on old times. Dan drove the truck around to the north side of the hut and we tailgated, looking out at the featureless horizon. I pulled my one-hitter from my purse, took half a puff, and offered it to Abe while Dan was around the corner peeing. Abe declined.

"Don't let Dan get into that," he said. "He'll be on top of the Quonset, buck naked, writing a letter to the Corinthians."

"It's good to keep in touch with the Corinthians. It's good to keep in touch in general."

Dan emerged from around the corner. "Get into what?" he asked. "You got some weed? Yes, please."

He had a puff of the one-hitter, coughing a few times, then opened another beer and joined us on the tailgate, gazing northward.

"Maybe we should've gone into the music business," Dan said.

"We're in the music business right now," Abe said. "We're sitting smack dab in the middle of the music business, as a matter of fact."

"Out here, twenty miles south of Burg?"

"What were you expecting?"

This gave Dan pause. "Where are all the liars, cheats, and thieves?"

"Where are all the hangers-on?" I asked, tongue-in-cheek, but neither brother caught on.

"I was hoping to be chewed up and spit out," Abe said. "More in debt than I am now, that's for sure."

"I was hoping to quickly go out of style and be made fun of for a couple decades."

"You know what disappoints me?" I said. "I go to Wal-Mart for a shrimp cocktail tray and don't see your names and faces on a T-shirt."

"It's not fair," Dan said.

"Just think," Abe said. "We could've been fully washed-up ten years ago by now."

"Yes!" Dan said. "We could've had it all."

Abe laughed. "Don't go rolling in the deep now. Mama don't allow no rollin' in the deep."

And away they went. To attempt to render the dialogue that followed would require once-innovative Modernist narrative techniques that fell out of general usage generations ago.

The brothers eventually set up their tents, pads, and pillows at far corners of the property. Bernfeld and Oliver had turned in an hour earlier. I got set up on a couch in the front room, a leg's length from the sweet spot, and found myself contemplating the rug; its origins, and why Bernfeld chose to keep it. Sentimental value was the only plausible answer. Maybe a niece had made it for him. If so, had that niece attended the Iowa School for the Blind? I couldn't see why not.

I switched off the lamp and chose not to fight sleep any longer, reflecting on my childhood desire to have a sibling of any kind. I would've accepted anyone with a pulse. The odds that a stork would've dropped a pair like the Haugenberrys on our porch were negative zero, but the thought experiments of having grown up with these dudes were irresistible. I'm certain they would've picked on me incessantly, instilling and inflating multiple psychological hang-ups. How opposite to my current state of affairs would my life be had I been raised with a pair of brothers like Abe and Dan?

These thoughts blurred into dreams, as they do.

6:30AM. Bernfeld had pork chops and a pan of scrambled eggs on the grill. I was the first to wander out to him. He asked me about my job. I kept things current, mentioning only the estate sale and the open mic.

"I guess I'm managing these guys," I said.

"You guess?"

"Is that what I'm doing?" It was more of a rhetorical question. "I've been booking their shows, lining up interviews, looking for opportunities. Is that what a manager does?"

"Sure," he said. "You're part agent, part manager."

"I don't have a business card," I said. "If I did, what would I put on that business card?"

"Name, contact information, and in unnecessary quotation marks: *Doer of Stuff.*"

"I like that."

"Some artists—many, actually—also require a handler," he said. "Someone to keep them out of trouble. Is this part of your job description?"

I thought on this for a moment. Despite their antics, both brothers were generally well-behaved, prompt, focused, and free of substance abuse issues. I mentioned this. "I'm not sure I'd be a good handler. I wouldn't hire me."

He asked what all we had in the works. I mentioned the Purgatory gig, the *Denver Post* article, and the potential videos.

"What's the big-picture, end-game goal here?" he asked. "Are we thinking regional superstardom? International obscurity? Weekend warrior status?"

"All of the above."

"It will never be enough, no matter what, as I'm sure you're aware."

I was half-sure I knew what he meant.

"You haven't asked me for advice, but I'll give you some anyway," he began, flipping a pork chop. "Focus on the *creating opportunities* aspect," he said. "Making an album these days does little more than create opportunities. Record sales are a thing of the past—chump change in comparison with the old model...

"...Create opportunities and experiences, live them to the fullest, don't cling too tightly to any perceived successes," he continued. "Pay no mind whatsoever to perceived successes. And, when it's all over, and it will be, you'll have whatever body of work you end up with, and a whole bunch of unreliable memories. I could go on and on. How many pork chops you want?"

Abe joined us, quickly going for a paper plate. "It's so quiet out here, you can hardly sleep," he said. "I'm used to the quiet, but this is a whole different level."

Bernfeld laughed. "You can almost hear a satellite pass over."

Dan emerged from the studio room drying his face with his shirt, and asked Abe if he'd gotten any sleep. "Too quiet. I had to fart just to make sure I hadn't gone deaf."

"AJ and I were just discussing the bigger picture," Bernfeld said, flipping a pork chop.

Neither brother had any reaction to this.

Bernfeld mentioned his schedule for the upcoming months. His limited availability after August put a slight rush on things, and they tentatively agreed to reconvene within the two weeks following the Purgatory show.

"At the rate you guys work, I don't see why we couldn't knock the rest of this out in a day or two."

And with that, we were on our way back to Denver. Bernfeld sent us with two CDs and two jump drives, each containing the three songs they'd finished, plus the others that they'd agreed to work on.

When I finally got cell service, I sent Gil an e-mail asking for videographer recommendations, then responded to the first few queries about Marc's furniture. You can only type so many e-mails into a cell phone with your index finger before the symptoms of confinement and mild rage come knocking.

We topped a hill on the south end of Byers and saw the peddler, set up in the same spot. Dan was adamant about stopping.

"Just for a sec. I've got a twenty-dollar bill for this fool."

We stopped, and Abe kept the truck running. Dan got out

and approached the peddler. He walked a straight line, but ended up a few feet off-target, holding the bill out as though he were offering it to an invisible man. The peddler shifted the few feet necessary to grab the bill. Any conversation they had was drowned out by the truck's engine and air conditioning, but it was brief.

Dan returned to the truck, and we drove away. Abe asked if the peddler had anything to say.

"He asked if we made it to P.F. Chang's in time."

An MCM collector arrived at Marc's door just before noon Monday. I'd spent an hour or more corresponding with him via e-mail and phone. A high-maintenance dude, this one, not afraid to assume I'd do anything he demanded in order to get furniture out the door. His overall manner was that of a poorly-managed, spoiled, entitled member of a royal family. His hair glistened, and he reeked of some exotic saccharine cologne. I assumed he could speak at length about falconry.

His travel itinerary that morning had included a flight from Aspen, then an Uber from the Centennial airport. I asked him how he planned to transport any furniture he might buy. He had no answer.

The focus of our previous correspondence had been on a sofa and chairs set, but his interests expanded once he saw everything else. He asked prices on several items, and I was able to answer with slightly elevated figures off the top of my head without consulting a spreadsheet.

Here's how it went:

How much?

Insert base price plus additional ten-percent markup.

I'll take it.

This continued through every room of the house, and after fifteen or twenty minutes I had a list of twenty pieces written down on a legal pad. I sat at the kitchen island and tallied them —just shy of forty-five thousand dollars.

He paid by Venmo with no haggling, and said his movers would be in touch with me. He returned to his waiting vehicle, and I never saw or heard from him again.

I double-checked the Venmo account. The balance stood at sixty grand, and that was just furniture sales. Most of the super-nice stuff was now sold, but there was at least another ten-to-fifteen grand remaining.

A man from a moving company contacted me within the hour, sounding suspicious about the whole matter. I agreed that it was a strange situation, but verified there were things to be moved, located at a real address. He arrived soon after in a small pickup truck to size-up the job. A large box truck arrived an hour later. By four o'clock, the movers had all of it out of the house.

The sale might've been cause for celebration, but I mostly felt violated. If the buyer had made some effort to ask about the history of the furniture, I might've felt differently. Not that I would've had any historically accurate answers for the guy, but I could've invented some. I was haunted by an image of Marc shaking his head in disappointment. I had to get out of the house and distract myself.

Gil called as I walked around City Park Lake. I agreed to meet him for dinner at a nearby vegan restaurant an hour later. This didn't allow me enough time to go to my apartment for a change of clothes, so my current ensemble would have to do. I could make excuses, and I did.

We got a table on the sidewalk in front of the restaurant. Gil wore a button-down shirt and crisp jeans, but nothing too ambitious. We ordered drinks and reviewed the events of the day. I began a very casual scan of the menu as Gil discussed the difficulties he was having getting in touch with the videographers he knew. "We may be out of luck this late in the game," he said. "Unless you're willing to pay short-notice pricing."

The word *seitan* began to pop from the menu, and being a diploma'd Lit major, I seized upon this detail. I remembered Bernfeld and Oliver's conversation about *The Divine Comedy*, and whether Gil had read it. I hadn't really planned on asking him, not right then anyway, but I did.

"Yes," he said. "All fourteen thousand-some lines of it. The hardest class I ever took."

I'd only read the *Inferno*, the first third of the whole, and mentioned this.

"In my family, it was expected that you know your Dante. A rite of passage, more or less."

I tried to think of an equivalent expectation in my family, but came up short.

"I was a business major, so an upper-level course on Dante was way over my head," he said. "But, I liked it. I managed a C plus."

I didn't feel the need to probe further. I asked Gil to tell me more about the two shows he'd e-mailed me about, and he gave a brief description of the headlining acts: a neo-traditionalist country singer from Houston, the other a soul singer from Detroit, both on big labels and on the rise. I noted the obvious dissimilarity between the two acts.

"The Haugenberrys can open for anybody," Gil said. "I think we should get them in front of everyone we can."

His use of "we" bothered me, and my instinct was to slam on the brakes. Gil seemed to sense this and pulled back a bit.

"This could be huge," he said. "This *will* be huge. It's the most unique, homegrown act I've seen in the thirty years I've been doing this. I'm offering to help—logistically, financially."

I expressed my appreciation, and then sat silent a little longer than I otherwise might have. I wasn't about to enter into any sort of agreement with him, yet, but I could mine him for information and ideas. The recording project was on track, and I had a few video ideas festering. Things needed to happen in a certain order, but maybe I hadn't thought of something.

Our drinks arrived, and I decided to skip the solid-food option. Gil ordered a Caesar salad with seitan. He asked if I'd considered putting a back-up band together.

"No," I said. "That sounds like an unnecessary can-of-worms."

"If you want to next-level this operation, I'd suggest a back-up band," he said. "I can make some calls, unless you have some people in mind."

I knew dozens of musicians, but only a couple I'd consider working with.

"You should look into a few Boulder and Fort Collins shows soon," he continued. "I can help with that. If you plan to do any sort of touring, I know a ton of people. Booking agents, publicists, etcetera. All the way to the top."

This all sounded wonderfully overwhelming. I hadn't considered the possibility of touring with the brothers, as it didn't seem likely they'd be interested, or could physically endure it. The Boulder and Fort Collins shows sounded doable and something we could agree to move on right then.

"What about merch?" he asked. "Do you have any?"

I told him about the T-shirts and posters, which I still needed to re-order.

"I'd suggest at least five different T-shirt designs, tank-tops, maybe a button-down. A couple different posters. A bumper sticker, Koozies, travel mugs, lighters. Hell, there's no end to what you can get branded these days. The more the merrier. It will all sell."

I could get Dan excited about designing all of this, but the up-front costs for a huge merch portfolio were out of my range. This presented itself as maybe what Gil meant by financial assistance.

Gil's salad arrived, and I ordered another vodka cran. We decided to move on the Boulder/Fort Collins shows. He'd contact his people in both cities and put a good word in, and then get me in touch with them. The merch situation seemed like the next thing to tackle, but I wasn't ready to ask Gil for money. Maybe I could find a way of fronting the money, maybe the brothers could chip in.

Conversation got wayward. Halfway into drink number two, I began to worry that I'd reached a certain threshold, so I switched to water. I hadn't gotten any sense from Gil that he was overstepping or attempting to take advantage of me. No evidence whatsoever that he was trying to seduce me or anything in that direction. No coercion, expectations, signs of duplicity. This was counter to all the advice and warnings I'd gotten. I decided to give him the benefit of the doubt henceforth, if he could maintain. I switched back to vodka cran, and tossed out this random rhetorical question:

"Reputations die hard, don't they?"

Gil laughed, sat back and rubbed his eyes. "They don't die at all, as far as I can tell. Maybe I'm impatient."

I wondered about the parameters of my reputation. Did I even have one? I must have something. I asked Gil what he knew, or had heard about me, and the casual turn of attention to me and mine seemed to be a relief to him.

"You're not to be fucked with, is all I've ever heard," he said. "Unless you wish to become a stock character Monday nights at Knights Errant. No thanks!"

Okay. I can work with this guy.

. . .

THE *DENVER POST* article dropped early Friday morning.

Wild Game
An Afternoon with Abe and Dan Haugenberry
by Kyle Nosodosteros | Columnist for the Denver Post

"These [expletive]s are everywhere!" Abe Haugenberry observes, tending to the meat on a portable Weber grill on his front porch. On the afternoon's menu: squirrel.

"The flavor isn't the best, and the texture even worse," adds Dan, Abe's elder brother by two years. "Nothing a little horseradish won't destroy."

You may have seen these two. If you've noticed two giants (Abe 7'1", Dan 7'2") walking South Broadway or the aisles of Home Depot this summer, odds are these are the guys—recently relocated from the Eastern Plains of Colorado to their old family home in the Baker neighborhood, a house they are currently in the process of renovating.

"I stopped at the Lo-Ball for a beer, got to talking to the booker, and a couple weeks later we were up on stage," Abe said, of their Denver debut. "Doing the ol' routine."

I happened to witness this performance: an anarchic mashup of the brothers Marx and Everly, spiraling toward a finale of Greco-Roman wrestling.

"Is it music? Is it comedy? Is it wrestling?" Dan asked, before taking a bite of skewered squirrel. "Of course it is. What else would it be?"

Their professional musical career began in the mid-eighties, on the sidewalk in front of their father's auto parts store in Burlington, CO—Abe age eight, Dan ten.

"We had about an hour's worth of songs, and when we

got through them, we'd take a break, then start all over again," Abe said. "Dad paid us five bucks a set, plus tips."

Word got out, and the brothers soon found themselves performing to a regular Saturday afternoon crowd of tailgaters. "An inclusive cross section of Eastern Coloradans," Abe said. "The regular gearhead customers, town drunks, country drunks, Spanish-speaking families, elderly women in house dresses. We had to get our [expletive] together and learn more songs to keep the people interested."

At this early point in the interview, Dan became violently ill on the front lawn. Abe continued as though nothing was the matter. "The rest of it grew out of boredom, angst, and maybe a little bit of sibling rivalry on Dan's part," Abe said. "I'll throw him under the bus any day of the week."

As the brothers navigated puberty and middle school, wrestling became part of the picture.

"Everybody's always assumed we were basketball players. But our PE teacher only knew how to wrestle. He didn't know [expletive] about basketball. We didn't care. You couldn't keep a ball inflated out there anyway with all the goatheads."

Dan returned to the porch, going for another skewer of squirrel. "What did I miss?"

The brothers went their separate ways after high school, each amassing an impressively diverse array of skill sets including farrier, electrician, hazmat trucker, HVAC technician "and about two dozen other things we aren't certified or licensed to do, but aren't afraid to charge money for," Abe added.

Dan became ill again, making it to the house restroom this time. Abe described their non-existent music career over the next two decades. "I didn't really miss it. It didn't miss me."

The passing of their father earlier this year inspired them to reunite. "The whole mess is cooked into our DNA," he said. "I can't speak for Dan, but I've been away from it long enough that it all feels new. The crowds seem to like it."

They're currently working on their first album, with sound engineer Herb Bernfeld, who currently runs a studio on the Eastern Plains. As for other plans?

"Our manager is a schemer," Abe said, referring to local legend, AJ Washburn, emcee of the long-running Lewd & Learned comedy open-mic at the Knights Errant Tavern. "She's got plans we don't even know about. All I can say is stay tuned."

Dan eventually returned to the porch, sweating profusely, red in the eyes, and pale. He picked up another squirrel from the grill and held it out toward me. "Have one, for cry-eye!" he said. "We've got plenty. Don't be shy."

The Haugenberrys perform at the Purgatory Ballroom, Saturday, August 13th at 9:00 p.m.

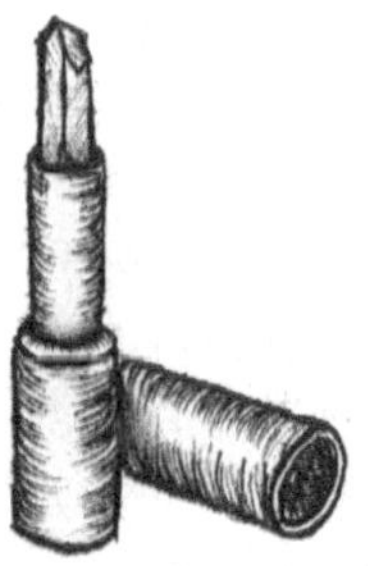

I WITNESSED the entire performance through a two-by-one-and-a-half inch GoPro camera screen, clipped to a handle attachment that resembled an alien proboscis as described in a Vonnegut novel.

The brothers took the stage and the heckling began before the first song.

"You're looking better, Dan!" someone shouted.

"Save the squirrels!" someone else shouted.

Dan adjusted his guitar. "We're on it," Dan said. "We've got a freezer full. Come getcha some."

Abe kicked off the first song: the Dave Edmunds tune that Bernfeld had played for us the previous weekend. They sounded almost too-professional. They'd learned something about mic placement during the recording sessions.

Seals & Crofts' "Hummingbird" was the second song, and they made it through the whole thing with no antics.

Ollie had texted me after we'd returned from Bernfeld's, suggesting the brothers do Harry Nilsson's "Without You." I forwarded it to Abe, not thinking much about it at the time.

They nailed it, all the high notes, and harmonies above the high notes. They ended the song abruptly, catching the audience off guard. A few moments of near silence passed before someone yelled "Well, sonofabitch" and the crowd blew up.

Abe knelt during the applause and began adjusting a sound effects processor foot pedal thingy that he'd added to the fray. Dan called him out on it.

"The fine citizens of Denver didn't come here to watch you dick around with some device," Dan said. "You don't see me checking my cell phone in the middle of the show."

Abe stood up. "This is no mere device," he said. "It's an existential effect box. This button makes you sound like you're trying too hard. This one makes you sound like you're pretending to be Frampton. This one makes you sound like your mother hates you and wishes you were dead. Craigslist. Forty bucks."

I did a quick pan of the crowd nearest the stage. Hirsh and friends were there, overdressed once again. A few faces I recognized from the previous shows, and a cluster of comedy night regulars. Oliver stood at the far end, near where Rikki was operating another GoPro camera. The enormity of the stage and the headlining act's lack of gear made for easy movement. I was mindful not to intrude too much, or impede the crowd's line of sight, but it became impossible after a while.

The brothers sang through one of Bernfeld's songs, and then the antics began—mic stealing, string cutting, unplugging of cables. Abe squirted some lighter fluid around Dan's feet and lit it. Dan spritzed some pepper spray at Abe as he sang "The Air That I Breathe." It was enough of a blast to send Abe backstage for a few minutes to recuperate. Dan made it most of the way through a Lightfoot song before Abe returned, sneaking up on Dan wielding a fire extinguisher. Abe aimed the nozzle at Dan's butt and let it blow full-blast. The force of it was enough to push Dan forward and eventually off the front of the stage.

Dan landed on his feet, but the four-foot drop to the dance floor was enough that he quickly lost his balance and ended up on his back. The neck of his guitar didn't survive the fall. He tossed it aside, and a member of the audience extended his hand to help Dan to his feet. A few others began shouting *fight, fight, fight* until the whole audience of several hundred joined in. Abe hopped down to the dance floor and the match was on.

Abe paused to rub his eyes, still under the influence of the pepper spray, and Dan took advantage of the distraction. Within seconds, Dan had Abe on the floor scrambling every which way. I had a perfect angle on it from the stage. Rikki was on the floor getting close-up footage.

The brothers were now entangled in a way that looked as though they might be waiting for the clock to run out. Abe began looking around in desperation. I realized I'd forgotten the coaches' whistle in my purse backstage. I immediately went for it and rushed back to the stage blowing it as loud as I could several times. It was too late, however. The brothers had already reached some sort of agreement to stop the match and reset. I felt kinda stupid, until I reminded myself of everything else that was going on.

After a few moments of crotch adjusting and stretching, they got into the referee's position, and when they looked ready, I blew the whistle. Within a couple of quick moves, Dan was on his back, arching and kicking. Abe had him in a headlock, from which there was no escape. Abe pulled a tube of lipstick from his back pocket and began spreading it on Dan's face with zero precision. After a few seconds of this, Abe slapped the floor and stood up. I blew the whistle again. Abe helped Dan to his feet and then climbed back up to the stage amid the applause.

"It is what it is," Abe told the crowd. "Should we sing one more?"

The crowd cheered. Dan made a slow climb up to the stage, smearing the lipstick with his shirtsleeve. His guitar resembled poorly-improvised archery equipment.

Abe began singing *a capella*, his guitar hanging at his side.

The song: "He Ain't Heavy (He's My Brother)". More impossibly high notes and harmonies, and the crowd ate it up. Instead of ending the song, they continued to sing as they turned and walked off the stage, a fade-out of sorts.

And that was it. Not quite forty-five minutes of entertainment. Not even close, really, but thirty minutes seemed like the natural lifespan of the act. I powered off the camera and rushed over to the merch table. I'd managed to replenish the supply of T-shirts and posters the previous day, for an additional rush charge. Several people asked to get their posters signed, but the brothers were nowhere to be seen. I sent Rikki off to find them, and while he was away, Hirsh and friends stopped by.

Hirsh asked how the estate sale was going, and I gave him the general update. He seemed pleased with it. I told him to stop over sometime during the upcoming week to see for himself.

"I just had a thought," Hirsh said, handing me a twenty-dollar bill in exchange for a shirt. "My niece is a producer at NBC. I'll get in touch with her and put in a good word. Maybe she can do something for you."

Hirsh certainly had a way of dropping life-changing news on me from the opposite side of a merch table. His record so far was an undisputed 1-0, so I had a slightly elevated inclination to get excited about this new possibility.

"Please do. I would be forever indebted."

He asked what we had online that he could send to his niece. I mentioned the Lo-Ball video, but suggested we wait until Rikki had the Purgatory video processed. He agreed, and I said I'd keep him updated. Without Rikki there to confirm, I estimated a week at most to have a final edit online.

The brothers eventually made their way to the table, impeded by several fans wanting a handshake, fist-bump, or a high-five. High-fives from a normal-sized person are an awkward proposition for a giant. If you recall Diana Ross and the Supremes' choreography for "Stop in the Name of Love", then that's what we're looking at. They entertained all requests, nonetheless.

They signed posters, and we sold out before the headliner took the stage, so we headed for the green room. It was time to take a load off.

Gil was there, speaking with the headliner's tour manager. Some sort of crisis was in progress. I inquired, and the tour manager said a vagrant had snuck onto their tour bus and passed out on a bench. The debate was whether to call an ambulance.

"I don't want cops sniffing around in there," the tour manager said.

"And I don't want cops anywhere near this place at any time," Gil said, scrolling on his phone, before turning to the brothers as though a revelation had presented itself. "What do you fellas charge for vagrant removal services?"

The brothers looked at each other and laughed. "Let's go have a look," Abe said.

We followed the tour manager out to the alley. He opened the bus door to assess the current situation.

"I'm guessing two-fifty, three hundred pounds, reeks of piss and schnapps," he said. "See what you think."

The brothers climbed into the bus and out of my line of sight. One of them started clapping and whooping, and the other joined in, at a volume no one could possibly sleep through. This went on for about a minute before Abe descended the stairs.

"Well," he said. "I once saved a cow stuck belly deep in mud, but never anything like this. Do you have any rope?"

Within minutes, Gil appeared with a roll of twine. It wasn't going to do. Abe suggested a heavy-duty extension cord, and after another few minutes, Gil appeared with a thick blaze orange cord. "Is twenty-five feet going to be enough?" he asked.

I managed a quick peek at the situation as Dan lifted and Abe ran the cable around the vagrant's arms, shoulders, and chest. It looked impossible in every way, and the odor was aggressive enough to force me out to the alley to avoid retching. The brothers followed soon after. The vagrant had apparently shit himself but was still breathing faintly.

"Now for the hard part," Abe said.

After much struggle, and several breaks for fresh air, they had the man to the front of the bus, ready to turn the corner and down the three steps to the ground. Gil and Rikki were at opposite ends of the alleyway on police lookout. Just as the vagrant's head and shoulders poked out of the bus, Rikki called my phone, alerting me that there was a cop circling the block, slowly, as though he were looking for something to do. I told the brothers.

"Let's get a move on then," Dan said. "No time for delicate moves."

Abe heaved backwards and Dan lifted and shoved the vagrant's legs until the body rolled out onto the rough, pothole-strewn asphalt.

"Let's drag him over by the fence," Dan said.

Moans and unintelligible verbiage came from the vagrant during the roll. The brothers were able to position the man so he was sitting upright against the chain link fence. Abe removed the extension cord harness, noting the pain the vagrant would experience when he regained consciousness: cuts, contusions, abrasions, possible dislocations and head trauma.

The vagrant was off the bus, so mission accomplished, but now what to do with him?

I called Gil and Rikki back from police watch, and without any debate, we decided to go back inside the venue to avoid attracting attention. I volunteered to call the paramedics, but not before the tour manager finished his attempt to purge the stench from the bus's interior.

I was into my second bottle of beer when the tour manager finally joined us in the green room. He went straight for the fridge, wiping his brow with his forearm. "I should've let those Peter Pans deal with this," he said, pointing in the direction of the stage. "You'd think that would be enough to teach them not to leave the bus unlocked, but you'd be wrong. Wrong, wrong, wrong."

Rikki nudged me, reminding me to call the paramedics, and so I did. After giving the dispatcher the location, and a completely plausible but heavily finessed account of the situation, she began asking questions that I couldn't answer without being at the vagrant's side. I left the green room and walked down the hall toward the back door with Rikki following. The music from the stage was loud enough that I asked the dispatcher to wait until I could get to a quieter spot.

I opened the back door and stepped out to the poorly lit alley. The vagrant should've been sitting directly in front of me, twenty feet away, but there was no sign of him.

"Are you still there?" the dispatcher asked.

Rikki and I took off in opposite directions, frantically searching for the guy, assuming he couldn't have wandered too far. Rikki had made it to one end of the alley and back and was now running to the other end.

"Are you still there?" the dispatcher asked.

I asked her to hold a moment as I looked behind the dumpsters and various bins and sheds in the immediate vicinity. Nothing. Rikki had reached the end of the alley and was now walking back toward me, with nothing to report, I assumed.

"Huh," I said to the dispatcher. "False alarm I guess."

She continued to ask questions, and I answered a few

before abruptly ending the call mid-sentence. The vagrant was gone, and the matter was off my hands.

Rikki and I returned to the green room.

"Are they on their way?" Abe asked.

"He's gone," I said.

"Dead?"

"Not there. Disappeared. Poof!"

No one believed me, even with Rikki to back up my account, and so everyone had to go see for themselves. Everyone but Gil, who remained sitting on a couch drinking a beer, amused by the whole situation. He turned to me.

"You're a comedian," he began. "Are you familiar with the term *comedy damage*?"

"Yes," I said.

"I've got *club owner damage*," he said. "Nothing affects me anymore. Not like it should."

I could relate.

"That entire situation could—*should have*—been handled differently," he continued. "The thing is, I knew that, and could have led that charge. We should've gotten the paramedics here right away, and had the pros deal with it. That would've been the more-ethical thing to do."

He took a drink of beer. "Instead, because of my club owner damage, I stepped back, looked at the bizarre set of variables involved, and chose to push for the alternative, which unfolded as it did. It was an almost perverted display of self-interest on my part."

He paused a moment, but didn't seem to be finished with his point, so I withheld comment.

"It was a more-amusing alternative. Impossible without those two giants. And so, we'll all walk away from this with a more interesting story to tell. But at whose expense? Maybe no one's. What would a couple of paramedics of average strength have done any differently?"

The thoughtful, confessional, philosophical side of Gil was blowing my mind. Here we were, less than a song removed from the episode, and he had an almost omniscient assessment of it at the ready.

"And now I'm sitting here rambling on and on. Club owner damage. The bum has disappeared. Am I concerned about his well-being? Yes I am," he said, standing from the couch. "But what can any of us do now? Nothing whatsoever."

He grabbed another beer, excusing himself to check on the box office.

"He'll turn up," he said.

THE *DENVER POST* article turned out to be a game-changer. By noon Monday, I had talent buyers from all the bigger venues and festivals across the state contacting me. I called Gil and he helped filter out the crap and criminals and prioritize what remained.

The most pressing opportunity was a Friday night main-stage opener at the Colorado State Fair only three weeks away. I replied with a yes, without having consulted the brothers. Surely, they wouldn't pass on that one, but it was clear that a sit-down meeting needed to happen to address gig offers, merch, and the idea of assembling a back-up band. I called Abe and left a message, then called Rikki and left a message.

MONDAY NIGHT, every business in a two-block radius from Knights Errant was closed due to a water main break and a power outage caused by the repair of the water main break. No one from the bar had bothered to call me, so I had to find out by going down there and seeing for myself. Not much to see, and even less to do aside from standing around looking useless, so I left.

I hadn't yet heard from Abe, so I decided to pay the brothers a visit. I parked across the street and could see Dan working at the drafting table. He noticed me and we met on the porch.

"The weekend proved to be too much for poor Abe," he said. "He's been down since yesterday."

"Down?"

"Probably something he picked up from that bum."

I noticed he was drinking a beer, on a Monday, which was a departure from long-standing tradition. He offered one to me, then walked to the kitchen. I snuck a quick glance at the ink drawing in-progress on the drafting table—a finely-detailed rendering of hundreds of paper matchbooks, as though someone had spilled a collection onto the paper. Dan caught me looking.

"Dad used to collect 'em," he said. "Every motel, gas

station, or restaurant he ever went to. There's four tubs of them out at the old place."

I asked him if he collected anything.

"No," he said, handing me the beer. "I've become philosophically opposed to collecting. The burden it puts on those you leave in your wake. What am I supposed to do with four tubs of matchbooks? Why me lord?"

I mentioned having a compact disc collection of about two hundred back in the early aughts. "All of it stolen from my car."

"Ouch."

"I never bought another CD," I said, taking a sip. "You might say I have a shoe collection, but that doesn't make me special."

"There are a lot of things that make you special, AJ," he said.

"What exactly do you mean by *special*," I said. "That's a loaded term."

"Yes, it is."

"It can be interpreted many different ways."

"Yes, it can."

"The mind tends to gravitate toward the less-flattering interpretations."

"Ooh, now you're onto something."

"Do you guys want to play the state fair?" I asked. "I already told them yes."

"When is it?"

"And we need to get four more T-shirt designs ready, and a logo for stickers, maybe some matchbooks. Maybe by the end of the weekend. Are you up to the task?"

Dan looked amused. "Sure."

I listed a half dozen of the venues and festivals that had contacted me. "And that's just for starters. What do you want me to tell them?"

"Let's do all of it," Dan said, without hesitation.

"Don't you think we should check with Abe first?"

"No."

"We should probably—"

Dan shook his head. "I know his schedule. It's the same as mine until we finish this house."

That was good enough for the time being, though I would confirm with Abe before agreeing to anything else. Our conversation seemed to set off an *ah-ha* moment for Dan, and he turned his attention back to his drawing. "The iron is hot, AJ. The iron is *hot*. That's what makes you special."

"The iron?"

"No, the heat."

"Oh, you stop it."

Had I just been hit on?

WHAT REMAINED of Marc's furniture sold at a rate of about one piece or set per day, slow enough to nudge me toward starting in on the autographs. I followed Walt's suggestion and began with the US presidents, and by mid-week had thirty pieces listed, from Biden back to LBJ. I could manage about fifteen listings per day before burnout set in and things got sloppy. At that rate, I estimated it would take the rest of my lifetime to list all the pieces individually. I needed a different plan.

Oliver came by to look at the records and audio equipment. He went straight for Marc's turntable.

"Wow," he said. "I've never actually seen one of these in the wild. A two-armed turntable. There it sits, almost mocking me."

He showed me how to operate it without setting off a Rube Goldberg machine of death and destruction. I asked why anyone would need a record player with two arms, and he explained one arm was for stereo, the other for mono. He didn't stop there, but that's all I really wanted to know. Jargon never sent my panties flying across a room.

We went downstairs, and I watched him flip through the first twenty or so albums. He offered to buy the whole collection right then. I wasn't sure he was serious, and he soon relieved my uncertainty. "I wish," he said. "I'd need to take out a second mortgage."

I had enough to do already, and no expertise with records, so negotiations took seconds. We came to the agreement that he'd grade and list the records for a ten percent cut, and he left with three tote bags of albums to take back to his shop.

Abe contacted me Wednesday morning, "feeling about eighty percent" he said, and good enough to head out to Bernfeld's that weekend to finish the recording. Dan had been drawing non-stop since my visit, having three T-shirt designs ready, the matchbook poster, and a few different logos. "We've gotten nothing done on the house in the meantime," he added.

We decided there was no good reason for me to accompany them to Bernfeld's. My back wouldn't survive the trip, and I wasn't necessary anyway. That, and I had a feeling I'd soon be visited by Hirsh and needed to show some due diligence with the sale. I was correct. He stopped over Friday, unannounced, in his jogging clothes.

"My, my. It's looking empty in here," he said.

"Kinda sad and lonely. I should've started with the small stuff."

He asked how things were going and I launched into more detail than was necessary. It didn't take more than a few minutes of TMI before I could see his interest waning.

"I contacted my niece," he said, inspecting some of the presidential autographs spread atop the kitchen island, "about an unrelated matter, but I talked up the brothers. I've got her interested."

We had agreed to wait until the new video edits were done before contacting the niece, and I almost mentioned it, mildly frustrated that our first impression on the niece might be less than perfect. There was no way to communicate this to Hirsh without sounding like an entitled, whiny bitch, so I held my tongue.

"And the Knights Errant is officially up for sale," Hirsh said, before doing some trunk-twister stretches. "That's the big news of the day."

"No way," I said, disheartened and a bit panicky, realizing my safety net was threatened. "How much? I can probably make it to the bank before they close."

"We're still working on that," he said. I asked if Charlie had any prospective buyers in mind.

"I'm not aware of anyone specific," Hirsh said. "I was hoping you might have some ideas. It would be nice to keep that place *in the family* as they say."

Gil was the first person that came to mind. Maybe the owner of the Lo-Ball, though he was barely an acquaintance.

"We've got a week or two before the MLS listing goes up," Hirsh said. "So, there's time to put some feelers out."

"I'll get right on that," I said, following him onto the porch.

"If you do find someone, have them contact me for now."

The almost inevitable scenario played out in my mind. The building would be sold to an out-of-state investor, scraped, and replaced by a T-Mobile store. I'm a huge fan of progress and change, in theory, but this wasn't going to do. Not in my backyard.

GIL and I met at the Knights Errant at noon the next day. One doesn't go there to "lunch" unless frozen pizza is your thing, or you prefer to drink your calories. I ordered a beer. Gil got a Diet Coke, noting he had a fifteen-hour workday ahead at the ballroom. He seemed preoccupied and antsy, so I skipped the small talk.

"I'm going to need you to buy this place," I said, remembering Ollie's comment about Gil's fundraising capabilities.

He stopped mid-sip on his soda, and looked at me, one eyebrow raised.

"It's up for sale in a couple weeks," I said. "And you know what that means in this part of town."

He laughed. "And you just want me to write a check?"

"Or Venmo." I placed my hands flat on the table and looked him straight in the eyes. "Now, I know what you're thinking."

"I wouldn't be surprised if you did!"

"It wouldn't exactly be *scaling up*."

"It would be a thousand more things to do."

"The building does need some work."

"I was hoping to get *out* of the nightclub business, not more into it."

"You'd be preserving a historical landmark."

"Hm."

"Just imagine, two years from now, you're driving by this spot, you're gonna look over and see a shiny new plastic Verizon Wireless store. You're gonna do a facepalm."

"A facepalm?"

I demonstrated the term in question. "Just like that."

He wasn't jumping at the opportunity like I half-expected him to. I didn't necessarily wish to become more involved with the business, but I knew I was the only person who could lead the charge to preserve it, so I got a little ahead of myself.

"How about you buy it, and I'll manage it. A partnership. Or we could co-own it, however that might work out. I could probably scrape something together. Donate some plasma, maybe work the streets a bit."

He looked slightly more interested in the partnership scenario, humming a little melody to himself and stabbing ice cubes with his straw as he mulled it over. I offered to put him in touch with Hirsh to get the details as they developed.

"Asking price hasn't been finalized," I said.

"I'm sure it will be offensive."

I suggested we might receive a "friends and family" deal, though I wasn't feeling too optimistic. Charlie wasn't susceptible to appeals of any kind when anything more than the cost of a single beer was on the line.

"So, what do you think, if the price isn't too ridiculous."

He thought for a moment, checked his watch, then stood from the booth, announcing his departure. "Would you be satisfied with a hard *maybe*?"

"I'll take it."

I called Dad as I drove back to my apartment. It'd been a few weeks since I'd checked on him. He didn't have any plans, so I packed a bag and made the trip, anticipating an overnighter.

He was in his usual spot when I entered the kitchen. The

sink was clean, and the concentration of air freshener was still noticeable, meaning the house cleaner had recently departed. Dad turned off the TV and stood from his chair.

"Well, sweetie. What have you gotten yourself into this week?" he asked.

"Do you want to buy a moderately successful Capitol Hill gay bar?"

"I wasn't planning on it."

I shared the limited information I had, and my predictions. "So, as of yesterday I'm in the historic landmark preservation business."

He listed all my ongoing projects as he understood them. "I'd say your plate is full."

"A plate is too small. One of those old fiberglass cafeteria trays maybe."

He suggested we go for a walk around the property before the rain started. I helped him out the door and down the steps to the driveway. "I can manage from here," he said. I opened the gate to the back acreage, and he slowly passed through.

"Do you know what a pizzle is?" he asked, pausing to inspect his cane.

"Not ringing a bell."

"The pecker of a bull," he said. "They make walking sticks out of them. Maybe I need to get one of those. Where do you suppose I'd find a pizzle cane?"

"Anything can be found online," I said. "If you prefer to buy local, there's Arvada Pizzle, or Littleton Pizzle Warehouse. There's more. Depends on the kind of shopping experience you prefer."

He veered to the left and gradually picked up the pace. "Speaking of giant peckers," he said. "How are your brothers doing? I read the article."

"Dad!"

He laughed. "Are you dating one of them yet?"

"I need to bring you to Grease Monkey to get your filters replaced."

"I've always done my own maintenance," he said. "Those assholes just want to up-sell you."

"No, I am not dating one of them. Strictly business."

"If you were to date one of them, which would you choose?"

"Dad!"

"From the article, it sounds like Dan might not have the stronger constitution. He sounds a bit sickly."

"That vomiting act was just a prank. They're always messing with people."

I told him about the episode with the flag peddler as we walked around the pond, both of us gathering bits of trash that'd blown in.

"Are they serious men?" he asked.

After twenty-five years of bringing boys home to Dad, I knew to expect this question, or some variation of it. "Absolutely," I said. "Professional, reliable, accountable."

"Would they take a bullet for you?"

"I haven't asked."

"Are they religious?"

"Not that I'm aware of."

"How are they at compartmentalization?"

I laughed, imagining myself on a blind date with some unwitting suitor and asking this before the waters and menus arrived. "That's a profound question."

"It does cut to the chase."

"Are you asking if they're well-adjusted?"

"Sure."

"As far as I can tell," I said. "Dan is the darker of the two. He's had some traumas. Slightly more introverted and unpredictable."

"And you're sure neither one has ever been married?"

"It's never come up. I'm sure it would have if it made any difference."

"How are they financially?"

"They both drive enormous, fairly new pickup trucks."

"I don't imagine they fit comfortably in anything else."

"That's true," I said, reminded of the cramped drive to Bernfeld's and back. I told him what little I knew aside from their pickups: the house in Denver, their parents' square mile of middle-of-nowhereness, and a couple other rental properties out east. "They seem to be doing pretty well. You don't ever hear them complain about being broke."

"You know who likes to complain about being broke?"

"Who?"

"Rich people."

"Oh, I knew that."

Dad stopped at one of the large rocks on the north side of the pond and sat down. "Here's what I'm thinking," he began. "You're what—forty-three, forty-four years old?"

"Sure am," I said, knowing exactly where this conversation was headed. I'd amassed two fists of trash but had nowhere to put it until we got back to the house. My bra was already full.

"You need to start thinking about your security," he said.

"C'mon, Dad. You know I think about that stuff all the time."

"These brothers sound decent. Why don't you snatch one of them up?"

"Snatch."

"Why not? You get along fine, they've got a sense of humor. What more do you want?"

"I don't know," I said, sitting on another large rock. "Things just don't seem to be moving that way."

"Moving what way."

"Chemistry. Mother Nature. Cupid."

"Maybe you need to be the one to pull the trigger."

"I haven't exactly walked through life assuming people are physically attracted to me."

"Oh, don't be ridiculous. Where did you get that idea?"

"Do you have all day?"

He pulled a can of chewing tobacco from his slacks pocket. "Okay, that's an erroneous position to start from, but let's start there anyway," he began, putting a pinch in his mouth. "You assume they're not attracted to you. You have no evidence that they are, or might be. That doesn't mean they aren't."

"So?"

"Make a leap of faith."

"Wait a minute," I said, shaking my head. "Who says I'm even attracted to them in that way?"

"They're handsome fellas! Abe reminds me of Clint Walker. Remember him? From the old TV show *Cheyenne.*"

"I have no idea."

"Dan, well, he looks like, I don't know. Clint Walker's older brother."

"Clint with a silent *N.* It seems wise to keep this a strictly business relationship for now. I don't want to mess things up."

Dad stuck out his index finger for emphasis. "However, there are limits to human reason."

"What?"

"You're being too rational, AJ."

"What kind of dad says that to their daughter."

"You've always over-learned your lessons. You need to mix things up a little."

"Ha."

"Just put a little something out there, something you can back out of in a hurry if need be."

"I'll think about it," I said, anxious to change the subject. "I'll keep you abreast. Not that there's anything to see here."

The thought of dating one of the brothers had been simmering the whole time. Abe was the obvious choice, as he seemed to be more receptive and affable toward me. Not that Dan made me feel like a nuisance, he was just more aloof, less present.

I remembered Rikki's summation of things, that the brothers seemed to be of a different species. There was truth to this, especially early on, but as I'd spent more time with them, it had become a less-convincing excuse. Maybe, just maybe, I'd think about trying to tear Abe away from the house alone for some kind of date. But when? What was the hurry?

Dad and I put in a solid hour of light yard work before the rain started. Not a heavy rain, but enough to suggest we stop what we were doing and shift our focus. Dad's focus shifted to bourbon. I found a bottle of chardonnay in the garage fridge that Dad couldn't explain but assumed was purchased by Mom and forgotten about. We eventually settled on the back patio overlooking the pond and meadow. Dad asked about the Knights Errant, and if I thought it would be worth the investment.

"A person could make a modest living off of that place," I said. "But that person isn't me."

"And why is that?"

"I don't have a million dollars, for one, and even if I did, owning a bar doesn't seem to be my destiny."

Dad laughed. "And you think you have control over that?"

"You can control what you can avoid. Am I right?"

He thought for a moment, taking a sip of bourbon. "Maybe you're the right person at the right time."

"I appreciate your optimism, but I just don't think I'm the gal for the job."

"Why don't you and I go have a look at the place tomorrow."

"Dad."

"Why not?"

"I wasn't serious when I asked you about buying the place."

"I know," he said. "You would've had a full business proposal printed out for me if you were. Let's just go have a look anyway. It won't hurt."

I conceded, for the time being, assuming he might feel differently when the time came to actually leave the house and make the drive. This led to a discussion of ways of making the business more successful. I had over ten years' worth of ideas pent up, and once my passionately elocuted list was exhausted, it occurred to me that I'd just sold myself as the right person for the job.

"Not that I'd want to be the one to do all of that," I said.

"I don't know, AJ. Who else is going to do it?"

Dad has a nostalgic tie to processed meat products dispensed from blister packs. I made him a bologna sandwich for dinner, and without warning, he was asleep in his recliner before seven. I thought to leave a note and drive back to Denver, as it was early enough to put some sort of Saturday night together. There wasn't much to do at Dad's place other than watch television or read *Shōgun*.

I wrote the note and went for my car, but guilt set in before I turned the key. If he woke up and I wasn't there, it would seem to him that I was rejecting his offer to take our trip in the morning. This would be a disappointment and would probably make him feel sad and abandoned. However attached to the idea he was, it was a source of excitement for him, and these were few and far between. I had to follow through.

Who was this Clint Walker fella? I had my laptop, so I returned to the patio and did an internet search. Boom. Dozens of mostly black-and-white images appeared. The resemblance was there. Clint also resembled Joaquin Phoenix and vise-versa, but I don't know that I'd compare Abe to Mr. Phoenix too closely.

I finished the bottle of chard and started another. After much digging, I found some episodes of *Cheyenne* online, and so I watched, misty, imagining Abe wandering the American West, dishing out frontier justice in the days after the Civil War.

DAD WOKE ME EARLY, informing me that he wasn't up to the task of making our trip to Denver that day. He didn't provide a specific reason, nor did I ask for one, as I was relieved our trip was off. "Maybe I need to switch to beer," he said, as he headed back toward the kitchen.

Waking up in the bedroom of your youth is an experience unique to itself. One could spend an excessive amount of time laying there reminiscing, remembering the Def Leppard and Mötley Crüe posters that once hung from the walls and ceiling, all the life-changing phone calls made or received while leaning against the headboard, thinking about the boys one may or may not have slept with in that bed when parents were out of town. One *could* do this, but not me. I sat up, noticeably hungover and dry-mouthed, ready to take on the day.

There was nothing to take on, however, just an infinite expanse of optional, non-pressing crap, and none of it enticing. The brothers were out at Bernfeld's and were unreachable. Gil had probably just gone to sleep, and there were no pending e-mails regarding Marc's furniture. Maybe I'd check in on Rikki, or drop by the record shop, but probably not.

It was going to be a day branded by the icy-hot iron of Nihilism, devoid of meaning—a concept that would have to wait until another, less-meaningless day. Dad and I agreed to reschedule our trip for the next weekend, and I left.

I'd just unlocked the door to my apartment when Abe called. I answered without hesitation, hoping it might turn my day around.

"How'd the recording go?" I asked.

"This is Dan. We're about an hour out. Abe isn't doing well."

There was phone noise and the usual cutting out. I held my phone out to check the time. Nine o'clock, which meant they'd left Bernfeld's sometime around six.

"The appendix is on the right side of the body, correct?" Dan asked.

"Yes, down by the hip bone."

"That's what I thought. It's not that then. He can't even keep water down."

Dan asked about hospitals, and I told him where I would go, which was in Aurora, on the east side of Denver, and closest to where they probably were.

"I'll keep you updated," he said, and hung up.

I would've been okay with a little more information, but that was it for the time being. Dan was probably driving a hundred miles an hour and under threat of being vomited on, so maybe he didn't need to be fussing with a smartphone.

Marc's house is twenty minutes closer to the hospital than my apartment, so I headed over there and waited. I couldn't muster enough ambition to do any work on the autographs or anything else, so I took a walk and found an antique store to wander through. Knights Errant opened at noon, and so that's where I found myself. Charlie was there, replacing a hose on the soda gun. It was the first time I'd seen him since learning about the sale, and I mentioned it.

"Appraiser is coming tomorrow, so I should have an idea in a few days, I suspect," he said.

"What are you going to do with yourself?"

"Moving to Boise. That's where the grandkids are."

"I've got a couple potential buyers," I said, before mentioning Gil. Charlie knew of him, but they'd never met. "And Roger Washburn. You're from Broomfield. You remember that guy?"

"I don't believe so."

"He was an administrator at the Rocky Flats plant back in the day. He was all over the news when the FBI raided the place."

"Interesting. What's he want with an old dump like this?"

"I think he wants to buy it for his daughter so she has something to do."

"Ha. Where did you find this guy?"

"He's my dad."

"Ah," he said. "I'd love to pass this place on to someone I know, but I need to take the highest offer."

"Of course."

So the friends-and-family deal was off the table. Not much else could be decided or moved on until the price was determined. If I could get a ballpark figure, then at least I'd have something to get Gil or Dad mentally prepared for. I asked Charlie if he had such a figure bouncing around his head.

"One to one-point-two million," he said. "Possibly more."

I'd made it back to Marc's front porch and was resting my eyes when Dan called. They were settled into a room. Abe was on an IV drip and was knocked out on morphine. Pancreatitis.

"He's more or less stable," Dan said. "Nothing too urgent, apparently, judging by how slow things are moving around here."

This seemed like comforting news.

"We all ate the same things," Dan said. "Abe hasn't had any beers since last weekend. They assumed this was alcohol related."

More tests were being ordered, including an ultrasound. "If that's all it is, he'll probably be in here four or five days."

I asked permission to visit, though I was already in my car, ready to pull out of my parking spot.

"Next of kin only," Dan said. "Why, and for how long, I don't know."

"Well, that's some horseshit." I turned off my car and began walking back to the porch.

"The good news is we pretty much finished the recording," Dan said. "We were planning on redoing a couple little spots today, but then this."

I'd confirmed two more shows that week, both several weeks away, so there was plenty of time for Abe to recover. If he was looking at four or five days in the hospital, then there was no reason to cancel or reschedule. We talked a bit more about the recording, until a nurse entered the room, and Dan said he had to go.

"I have a hunch our wrestling days are over," he said. "Just a hunch."

"I thought that might be the case."

"I hope that doesn't void any contracts."

"Nah," I said. "It's just...well, just a bummer."

"We'll make up for it."

AN E-MAIL NOTIFICATION beeped on my phone first thing Monday, and in an effort to open my laptop as fast as possible, I knocked over a coffee mug, sending eight ounces of aggressive stain-causing Colombian Blend across the island in all directions—a model-train-scale tsunami of Juan Valdez. The only things that stood in its way were a salt and pepper shaker, and a spread of documents containing the autographs of James Madison, Thomas Jefferson, John Adams, and George Washington.

Fortunately, they were all mostly-enclosed in Mylar envelopes. The tops of the envelopes weren't sealed, however, allowing a small amount of coffee to intrude. I panicked, peeling each of them from the granite, shaking them dry. When the crisis was over, James Madison was the only casualty, the handwritten letter suffering a small stain in its upper right corner.

This is why we can't have nice things. There was no reason for me to mention this episode to anyone, ever, I decided.

All of this because of a routine e-mail notification.

It turned out to be the opposite of a routine e-mail, however, from someone named Jessica Hirsh. I opened it and was immediately drawn to the NBC peacock insignia at the bottom of the message. It was brief, simply stating that her uncle Don had turned her on to the Haugenberry act, and that she loved it. Please give her a call at my convenience.

The autographs and envelopes needed to leave the room first thing. There was no telling what kind of spasmodic behaviors my body was capable of in the face of game-changing news. I placed them back in the safe and went to the front porch.

This phone call required mental preparation and instant access to information real and imaginary. I brought up the Haugenberry website and was surprised to find some of the Purgatory footage uploaded. I watched a few minutes of it, just to get the gist. It was superior to the Lo-Ball footage in some ways but lacked much of the chaos and unpolished charm. I assumed Jessica had watched both and could make up her own mind about it.

I called, and she answered within a couple of rings. Her voice was deeper than expected. After some brief intros and niceties, she got to the point.

"This stuff is gold!" she said. "And that *Denver Post* write-up. More gold."

It sounded like a compliment, but it seemed odd to thank her, so I just agreed with her.

"You can't *not* watch it once it gets going," I said.

"I'd love to see this in person."

I mentioned the next gig on the schedule, only a few weeks away. "If you're into state fairs."

"Oh, the smells!" she said.

"And the belt buckles."

"Anyway," she said. "There are a few challenges here. Time format for one. Is there a way to condense this into a four-minute time slot?"

I'd thought about this a hundred times probably, all of it adding up to nothing. "That's not something we've had to do yet, but anything is possible with these two."

"And the element of surprise, let's just call it that—how much of their act is planned?"

"They don't tell me."

"The NBC legal department doesn't like surprises."

I asked for some clarification.

"If a hairspray can explodes or a cameraman gets blinded by fire extinguisher dust, it's my job on the line."

She'd seen both videos.

"Understood," I said.

"Do you have a record to promote?"

"We do, actually," I said, reaching for some imaginary numbers. "We're planning a mid-September release date."

"Great. Well, if you can get a four-minute condensed version to me, then I think, I *hope* we'll be in business."

"We're on it."

"Jimmy's seen the videos. He's a fan. I think we just need to groom and finesse a bit, without it seeming groomed and finessed."

Jimmy Fallon, I assumed. There was no way of asking for confirmation of this without sounding like a celebrity-obsessed fangirl, so I let it ride. I mentioned Abe being out of town in place of him being in the hospital—too sad-sounding—but we could get a video demo to her in a couple of weeks. With no further ado, we thanked each other and said our goodbyes.

I stood from the patio chaise, walked to the edge of the stairs and howled. Two *woooos*, the second one slightly shorter than the first.

The brothers needed to hear this news immediately. So, I called Dan, and just started talking without asking about Abe's well-being.

"I just got off the phone with a *Tonight Show* producer," I said. "You guys wanna be on the *Tonight Show*? Of course you do. We need to get a four-minute demo video together."

No response from Dan, whatsoever.

"Hello?" I said.

"You'd better come up here," Dan said.

"Is everything okay? Will they let me in the room?"

"Just come up here."

I left Marc's house immediately, failing to set the alarm, or bring my laptop inside.

I could tell the news wasn't going to be good, there was just no way, and no use being Pollyannish about it. The bipolarity of my emotions had me completely disoriented. I probably shouldn't have been driving, as things like stop signs and stop lights didn't seem to have the same effect they usually do.

I parked and went through security where they gave me a face mask and the room number. The anxiety and dread brought on short spells of light-headedness. I had to hold onto the rail in the elevator I shared with a young boy in a wheelchair, obviously in much worse shape than I. All of this was peppered by fantasies of walking through the doors of 30 Rockefeller and how the Haugenberrys' four-minute *Tonight Show* appearance might unfold. It was a weird, wayward train of thoughts, if you could call it a train. More like a pack of clowns on roller-skates playing grabass.

I knocked on the door and waited. Dan eventually answered, having assumed I was just going to give a warning knock and walk in like nurses do. Abe was sleeping, his feet hanging off the bed a couple inches. I'd last seen him a mere eight days previous and he was noticeably off-color and thinner. Dan looked fatigued, puffy around the eyes.

"Well, what do we do," he said. "Go for a walk?"

"Whatever you want."

"Abe's in and out. Fifteen minutes on, an hour off, ten minutes on, three hours off. I need some fresh air."

We went for the elevators. Dan wasn't ready to tell me. Instead, he asked about my conversation with Jessica the NBC producer, and there was just enough info about that to get us outside and into a park-like area with flower gardens and fountains. We found a pair of benches, facing each other, and sat.

Dan took a deep breath, looking at the sky.

"Wow," he said. "*The Tonight Show*. Abe will get a kick out of that. Dad used to let us stay up late to watch Johnny Carson. He considered it a part of our formal education."

"I remember his final show, with Bette Midler. I bawled my eyes out."

"Oh, yes. If I'd been watching alone, I would have bawled my eyes out too," he said, shifting his weight. "But, of course, a boy couldn't do that back then."

This brought on a few moments of contemplative silence. I happened to know quite a bit about both Johnny and Bette, having been significantly moved by the aforementioned episode, which led to further research into their careers. This didn't seem like the time to sound like a know-it-all, so I just let the traffic noise do its thing. Canada geese lurked behind Dan, as he shifted his weight again.

"It's bad, AJ," he began. "I'm sure you've guessed that already. We wouldn't be sitting here."

"I'm prepared. Cancer, I'm guessing."

"Late, late."

"Pancreas?"

"And its neighbors. He's looking at months. And that's with chemo and whatever other snake oil they can pour on it," he said.

"Ugh."

"Maybe we can get Stevie Nicks to stop by to burn some shit and do a little dance."

There's a time to laugh, but maybe this wasn't one of those times. I couldn't help it. "I'll get the Make-A-Wish Foundation on the phone right now."

"Anyway, he's going to want you around," Dan said. "You make him laugh and he trusts you."

This was the moment my stomach finally dropped all the way to the floor. My dad's voice echoed in my head. *What more do you want?* it said.

"Hell, I'm surprised he hasn't asked you out already," Dan said.

I didn't know how to respond to this voluntarily, though my adrenal gland kicked into action—that ol' playground feeling you get when you find out a boy likes you. I just stared blankly at the flower garden.

"Anyway, that's the deal," Dan said.

His eyes wandered for a moment, then he stood and turned his attention to the geese. "What the fuck you looking at!" he shouted, stomping one foot forward quickly, as though he were trying to psych the geese out. They didn't flinch, so Dan ran straight through the middle of them. The birds fled in every direction, all worked up, looking like they might faint from all the fuss. Dan focused on one of the larger birds, chasing it twenty or thirty yards until they both gave up, as though an imaginary ball had gone out of bounds.

Abe was still knocked out when we returned to the room. The TV was on, which meant he'd been awake for some amount of time while we were gone.

"We haven't gotten too far in discussions about the future," Dan said. "He doesn't stay awake long enough and can barely talk when he *is* awake."

It was nearing lunchtime, so I offered to get some take-out. As we discussed our options, a doctor and nurse entered, announcing the immediate need for surgery. A tumor was obstructing Abe's pancreatic duct.

Everything moved quickly after that. Dan signed some forms on a tablet, and Abe was rolling down the hallway within five minutes. The surgery would take two or three hours, depending on what they found. Dan asked when Abe might be able to go home.

"Too early to say," the doc said.

After a couple minutes of sitting in the room with nothing to do, Dan suggested we leave the hospital for a while.

So, we did, in Dan's truck. We didn't have a destination, not one that I was aware of. We drove west on Colfax, and I suggested some things I thought Dan might want to do, maybe go to a record store, or a movie, or a restaurant. None of it interested him.

"How about a dive bar," he said. "With air conditioning and dim lights."

I knew just the place. Neither brother had been to Knights Errant. Had I somehow neglected to invite them to comedy night? I couldn't remember.

The barroom was empty except for the bartender, another new hire. I guessed she was probably in her mid-twenties, with sleeve tattoos, multiple piercings, and shoulder-length hair of many colors. Dan commented on this as we sat in the poorly lit back corner booth.

"I don't get any of it," he said. "Looks like she's been through the spank line of a hundred native tribes. And the hair—you need to be careful with the hair dye. That's an Easter egg decorating catastrophe."

The ghost of George Haugenberry perhaps? I decided to let him go off on any tangent he wished. There was plenty of time to deal with the pressing issues. When he was ready to go there, we'd go there, and we got there sometime into my second pint, and his third pitcher.

"I've got some phone calls to make," he said. "I probably should make a list."

I had a small spiral notebook and pen in my purse. I placed them on the table and offered to do the writing. Childhood friends, schoolteachers, former employers, neighbors. The list filled two of the small pages. He didn't mention a single relative in the twenty-five-person list, and I asked about it.

"One uncle, on mom's side, sitting in a nursing home in Sacramento. Alzheimer's," he said. "That phone call is coming any day now."

He grabbed the notebook and began reviewing it. "Goddamn. That's a lot of calls. I don't know if I'm up to it."

I suggested sending an e-mail.

"Half of these prairie-billies don't even have a cell phone," he said.

"What about the other half?"

"I guess I could send an e-mail to a few of them. Of course, I'd have to call them anyway to get their e-mail addresses."

I offered to write the actual e-mail, thinking maybe he'd prefer not to do it, and I was correct. We had a brief discussion about when I would write it. Not right then, was all we decided on.

I took back the notebook. "Who are the most gossipy, chatty people on this list?" I asked. "Maybe we can get them to do a lot of the work."

Dan named two people immediately, and another two with slightly less conviction. I circled their names.

"If you called these four people, would they be able to cover the rest of this list?"

"Probably so," he said.

"Bam. There you go. Four phone calls."

"I can handle that."

"We're going to get through this, Dan."

ABE WAS BACK in the room just before sundown. The tumor had been removed, along with some other areas of malignancy. There was no telling when he would wake up, but the sooner the better, the doctor said.

Dan slept, passed out on a recliner facing the window. I didn't keep track of how many pitchers he'd put down that afternoon, but our tab was just shy of a hundred dollars before tip, only fifteen of that my doing. I didn't enjoy having to drive the enormous pickup back to the hospital. I felt like Lily Tomlin in that huge rocking chair.

With the room finally emptied of medical professionals, I moved a chair to Abe's bedside and placed my hand on his arm. I'd held back tears for the most part until then. Our extraordinary run of good fortune was over. There would be no more gigs, no *Tonight Show*. It was the end of what would've been a torrent of possibilities and opportunities, the stuff dreams are made of.

I sat and cried for who knows how long. There's no need to measure such things. The news was what it was, and it saddened me to think Dan and I knew more about Abe's predicament than Abe did at that point. All I really wanted at that moment was to hear Abe's voice.

I had some phone calls of my own to make. Dad was first in line, but it was too late to call by the time I made it back to Marc's porch that night. I texted Rikki to check if he was awake, and he called me back right away. Loud music played in the background, suggesting he might be at a bar, mixing it up with the general public and staying out of his own head. Wrong. It was his home stereo.

I told him the known knowns and the known unknowns regarding Abe.

"Oh, for fuckssake," he said, taking a moment to let it sink in. "Now what?"

"I don't know."

"How are *you* doing?"

I mentioned the conversation with the NBC producer that morning. "The best of all news and the worst in the same day. The same hour, actually."

"Do I need to take you to a karaoke bar?" he asked. "That's my solution for everything, you know."

"No. I'm not presentable."

He asked if there was anything he could do to help, and nothing came to mind, aside from just being present. I remembered the four-minute video Jessica at NBC requested. Had I not received the news about Abe that morning, this is what I would've called Rikki about. I asked if he could throw an edit together.

"Of course," he said.

"Just in case this all turns in another direction."

"You never know."

"This whole thing has been one improbable event after another."

"To say the least."

"Should we plan on things continuing in that fashion?"

"Absolutely."

We were edging toward the topic of a book Rikki had turned me onto years ago. "We need to expose ourselves to the Black Swan." I said.

"You can't win if you don't play."

"It's time to strip naked and put our dusters on."

THE NEXT MORNING, as I was beginning to think about getting ready to start on the file cabinets of autographs, Dan called.

"He's awake," Dan said. "It hurts to talk, and he's in and out, but he's up."

"Awesome," I said, before asking if there was any new info from the doctors.

"Not really," he said. "He's only doing handwritten communication or thumbs up thumbs down," Dan said. "His lung function is crap because of the morphine."

I asked if it would be okay to come up there in an hour or so.

"I don't know," he said. "I'd better ask him first. Now he's asleep again."

"Have him text me when he wakes up."

That text arrived two hours later. Not a text, but a familiar black and white photograph of a shirtless fat guy in sunglasses getting shot in the stomach with a cannonball. I expected another text to follow, maybe a comment about the image, but it didn't come. My first instinct was to ask him how he was feeling, but then I looked back at the photograph he sent.

Can I bring you anything?

I'm good. Dan brought some books

Is it okay if I come visit?

Doctor sez I shouldn't laugh for a couple days,
so probly not!

I'll behave. I promise

How about tomorrow?

This wasn't the answer I wished to receive, but it'd have to do. Abe was alive and mentally with it, despite the cannonball to the stomach and morphine fog. It was enough of a relief to allow me to return to the intimidating, ominous file cabinets.

Remember those letters from the afterlife that Marc promised? I still hadn't found one. I opened the first file folder in the A-F cabinet—*Aaron, Hank*—and there one was. I went to the kitchen island and read it.

It lacked the charms of the first letter, but it was helpful, offering suggestions on how to approach the collection. Half of the autographs were sports-related, and half of those were specific to Denver sports teams. He suggested I separate the sports figures from the politicians, the movie stars from the criminals, etcetera—basically how things should've been orga- nized from the start, according to autograph expert Walt Flickinger.

The chore of sorting and segregating seemed like too much work to tackle alone. I'd need to contact Walt and maybe offer him a hundred bucks to come help me for an afternoon. After looking through the first fifty or so folders, maybe one name out of four was familiar to me. I decided to remove the familiar names and set them aside, leaving the unfamiliar names for Walt to deal with.

Marc's letter ended with this:

Imagine a sexual climax while approaching the speed of light—St. Augustine meets Einstein...

I'll get right on that, Marc, I thought. Maybe all this afterlife gibberish would add up to something once I'd found the rest of the messages. Or, maybe just a scavenger hunt off the edge of a cliff.

The first cabinet took an hour to get through. My eyes needed a break, so I refilled my coffee and went for the porch. A paper copy of the *Denver Post* teetered at the edge of the top step, a paperboy's equivalent of a hole-in-one. I brought it to the chaise and had a look at the previous day's events. A full-page ad for the Colorado State Fair greeted me near the end of the first section, which included a list of musical acts, the Haugenberrys among them. *Crap*, I needed to contact them right away.

I texted Abe, holding onto some hope of not having to cancel, but expecting the reality of things.

He texted back, *No chance.*

My e-mail to the State Fair folks became the e-mail I'd eventually give to Dan to send to his people, minus any calls to action. There was no rescheduling to be done with the fair, since it was a once-a-year event, so I just laid out the facts.

Gil called. Did I want to do lunch, he asked. No, I didn't want to sit at a restaurant. We agreed that he'd pick up some Greek food and bring it over.

He arrived an hour later, and as soon as he emerged from his car, I knew something was off. His long hair was gone. I could see the entirety of the back of his neck from where I sat. I walked to the edge of the porch, making imaginary binoculars with my hands.

"Is that Gil Barbieri? Of Rutgers University?"

"It was time," he said, smiling, shaking his head.

"I'm guessing you had an epiphany."

"More than one," he said, setting the food on a table next to the chaise. We made eye contact.

"You don't look okay," he said.

"This is my barely-keeping-it-together face."

I handed him my laptop so he could read the e-mail I'd been preparing.

"Wow," he said, wide-eyed. "That is..."

I waited for him to finish the sentence, but that was the end of it. We sat silent for a while, watching the usual traffic, dog-walkers, and joggers. There were Canada geese in the distance. He eventually opened the bags of food and began arranging the clamshells on the table. "I got a little bit of everything, falafel, gyros, dolmas, salad."

I thanked him, noting that I hadn't eaten anything since the previous morning. "The Griever's Diet has kicked in."

I went to the kitchen for some real plates and silverware. He was eating a dolma, looking almost pissed off when I returned. I assumed he had some sort of agenda, but maybe now wasn't the time, in light of the news about Abe. It seemed I was in charge of what was appropriate subject matter for conversation.

"So, the hair," I said. "The back of your neck hasn't seen daylight since when, 1980?"

"More like 1967," he said. "I've always had long hair. My parents were hippies. Freaks, to be more precise."

"What's the difference?"

He thought a moment as he chewed his dolma. "Zappa-heads versus Deadheads."

"I don't get the distinction."

"It's not that important."

"Sure it is."

He looked amused, and after a moment of thought-orga-nization, he explained it this way: freaks were more of an ironic, self-aware version of the hippie, less prone to the quackery of spiritualists and the other trappings of the hippy movement.

"That's how I see it, anyway," he said. "Does that help?"

"Sure," I said. "Anything to distract me from this." I pointed at the e-mail on my laptop screen.

"Ugh. Just when things were really starting to kick ass."

I told him about the phone call with Jessica the NBC producer.

"What?" he said, standing from the cast iron bench as though it had suddenly become electrified. "Motherfucker!" he shouted, attracting the attention of a passing racewalker, who gave us a side-eye scowl. Gil waited until the racewalker was out of earshot. "I can't believe people still do that shit. Race-walking. Do it in the privacy of your own home at least. Don't force your ill-conceived retro fad exercise jackassery on the public."

"Agreed."

"See, a hippy would race-walk. A freak would run circles around the hippy and heckle. Both of them getting exercise, at the end of the day."

"I get it now," I said, putting a money-shot of tzatziki sauce on my gyro.

"So, what does this have to do with me cutting my hair?" he asked. "I was sitting at my desk about two-thirty Monday morning. I popped a gummy and flipped on the TV. *Born on the Fourth of July* was on, you know, with Tom Cruise. Man, what a heavy-handed movie…"

"…anyway, the gummy kicks in, kicks in some more, and here comes Tom and the boys rolling around in their wheel-chairs all fired up, I happen to look over at the microwave and catch my reflection, and I thought to myself *man, that's what I probably look like to most people*, and I'm not nearly as good-looking as Tom Cruise. And he was *trying* to look like crap."

"Makes sense."

"I paid one of my bartenders thirty bucks to hack it off, right there in my office. Cheap ass, dollar store office scissors."

"Makes perfect sense to me."

"I'm gonna be talking with bankers and lawyers in the near future. So, I figured I oughtta lose a couple of the rough edges."

"And why are you going to be talking with bankers and lawyers?"

"I may have talked myself into buying the Knights," he said.

This was good news, for once. "Please tell me Tom Cruise had something to do with it."

"No, but I'd let him jump on my couch."

I told him the appraiser was probably working on the project as we spoke. Gil mentioned a real estate buddy who'd run some comps on buildings and businesses in the area. "I could probably pull it off, unless there's a bidding war. He doesn't expect one, or much of one. The market has cooled. Interest rates are way up."

I texted him Hirsh's phone number.

"Have you heard of these zero-alcohol bars that've been popping up?"

"I saw an article a few months ago. Didn't read it," I said. "Seemed like an April Fools' kind of thing."

"Oh, they're real. I went to one last week. Surprisingly busy for a weeknight. Couldn't believe it."

My gyro was being temperamental, shooting tzatziki sauce in every direction. I set it down and wiped the sauce trails off my forearms. "Don't tell me you're thinking of turning Knights into an alcohol-free bar."

"It's just a thought," he said. "There isn't one on this side of town, yet."

Nothing about my facial expression or body language suggested that I liked this idea, and he could sense it. I began to think of another topic to discuss.

"Why don't I take you out to one," he said. "You'll be surprised."

My resistance to the idea seemed to take on a life of its own, and I suddenly felt old-fashioned, conservative, set in my ways, which was offensive to me. I begrudgingly agreed to join him. "Someday," I said.

He smirked, and I could tell he was already assembling some sort of scheme to get me into this no-alcohol bar. Whatevs. I was over it for the time being. A change of subject needed to happen. He was wearing the same shirt he'd worn the night of the Haugenberry's Purgatory gig.

"I wonder whatever happened to that vagrant," I said. "Have you seen him around the 'hood?"

He cringed and shifted his weight. I expected him to volunteer some information, but no.

"Well, let's have it," I said.

"Nah," he said. "It's not...Maybe some other time."

It occurred to me that the episode with the vagrant had become the turning point of our good fortune, and this made it more significant than it probably was. It warranted some closure.

"C'mon, Gil."

"Nah. I'd prefer not to talk about it."

Whatever info he had wasn't sitting right with him, though I was suspicious he was now using it as leverage of some sort.

"How about you tell me over some non-alcoholic drinks at some lame zero-alcohol bar," I said.

And this is how Gil gets his way.

ABE TEXTED THE NEXT MORNING, giving me the okay to come visit after noon. At 11:50, I was in the hospital elevator with a tote bag of pre-owned DVDs—Dean Martin roasts, and a box set of *Tonight Show with Johnny Carson* that I'd found at a thrift store on my way to the hospital.

I exited the elevator and walked past the break room, where Dan was preparing a drink, lost in thought. I watched him for a moment.

"A little mid-day tea-bagging, Mr. Haugenberry?" I said, in a British accent.

It spooked him a little, but he adapted.

"Oooh yes," he said, breathy, dipping a tea bag into a small paper cup of steaming water. "Don't stop, *don't stop.*"

The nurses' station was adjacent to the break room, and I got the sense that Dan and I were being overheard, so I lowered my voice, asking how Abe was doing.

"They gave him the talk last night," Dan said. "So, he knows what's up."

"Ooof."

"He seems to be in less pain today, though. They've backed off the morphine a bit."

I followed Dan into the room. Abe was breathing into some

sort of handheld, toy-like lung capacity measurement apparatus. He set it aside once he noticed me.

"*The Tonight Show*," Abe said, just above a whisper, but looking elated.

I held the bag of DVDs out toward him. "A box set. How did you know?"

"I told him about your phone call with what's-her-face from NBC," Dan said.

"Oh, that," I said, setting the bag on a tray table. "Yes, the *Tonight Show*. Can you believe it?"

He asked how I managed to pull it off, and I told the truth. "I just happen to know someone. I didn't have to slay any dragons or anything."

Abe spoke in broken sentences, his lung capacity still less than normal. He was more chipper than I'd expected, given the news he'd recently received. Maybe it hadn't sunk in. I could see small containers of applesauce and Jell-O in the trashcan, which meant he was eating *something* at least.

"We need to get you out of here so we can make a video," I said. "NBC wants a four-minute short."

Abe smiled and shook his head. "You don't stop...do you."

Dan volunteered to drive somewhere for food. "I'm thinking Zimbabwean, maybe Mozambican."

"Of course you are," I said. And with that, Dan was gone. Another impulsive exit, leaving Abe and I to ourselves.

I moved a chair to Abe's bedside and sat. We looked at each other, silent, for a few moments. I set my hand on his forearm.

"Well, shit," Abe said. "And I was just...about to....ask you on a date."

I smiled and wiped away a tear with my thumb.

"Where were you planning on taking me?" I asked. "Assuming I said yes."

"Hmm," he said, looking at the ceiling. "A food

truck…maybe one of those…rent-to-own stores…preferably…on the same block."

"That sounds lovely," I said.

"Then maybe…if it goes well…we could go…for a walk along…Sand Creek…maybe split…a can of…Copenhagen."

"What should I wear?"

"Surprise me."

"What about you?"

"Z Cavaricci…maybe a…hi-viz…safety vest."

"Oh, what are the social pages going to say?"

"Game over!"

I let the visuals play out in my head as I reached for the bag of DVDs. I hadn't arrived with a comedic agenda, assuming it was still painful for Abe to laugh. He obviously didn't care. I set a small stack of the Dean Martin roasts on the bed and asked if he'd ever watched any of them.

"No. Just the…late-night…infomercials."

"Relentless insults. These are good inspiration," I said, inspecting one of the cases. "If you're ever in need."

"Dan's face…is inspiration…enough."

I could tell he wasn't physically able to withstand his half of a long conversation, so I filled him in on the events of the previous week, the news about the Knights Errant, Marc's sale, the gig offers I'd received.

"We finished…the recording," he said.

I asked him if he was happy with it, and he gave the thumbs up with his right hand, then the left. "I'd like…to do…another one…our own…songs."

"Heck yeah," I said.

"I got to…keep on…doing something," he said. "Not going to…sit around…watching reruns…the rest of my life."

He closed his eyes and fell asleep. We hadn't gotten around to *the talk. Give him a few more days*, I told myself as I sat and watched him, imagining our first date on the banks of Sand

Creek, the moonlight reflecting off his vest, as we took turns spitting Copenhagen into the weeds.

I called Bernfeld first thing Thursday. Dan had been keeping him updated about Abe. He planned to make a trip to Denver the coming Saturday to visit and hand-deliver the finished mixes. I mentioned Abe's desire to make another album of original songs and we discussed some options that wouldn't require making the long drive out to his Dust Bowl studio. This would be no problem. The only bottleneck: the original songs.

I had appointments scattered throughout the day, frequent enough to prevent my visiting the hospital. Walt had tipped off a rare book dealer from Salt Lake City about Marc's collection and he was *en route*. Though this went against my fiduciary duty, I wasn't ready to sell the books yet, and I'd considered keeping them. I didn't *need* to sell them to the dealer and made no promises. He just wanted to look, he assured me.

Dan called mid-morning. The sight of his name on my phone brought on a sense of dread and anxiety, a feeling that wasn't there less than a week previous, and this made me sad. I answered, expecting bad news, but this wasn't the case. Abe was doing better. I heard the strumming of a guitar, and he put me on speakerphone.

"We finished a song," Dan said. "Abe wrote most of it. You ready?"

He began playing, and it sounded more like a Great American Songbook standard than a rock or mellow gold song—something Louis Armstrong or Ella Fitzgerald might've recorded. The repeated line of the song was *this is my ticket out of this town*. Many stops and starts and do-overs later, the short song ended. It needed work, but it was a good first draft.

"Is the Vegas ending too much?" Dan asked. "That was my idea, depending on what you have to say about it."

"I love it."

"Yes, it adds a bit of glitter and showbiz to an otherwise sad affair. Gotta go. We're on a roll."

The book dealer arrived early afternoon and spent a solid hour looking through the collection. When he was finished, he removed his latex gloves, and shoved them in his jeans pocket.

"Impressive," he said, heading for the front door. "There isn't a book on that shelf worth less than five hundred bucks. I appreciate you letting me look."

Was that it? No offer to buy, or to refer to other dealers or collectors? A waste of a ten-hour drive, it seemed to me, and a waste of *my* time. Maybe there was something I didn't know.

"I just like the hunt," he said. "There's a signed first edition of the Old Testament sitting in a thrift store somewhere, and I'm going to find it."

Dan called shortly after. The sight of his name on my phone didn't bother me this time.

"Here's another one," he said. "Sort of a cowboy trail song. Clippity clop, clippity clop."

Fuck y'all for suckin'
At doin' what you do
My middle finger's pointing
At you and you and you
All y'all standing behind me
This one's for you
Fuck y'all for suckin'
At doin' what you do

"What do you think?" Dan asked.

"That's it? That's all?"

"We're thinking so. Gotta go. I just had another idea."

A pair of early-fifties Eames-Herman Miller fiberglass armchairs sold late afternoon—the last of the good stuff in terms of collectible MCM pieces. The rest of the furniture would wait until the in-person public sale. Oliver stopped by and grabbed a few more totes of records, and I had all of the autographs separated into *Names I Recognize* and *Stuff For Walt To Deal With*. A productive day.

Some porch time was in order, so that's where I went, with a jar of chardonnay. It'd been a couple hours since I heard a new song from the brothers, so I called Dan. He answered, speaking quietly. Abe was sleeping.

"He was up most of the day," Dan said. "I'll bet he sleeps through the night."

I asked for any updates from the doctors. They thought Abe might be able to go home early the next week.

"And, speaking of going home," Dan said. "I need to get out of here. Where you at?"

I told him, and a half-hour later, he was where I was. We sat quiet for a while, taking in the typical scenes at the park. He'd picked up a twelve-pack of beer on the way. "Can't wait to get out of that place," he said. I asked what the doctor's plan was.

"They're going to let him heal up first, then off to the oncologist."

I offered to assist with getting Abe to and from the many appointments and treatments in his future. Dan thanked me. "We'll just take them one day at a time."

"Have you made your four phone calls?" I asked.

"Only two," he said. "We've got a couple visitors coming this weekend."

A homeless man entered our line of sight, on the sidewalk across the street, westbound, moving from discarded cigarette butt to cigarette butt, smoking the one or two puffs remaining on each one before tossing it into the street and moving onto the next. The man had a sort of Fred Astaire strut. Dan laughed. "God bless America," he said.

"I'm not much of a theater goer," I said. "But I've seen a

lot of cutting-edge stuff sitting here. This one looks like a perverted re-imagining of *Hansel & Gretel.*"

"You should make the movie. Gil could play the homeless man."

The man did resemble Gil, a sunburned, dilapidated doppelganger or close relative. I mentioned Gil's haircut and told the story behind it.

"Well, good," Dan said. "He looked like a photobomber in search of an old Metallica poster."

"Nailed it."

I mentioned the tour bus vagrant, and that Gil knew something he wouldn't tell me.

"Do we need to go shake him down?"

I mentioned the date I had with Gil, which had yet to be scheduled.

"A zero-alcohol bar?"

"Yes."

He shook his head but had nothing to say about it. We watched the cigarette butt chaser and talked about the recording options Bernfeld mentioned. It'd be a couple weeks at least before Abe would be able to sing, and then not at full-strength even then, and maybe never again. I mentioned the brief conversation I had with Abe the night before, and the album of originals.

"That's what he wants," Dan said. "I think he's finally found something he loves to do."

"Recording?"

"Writing and recording. I've never seen him so excited," he said. "It's a shame he didn't figure that out about twenty-five years ago."

I asked if their dad ever brought up the idea of doing a recording back in the day.

"Nah. Not that I can remember. Too expensive probably."

My jar needed a refill, and some music was in order, so I

excused myself from the porch. Marc's stereo was still parked on the jazz station, so I turned that up, got my refill and returned to the chaise.

"Have you found your calling, Dan?" I asked, at least a little bit in jest.

He laughed. "Do I look like I've found my calling?"

I waited for him to continue. "What about you, AJ."

"I don't know," I began. "And the more often I think about it, the less time I spend thinking about it when I do. Does that make any sense?"

He pointed at the cigarette chaser, who was now doing the moonwalk. "Yes. Anything makes sense at this point."

"Managing a couple of singing giants felt pretty close, though."

"The *Tonight Show.*"

"I'm thinking we'll move forward with it," I said.

Dan looked puzzled.

"Abe will have some good weeks and bad weeks," I said. "I've been through this before with my mom. With any luck, we'll get the call on a good week. You up for it?"

"Luck."

"It'll give Abe something to look forward to, at least. If it doesn't happen, it doesn't happen."

He thought a moment, before crushing his empty can underfoot. "What are the chances of getting couch time? I want Abe and I to sit on Mr. Fallon's couch and give him shit."

"I'll look into it."

"That's what Abe would want. *That's* the mountaintop."

Sand Creek. One of Denver's lesser-celebrated waterways, flowing southeast to northwest until it converges with the South Platte River, which then cuts northeast. It meanders through the industrial zones of the city where fresh air mingles with the stench of oil refinery, massive wastewater treatment complexes, and recycling centers. If you wish to race-walk through an official EPA Superfund site, this is the trail for you.

The creek entered my dream in the last moments before I woke Friday. I decided this was a sign. Abe had placed it there, just to mess with me.

As I waited for coffee to brew I consulted an online Denver Parks & Rec trail map. The eastern stretches of the trail, furthest from the stink and industrial waste, probably weren't too bad, I figured.

The dirt parking lot was empty. I put on a baseball cap and sunglasses, locked the car, and had a brief look at the map posted at the trail access point. The completed, concrete trail continued east for not very far, before becoming the dashed line of "future trail."

Here's the part where AJ ventures into nature to find her soul, I thought to myself as I set off, prepared for maybe a half-hour round trip. A dumb and fleeting sense of pride came over me, and an even dumber bout of self-congratulation for doing something outside my usual routine.

I needed to adapt, scheme, and get a new plan together. How to approach Jessica at NBC was priority number one. Should I tell her about Abe's prognosis, play the sympathy card, and try to expedite things? Should I proceed as though nothing was wrong? Some combination of the two? Could we still make that four-minute short?

The concrete trail ended a city block's distance from the parking lot. I traversed some construction debris and continued along the pre-existing dirt path. It narrowed after a while, increasingly weed-infested, but still wide enough for a single-file line to pass through.

As I approached a fork in the path, a faint, foul stench hit me. It seemed to be wafting from somewhere and something closer to the creek itself, which was now completely obscured by eye-level cattails. I veered that way, and within a few steps, I found something I knew Rikki would be interested in.

I called him immediately, tracing my steps back to the fork. My adrenal gland was having an orgasm. No answer, so I called again. No answer, so I called again, on and on. I'd made it back to the concrete before he answered. He'd been in the shower. I told him where I was, a simplified version of why, and then mentioned the dead body.

He began asking a series of specific questions as though he'd been preparing for this moment all his life: was there anyone else on the trail? Any chance the body could be seen from an overpass, hill, or retaining wall? Had any scavengers gotten to it?

"What about the stage of decomposition?" he asked.

"I don't know," I said. "I don't know the jargon."

"Fresh? Blue and festering?"

"Definitely blue and festering."

"Good to know," he said, before insisting I remain at the

trailhead and do everything in my power to keep others from going anywhere near the body.

"What am I supposed to tell people?" I asked.

"Improvise."

"May I ask what I'm signing up for here?"

"Don't go anywhere, don't call the cops, don't call anybody. I'll be there in thirty, forty minutes tops."

The parking lot was still empty when I made it back to my car. This bought me some time to attempt to reverse-engineer the conversation I'd just had. I'd called Rikki only to unburden myself from the shock and horror of my gruesome discovery. The speed and ease at which he'd produced the phrase *blue and festering* disturbed me nearly as much as the body itself.

An Aurora Parks & Rec truck entered the lot, sending me into panic mode. I still hadn't devised a strategy to keep people away from the body. I could tell lies all day to regular citizens, but what could I say to a park ranger? Fortunately, I didn't have to say anything. He said hi, I said hi, then he emptied the trash barrel and took off.

I was prepared by the time the second threat arrived. I didn't even let the woman get out of her SUV. Don't go east on the trail, I told her, warning about a deranged man waving a hunting knife and a broken bottle. The cops were on the way, I told her.

The woman and her SUV were completely out of sight in under a minute.

Rikki arrived at the half-hour mark, as promised, followed by a shiny white passenger van. I stepped out of my car to size up the situation. Five men in Cabernet-colored robes exited the van. All of them were at least one half East Asian and generally dark-complected. I estimated their age range as between forty and sixty. They appeared anxious, ready to move.

"Where are we headed?" Rikki asked. No hellos, introductions, or weather observations.

"This way," I said, taking the lead, setting off on the concrete trail. My pace wasn't fast enough for the men, and their following so close soon became mildly annoying. I stopped and pointed east.

"At the end of the concrete, keep going straight on the dirt path for about fifty yards," I said. "There'll be a fork in the path. Go left, toward the creek. You'll know by then."

The men put their hands together as if to pray and bowed slightly before scurrying away—race-walking almost, without all the chicken-dance upper-body foolishness.

Rikki didn't join them.

"What exactly is going on here?" I said.

"Meditation on the Corpse," Rikki said.

"And I'm supposed to know what that is?"

The men had reached the end of the concrete and were gradually disappearing into the cattails and thistle. Rikki asked if there was access to the area from the other side. I didn't know for sure.

"I'm going to go check it out," he said, beginning to walk away. "You stay here and keep watch."

"Oh, for chrissakes," I said. "This better be worth my time."

He spun around and walked backwards a few paces. "You've done these men a great service. You'll be rewarded," he said, before turning back around and speeding up his pace.

"Now, or in the afterlife?"

"Yes," he said.

"Oh, c'mon Rikki," I shouted. "I used the Oxford comma. You heard it."

He was too distant by this time to respond and was soon deep into the future trail. I looked around for a high spot or perch where I could possibly get an overview of things. There was a mostly-dead cottonwood tree close to the end of the concrete that looked promising. I scaled it a few feet. I could see Rikki's head bobbing up and down in the distance but couldn't spot the monks or the body with any certainty.

After a minute Rikki turned around and was now walking back. I climbed down to the dirt and waited for him at the edge of the concrete.

"I don't think anybody's gonna be wandering in from that side," he said. "We should head back to the parking lot."

I wasn't used to Rikki acting like a team leader, and it was amusing, almost laughable. I followed him back to the lot, and went for my car and water bottle. Rikki popped the hood of his car, lifted it, and snapped the kickstand thingy into place. I expected him to check the oil or washer fluid levels, but no, he'd just opened his hood for shits.

"Plausible deniability," he said. "If a cop or ranger stops here, we need to look like we have a reason to be loitering."

"Ah."

His phone rang, and he answered it. *Yes, we're here. All good so far. Hurry.* He returned his phone to his back pocket.

"Who was that?"

"Broomfield monks."

"Sweet Jesus," I said. "Is this some kind of mass pilgrimage?"

"It could get out of hand. Hard to say."

Now that things were temporarily under control, I asked again what was going on.

"If you'll allow me to *mansplain*," he began. "Meditation on the Corpse is a central practice in the Buddhist tradition. The thing is, it's difficult to access an actual corpse in the United States, the death industry being what it is."

"Couldn't you just sneak into a funeral home?"

He looked at me like I was crazy. "Hell no, that's not...that's just ridiculous on many levels."

I decided to keep going. "Walk into a funeral home, check the name on the marquee, and start introducing yourself around—*I'm so-and-so's Buddhist Asian friend. Mind if I take a gander?* Boom. There's your corpse."

"Good lord. No. Just no."

Another van arrived, carrying another group of monks. Ten this time. Six Asians, and four pasty, emaciated white dudes. Rikki gave them the run-down. They did prayer-hands and bowed in my direction first, then Rikki's, before hitting the trail. None of the monks carried a backpack or anything that might contain the essentials. I mentioned this to Rikki.

"These men can go days without food and water," he said.

"How long will this continue?" I asked.

"The cops will run them out eventually," Rikki said. He pointed at a neighborhood to the north of the creek. "Some ol' busybody over there will call the authorities once she notices the swarm."

Three more vans, a car, then another two vans rolled up, bringing the total to eighty-nine monks. It was 9:45AM, and only a matter of time before a ranger or police officer was bound to arrive. The heat of the day was starting to assert itself. Rikki spotted an approaching Parks & Rec truck in the distance and closed his hood as the truck turned into the parking lot.

"Let's look like we're leaving," Rikki said.

The truck parked directly behind our cars, preventing us from backing out. The tinted driver's side window rolled down and the ranger took a quick look at us.

"I hear there's a party going on around here," he said.

"Dudes in robes," Rikki said, pointing toward the area of interest. "They've all been walking that way."

The ranger pulled forward slowly, parking behind a couple of the vans. He got out and began writing license plate numbers in a small notebook.

"Dudes in robes," he said, smiling. "Dudes in robes. Suppose we've got a little satan-worshipper's convention going on this morning? A baptism perhaps? If that's the case, Sand Creek seems like the right choice."

Rikki mentioned there were "maybe fifty" robed dudes. "Most of them looked Asian. Most of them older."

"Huh," the ranger said, looking at the sky for a moment. "Asians. Were any of them carrying anything?"

"No," Rikki said. "Not that I saw."

The ranger wrote in his notebook again, speaking slowly—taking his own dictation, basically. "Roughly fifty empty-handed Asian geezers performing a satanic baptism on Sand Creek southeast of the east terminal parking lot 9:50 in the morning. I like it!"

By now it was clear the ranger didn't give a single damn about what was going on. "I'd better go check on things. You two coming with?"

Rikki and I looked at each other and shrugged. "Why not," Rikki said. I agreed, hoping to at least get a cell phone pic of the gathering. We followed the ranger, making small talk as we went. A low, monotone hum was audible by the time we reached the future trail. The ranger stopped and put his index finger to his lips. "Shhh," he began. "Those are satanic chants. They're chanting in Satanese."

He continued into the cattails, and we followed, trying to hold back laughter. I wondered if—suspected even—he knew what we'd been up to the whole time and was now just messing with us. Maybe he had *park ranger damage.*

Had we done anything illegal? Failure to report a dead body? In one sense, I'd say we'd done a damn good job of reporting a dead body. We had eighty-nine uniformed Buddhist monks on the scene within an hour, representing an authority—one could argue—infinitely higher than the Aurora Police Department.

We arrived at the fork, the chanting now very loud, like a forest of baritone cicadas. The ranger continued toward the gathering. Rikki gestured for me to hold back. "I don't want them to see us," he whispered.

The ranger stopped and observed, his arms folded. The aroma of burning incense took the edge off the stench, but just barely. The chanting continued, uninterrupted. He stood there for a couple more minutes before taking a few cell phone photos of the proceedings. The monks were ignoring him, no doubt about it, and he knew it. He spun around, and with a smile on his face, walked toward Rikki and me, still at the fork.

"What to do, what to do," he said, passing us, moving toward the concrete trail. There was a spring to his step, and a jiggle to his belly. "I hate to spoil a party."

We followed him back. At least two police cars had arrived at the parking lot while we'd been away. The ranger hurried ahead to fill them in. Rikki's and my pace slowed, as we hoped anything the ranger had to say to the cops would clear us of any possible connection to the gathering and we could just pack up and leave.

This turned out to be the case, for the most part. We had to provide our IDs and answer the same questions the ranger had asked us earlier. Two of the cops followed the ranger to the gathering, while two stayed behind inspecting the vans and securing the scene.

Rikki and I were free to go, as far as we could tell, and so we took full advantage of the opportunity before the cops had a chance to think up any further questions, or otherwise get *inspired*.

I needed the ranger to forward me the photos he'd taken, and that little hiccup prevented me from peeling out of the parking lot right then. Rikki was long gone by the time I had a plan together. I couldn't leave a note on the ranger's truck. The cops would see it, and that'd probably raise suspicion. I'd have to hunt the ranger down somehow and ask him for the photo later.

I made my way to I-70 imagining what was going on at the meditation; how the cops were handling it, but mostly how the eighty-nine monks were reacting. Would the cops issue citations? Would they do anything with the body, or just push it into the creek and hope for the best? Those were questions for the ranger.

The first vanload of monks, I estimated, had a little over an hour with the body. The last monks to arrive maybe had fifteen or twenty minutes. Was this enough? How much meditational progress could one make in this amount of time? How long would they have stayed there if uninterrupted? Those were questions for Rikki.

The images of the monks bowing toward me played in my mind, and I wondered about the economy of karma. My discovery of the body had been serendipitous. However, I'd communicated it to Rikki, who then communicated it to the monks. I was the instigator, of sorts, and since I had nothing to do with the breaking-up of the gathering, I figure I'd earned maximum karma for my efforts. A solid A-plus. One hundred karmas. How would these be dished out in the real world?

GIL CALLED WHILE I was inching along the interstate, stuck in traffic, air-conditioned Purina Puppy Chow atoms blasting in my face.

"May I vent for a moment?" he asked.

"Of course," I said. "Please do."

He explained how the band who'd been scheduled to play at Purgatory that night canceled, without a compelling reason.

"This shit happens more and more often. Pissed-off fans, refunds. I'm out an entire Friday night of bar revenue. I'm over it."

"Club owner damage," I said.

"Exactly."

I assumed since the band canceled, he might have the evening free. "How about we hit up that zero-alcohol bar tonight?" I asked.

"How about we hit up a nothing-but-alcohol bar tonight?"

"It's a date."

There was no way I was going to meet him without solid visual evidence of what I'd experienced that morning. An internet search for park rangers was fruitless, but I did find the number for the Aurora office. I called and asked the receptionist if she could tell me which ranger patrolled that area of Sand Creek. She couldn't say for sure and wasn't too forthcoming with speculation. I gave her a brief physical description, and she said who she thought it probably was. I asked if she could put me in contact with him, and she gave me a phone number.

I called and could tell immediately that it was the right guy. I explained to him who I was, and he filled me in on how everything unfolded after the police interrupted. The monks had simply up and left, no conflict or resistance, barely any back and forth whatsoever. No citations were written, no arrests, nothing of the sort. Nothing about the dead guy. A news helicopter had hovered over most of the evacuation.

"Check the local news tonight," he said. "Time to dust off the old VCR."

I asked about the pictures he'd taken, and if he'd send them to me, in case the helicopter footage didn't make the news.

"Absolutely."

He didn't sound too busy, or anxious to get off the phone. I asked him how the rest of his workday was shaping up. He laughed.

"Dead as a doornail," he said. "This morning was more action than I'll see the rest of this year, and probably most of next."

I decided to freestyle a bit, telling him a few lies about myself and the research I'd done in the couple hours since the evacuation.

"These Buddhists are a bit hard-up for corpses, it turns out," I said. "They don't like them preserved, embalmed, any of that. Fresh or rotting, out in nature, just like that one today. That's the way they like 'em."

"No kidding."

"*Meditation on the Corpse* is what they call it. A centuries-old tradition. Very common in Asian countries."

"Well, I'll be."

I asked him how often he ran across dead bodies in his line of work.

"Oh, I don't know. One or two a year," he said. "But I'm lazy. I don't like to get out of the truck that much. Some of these younger guys probably find one or two a month. Homeless drunks and druggies, almost always."

"I'm just thinking hypothetically," I said. "But one *could almost* start a side business."

He had a hearty laugh at this. "I'll be damned if that isn't the best idea I've heard in a good long while."

"Just thinking hypothetically."

"Maybe this'll get me off my fat butt and out on the trails a bit more."

"A little bit of exercise never hurts. I don't get out much myself, to be honest."

"Well, Miss Washburn, it's been good talking to you, and I'll send those photos soon as we hang up."

And that was it. I didn't expect him to agree to any sort of corpse-scouting partnership. The absurdity of the idea was all I was really concerned about. Maybe it'd get him out on the trails a bit more. If so, then good for him. I'd feel confident that I hadn't just wasted one of my precious karmas.

I called Rikki to tell him about my conversation with the ranger, mentioning the news helicopter.

"*News-watching party,*" he said, sounding exactly like Richard Simmons.

I wasn't sure which of the five local stations had captured the footage.

"They all use the same traffic-copter," Rikki said. "I'd guess Fox 31 would be most likely to run the story."

After texting just about everyone I knew, I found myself on Rikki's couch, in front of his big screen, anxiously waiting for commercials to pass. Hank Ajax, Dealin' Doug, Jake Jabs—the household names of Colorado.

A bit of weather, sports, and there it was. *Mysterious Gathering on Sand Creek* was the bottom-of-screen headline. The helicopter footage wasn't all that compelling, really, just an amorphous mass of robed men near a creek. Ten seconds of it. No on-the-ground reporting, interviews with police, or anything we didn't already know. No mention of the dead body, of course. That would be too disturbing.

Rikki turned to me when the fifteen-second segment was over. "Well," he said. "That came and went."

"We made the news, Rikki. Soak it up!"

I called Abe first. He answered right away, and I could hear the TV was on in his hospital room.

"Did you see it?" I asked.

"What, those cult members at the creek?" He sounded almost back to normal, talking at his usual volume, and in full sentences.

"Buddhists."

"What about it?"

"That was your fault."

"What?"

I told him about my dream and blamed him for placing

Sand Creek in it. "I wouldn't have gone there otherwise. Zero probability."

"I'm not following."

I gave him the most abridged account as possible, avoiding any mention of the corpse. "So, I go for a walk. A little somethin-somethin happens, a little of this and that, and all of a sudden there are eighty-nine Buddhists meditating in the cattails and a news copter overhead."

"Okay."

"The Butterfly Effect," I said. "You make a joke about Sand Creek one day and, well, you just saw the rest on Fox 31."

"You're out of your mind."

He told me he'd been taking short walks around the halls and eating solid foods. The doctors thought he could go home in a couple days. One of his high school teachers and a high school-era ex-girlfriend had visited that day. "It was like they were teleported from two lifetimes ago," he said. "We didn't have a whole hell of a lot to talk about."

A doctor entered his room, so he promised to call me back.

"The Butterfly Effect," he said, in a contemplative tone, before we hung up. "That's the one where the butterfly farts in a crowded theater."

"Yes, that's the one. You get me, Abe."

GIL and I started the night at the Lo-Ball. He didn't know it yet, but I had plans for him, a test of sorts. If he passed, then I was confident I could talk him into just about anything. Conversation turned immediately to the Knights Errant. He'd talked to Hirsh that day, and a realtor.

"One point three million," Gil said. "Offensive. Repulsive even, but expected."

"Are you gonna go for it?"

"I already did."

This was exciting. I put my hand up for a high five, but he didn't match me.

"Not a done deal yet," he said. "Just waiting to be outbid."

We talked about the business and the building, and changes that needed to happen. Fairly minor stuff, really. Charlie's set-it-and-forget-it attitude had let the place grow stale over the years. A fresh set of eyes, some new paint, and updated furniture could almost be enough. The barely-utilized upstairs could be converted into any number of uses. We got way ahead of ourselves on that.

A band began to play, and it was too much to talk over, so we left. The dilapidated tavern across the street seemed suitable. It never had any bands, just an old-school 45rpm jukebox with one speaker. We got a booth, and I went for a pitcher of beer and two glasses. A few of the country band members from the Haugenberry's second Lo-Ball gig were bellied up to the bar. They recognized me. We exchanged nods and waves. Basically everything in my world had changed since that night, and I really didn't want to review it with any of them.

Gil was scrolling on his phone as I returned to the booth, determined to get him to tell me what he knew about the tour bus vagrant. Other than the text about watching the news, I hadn't said anything about my day. He mentioned my text. "I didn't get a chance to watch," he said. "What was that about?"

I lied. "Oh. False alarm."

He seemed satisfied, so I asked him about the vagrant. He looked disturbed, and took a deep breath. "Well, he turned up. The guy was hell-bent on going on tour."

"Turned up where?"

"He somehow managed to crawl into one of the undercarriage compartments of their bus," Gil said. "They got all the way to a truck stop in Ogallala before they figured it out."

"After all that fuss about locking doors," I said. "Was he still alive?"

"Not even close."

"Then what?"

"They parked between a couple semi-trailers, rolled him out onto the ground and left him for someone else to find."

"That's awful."

"Textbook tour manager damage," Gil said. "No 911 call, nothing. He didn't want to be late for their Sunday afternoon gig in Omaha."

"And the juggernaut of commerce rolls on."

He looked convincingly bummed out; sunken posture, wandering focus of the eyes. "It's been bugging me. I could've changed the whole outcome."

I reminded him that we did call 911 after removing the vagrant from the bus. We'd made an effort.

Gil took a sip of his beer and made a sour face. "This beer is *way* off," he said. "*Way off.* They need to clean their tap lines. Disgusting. I wouldn't be surprised if this whole room dies of dysentery."

I took a quick sniff of my glass, still mostly foam, but couldn't detect anything unusual. The jukebox started playing a country song that Gil recognized, and this agitated him. He brought the pitcher back to the bar, told the bartender the deal, then gestured for me to follow him.

You don't have to call me darlin', Darlene, the jukebox sang.

"Things ain't gettin' any better around this joint tonight," he said, as I followed him out to the sidewalk. We stood for a moment, looking in every direction for what to do and where to go next. We were right in the center of heavy foot traffic. I suggested we go to a club called Stellas that was a couple blocks away. It was the cleanest, shiniest bar in the neighborhood. Some friends of mine were DJing there.

We entered the place. Gil had never been there and noticed the line of salon chairs to the right of the front door where people were giving and receiving pedicures. One of the pedicurists noticed Gil and smiled at him, giving him a quick, enthusiastic wave as she put one tool down and picked up another. He waved back, and then followed me to the bar.

"Who is *that?*" I asked, as we waited for a bartender.

"That's who I go to," he said. "Jolene. She runs a shop by the Brown Palace."

Well, crap. There went my nefarious plan to coerce Gil into getting a pedicure. The potential tests of limits, personality, and possibility—gone. We ordered drinks and settled at a small round table near the window looking out to the street. He stabbed at the ice in his glass with the straw.

"So, if I end up buying the bar, are you going to manage it for me?"

I'd already considered this possibility quite a bit. Was I

overly excited about it? Not really, just another stepping stone in a forever of them. I had a month, maybe ninety days, before wrapping up the estate sale, and having to re-acclimate to the doldrums of the normal economy.

"I need a job with benefits," I said. "Health insurance, at the *very* least. I've got *issues*."

"Done," he said, before describing the portfolio of benefits his core crew had at Purgatory. This was mildly enticing.

"Are you going to let me do whatever I want with the place?" I asked. It was a bold question, sure.

"I can't agree to that."

"Why?"

"I barely know you," he said, stabbing his ice. "And vise-versa."

"You know me, Gil," I said. "Improviser, enthusiast, opportunist. I don't have an ill-intention in my entire body. An impeccable track record of kicking specific and certain ass."

He laughed. "Ok, I'll let you do whatever you want with the place—with an asterisk."

I knew this was probably an empty promise, but I just wanted to hear him say it.

"I can give you a *hard maybe*," I said. "But first, you need to tell me more about your friend Jolene."

"I go see her every couple months," he said. "She's an excellent listener, possibly a genius in that domain."

I touched my finger to my lips and attempted to look like I was trying to solve a dime store mystery. "Gil Barbieri gets a pedicure every two months. Who would've guessed?"

"I have *issues*, AJ. I need to take care of my feet."

WALT and I met at Marc's first thing Saturday morning. I needed to get the autograph project under control. The presidential stuff was listed, and selling, but the other ninety-five percent of it had just been sitting idle. Life had gotten too complicated, and the autographs had taken on the aura of being a nuisance. I wished Walt would just take over the rest of it, for a percentage of sales. This is what I planned to offer him at the end of his visit. But first, I wanted to see what he could do with the remaining collection.

He moved fast, sorting through the names I didn't recognize, separating and segregating. At the end of the first hour, he'd made it through one of the three unsorted file cabinets. Stacks of file folders were strewn about the den floor. Four of them were noticeably thicker than the others. "Broncos, Nuggets, Rockies, Avalanche," he said, pointing to each stack, suggesting I sell them in bulk, to make life easier. That's what I wanted to hear.

By noon, he'd gone through the whole mess, reorganized and refilled the cabinets. The Denver sports team autographs filled almost two of them, that he suggested I sell as a lot.

This had instantly cut my job in half, enough so that I decided to wait to offer him the opportunity to take over the project. Another two drawers of files he suggested I throw away, leaving me with one and a half cabinets of autographs to contend with. This I could handle.

I paid him a hundred bucks, and asked him if there were any autographs he wanted to take with him. He refused, saying he'd keep an eye on the auction listings.

Dan called soon after Walt left, inviting me to come visit.

I was at Abe's hospital room door within a half-hour, giving the courtesy knock and letting myself in. Bernfeld was there. We hugged. Abe was wearing headphones, staring intensely at a laptop screen.

"The final mixes," Bernfeld said, reaching into his pocket, pulling out a jump drive, which he handed to me. "A fine collection of songs, if you ask me."

Abe removed the headphones. "Sounds great. Now what? How long does it take to get records made?"

"Vinyl records?" Bernfeld asked.

"Yes. Old-school vinyl records."

"There's about a six to eight month wait list, last I heard," Bernfeld said. This had a certain sting to it, as this time frame happened to be the same one the doctors had given Abe a few nights previous. "Unless you have deep pockets. Taylor Swift could probably have a record pressed and in the shrink-wrap by Monday."

"Let's call her up," Abe said. Dan had his back turned to us, gazing out the window. Abe tossed an empty applesauce container at him. "Dan! Taylor Swift. Get her on the phone."

Bernfeld suggested we get some cover art together, liner notes, and whatnot and just plan on uploading to the music streaming sites. He was the only one in the room who knew how to go about doing this, aside from the artwork. Dan and Rikki could take care of that.

We tossed around some ideas for the cover, and possible titles for the album. Nothing stuck. Dan didn't want to use anything he'd already drawn. We'd all need to sleep on the idea, seemed to be the consensus.

A doctor and nurse entered, casually noting the small party we had going on, suggesting we might look into getting a bigger room. Abe cut through the small talk.

"So, doc," he said. "When this is all over, I want my body torn to shreds by vultures. How can we make that happen?"

The doctor laughed. "I'm afraid that probably won't be an option."

"Why not?"

The doctor explained how chemotherapy adds "a certain level of toxicity to the body."

"You don't want to do harm to the birds," the doc said.

Abe looked offended. "Who says? Did you know that vultures shit on their legs to control their body temperature?"

The doctor looked around at the rest of us, red in the face. "I did not know that," she said.

"Humans sweat, dogs pant, vultures shit on their legs," Abe continued.

The doctor poked around with her stethoscope and checked his surgical scar. "The good news is we can probably send you home tomorrow. I'd like to watch you do a couple laps first. Are you up for it?"

He stood from the bed, slow but steady. The nurse placed a walker in front of him. It was far too short to be of any use. "I don't need this thing," Abe said. "I can use Dan's shoulder."

Bernfeld and I followed the brothers as they moved out to the hallway and began their walk, the nurse alongside guiding the IV stand. It was a poignant sight, one brother helping the other, sans Zippo or pepper spray.

"You look like an old biker chick after a long weekend in Sturgis," Dan said.

Abe took his hand off Dan's shoulder. "Every once in a while, you're right about something."

He did two successful laps and offered to do a third. The doctor was satisfied with two, but told him he could keep going if he wished. He decided to return to the room, so we followed him. We talked about the album a bit more. Dan would get artwork to Rikki, who would then digitize it, and send to Bernfeld to use for the streaming site uploads. Simple enough, and with that settled, Bernfeld made his exit.

It occurred to me that there wasn't a bed at the Haugenberry house. If Abe was going home the following day, he'd need a bed. A tent in the backyard wasn't going to do. I offered up the guest bed at my dad's place. We'd just need to go pick it up.

"I'll have one delivered," Dan said. "A California King with a twin on the end. Sound good, Abe?"

Abe had fallen asleep.

THE DENVER SPORTS autographs were gone before noon Sunday. All two file cabinets' worth, and the cabinets. Walt had suggested I ask four thousand, and accept three. I got three-and-a-half from a couple of tipsy older guys in golf attire. My workday was done.

I had six drawers of autographs to get through and estimated it would take a week per drawer to get them listed on eBay. Oliver was about half done with the records. Most of the furniture was gone. There were the books still, but I hadn't convinced myself which way to go with those. I estimated a total of seven weeks remaining until the in-person sale, and then another week of cleanup. Maybe I could hire someone else to do that.

Dan called to let me know they were on their way home. He asked if I'd go to the grocery store and get some things for Abe, light stuff—applesauce, oatmeal, salads. I did, and arrived at their door with two hundred dollars worth of light stuff. Dan assembled bed frames in the living room while I stocked the fridge and pantry. Abe filled me in on the week ahead: oncologist appointment first thing Monday, and his first chemo treatment Tuesday. A few visitors were due to arrive later in the week, depending on how he felt.

The living room remained bleak: Dan's drafting table and the beds. No TV, stereo, side tables, lounge chairs. We needed to fix that before any visitors arrived. Dan gave me his credit card and sent me on a shopping spree in his truck. I made two trips: one for a big screen TV, the other for some tables and chairs. By late-afternoon we had the furniture assembled and the TV on a wall mount. Rikki stopped by with a DVD player and got the TV set up for streaming.

We ordered pizzas and watched episode one of *Little House on the Prairie*, because, well, that's what Abe wanted to watch. He heckled the actors before they even had a chance to do anything—Laura Ingalls running down the hill in the long grass. "No one's going to marry you, Laura. Wash your damn feet," Abe shouted. "You smell like a can of sardines that's been sprayed by a cat."

Dan joined in, and Rikki eventually. It got brutal.

Abe was asleep by the end of the episode. We quietly cleaned up the dinner mess, and Rikki and I made our exit. Dan announced his plan to go get some beer and begin working on the cover art.

"I should have something for you in the morning," he said.

Rikki and I were at the sidewalk. "Take your time," I said.

Dan stopped at the edge of the porch. "I wish we had some."

Gil called first thing Monday. He'd been outbid.

"By a hundred thousand dollars," he said. "I can't swing it."

I asked who outbid him, but he didn't know. "Didn't you ask?"

"The realtor wouldn't say. Probably better that I don't know," he said.

"And why is that?"

"Let's just say *something* happened to the guy, they're gonna come straight for me. Someone's always got an eye on the Italian from New Jersey."

This sounded a bit dramatic, but I let it slide. I offered to get my dad involved, and we could put in another bid.

"I don't know, AJ," he said. "That would be more complicated than you think, and we don't have time."

Time.

"So that's it?" I said.

"Afraid so."

"Unless *something* happens to this guy," I said.

"Yes."

I called Charlie immediately for more details. He'd been expecting me, but claimed to know nothing about the mystery bidder. "I have to do what I have to do," he said. "We'll wait a couple days for another bid to come in, but then it's time to pull the trigger."

"Ugh."

"I'm sorry, AJ."

"Can I keep the sign at least?"

He laughed. "I'll check into that."

By the time I reached Marc's front door, the prospect of saving Knights Errant was completely out of reach. I didn't have the private low-orbit rocketship money required help Gil outbid the mystery man, and even if I did, that would probably get outbid.

A shitty start to the week. Wildfire smoke was heavy enough that I couldn't see the lake across the street from Marc's. No joggers, dog walkers, cigarette butt chasers. I started on the first drawer of autographs, determined to go at it until I collapsed, or got too drunk, then collapsed.

Dan sent a photo of the cover art he'd created. It was okay, but it didn't have the grab-you-by-the-collar-and-shake quality I hoped for. Not that I had any better ideas. I spent much of the rest of the day trying to think of some, but it just wasn't happening.

I found a signed eight-by-ten photo of Michael Landon that I set aside for Abe. When five o'clock came around, I locked up, and drove to the Haugenberry's.

He sat upright in his bed, and I hid the photo behind my back. "I brought something for you. A signed photograph. I'll give you three guesses."

And with no hesitation, he produced three names rapid-fire. "Slobodan Milosevic. Darrel Strawberry. The old lady sitting in the window on *227*."

"No, no, and no," I said, revealing the photo. "You can keep this."

"The finest head of hair ever placed on a white man."

"It's pretty remarkable."

"I'll be losing all of mine soon," he said. "Can you find a Michael Landon wig online, you think?"

"I'll find one."

I asked about the oncologist appointment. He said it went okay. "First treatment tomorrow. I'll be feeling like shit the rest of the week, it sounds like. Exactly how shitty is unclear. Will I be able to do anything but lay here?"

I recalled my mother's experience with chemo and radiation and didn't have any good news for him. I offered to make him dinner, but he refused.

"I'm thinking an episode of *Little House*, and a nap."

"Fair enough."

We watched episode eight, until Abe fell asleep. No heckling, unfortunately. I kissed him on the forehead and gathered my things. A spiral notebook rested on his side table. He'd written in Sharpie on its cover: MY AFFAIRS, IN ORDER.

There was no going outside the rest of the week. Too much smoke. I dug up my trusty ol' cloth pandemic mask and started wearing it again. By late afternoon Thursday, I'd powered through the first drawer of autographs. The last item in the drawer: a voided check from Larry Hagman. I thought Abe might like this as well, so I saved it for him.

I didn't hear from Abe at all that week, just a few brief texts describing how awful he felt. I wanted to talk to him but had to remind myself what it feels like to be wiped out with the flu, having no energy for conversation. I texted him before leaving Marc's, asking if he wanted me to bring him anything. *No*, he replied. *Feeling a little better tho. Stop by tomorrow.*

Dan called first thing Friday. He could barely get a word out.

"He's gone."

I was speechless. My body felt like an old CRT television

being turned off, all the light and sound shrinking to a single point, then disappearing.

"You still there?" Dan asked.

"Yes. What do you mean he's gone?"

"Passed in his sleep at least. Eyes closed."

"No."

"EMTs think probably a blood clot from the surgery."

I could hear the familiar beeps of his truck, which meant he was preparing to drive somewhere. "Let me call you when we get where we're going."

My back hit my bed, and I cried and cried. Not so much for Abe, but for Dan. He had nobody left, the end of his family line. I tried to console myself with stupid little thoughts painted in cursive on planks you hang in the hallways of your mind. *At least he died peacefully, at least he didn't have to suffer long.*

I brewed coffee and looked out the window. A storm had passed through overnight and the air was fresh. The smoke had cleared, and you could see the mountains. I filled my travel mug and went for a walk.

Rikki was sitting on his front lawn, digging weeds out of his flower beds. He stood when he noticed me and the shape I was in. We hugged for a while. He didn't ask what the matter was right away, and that was fine. I let go of him because I had to sneeze.

"Is it Abe," he asked.

I nodded, and sneezed again, before sitting on Rikki's porch step. He sat next to me and grabbed my hand. "I'm sorry."

We watched the traffic, the joggers, the bicyclists, neither one of us saying much of anything. He offered to make me a bagel.

"No thanks," I said. "Let's finish with these weeds."

And so that's what we did for the next hour or so. We

finished the weeds and still no call from Dan, so I suggested we find another yard project to distract us.

"We've got some good momentum," I said. We pruned bushes, raked the lawn, Rikki touched up some paint on his back porch railing. The heat eventually kicked in, and we retreated to the shade of the front porch.

"Thanks, Rikki. That's just what I needed," I said, checking my phone. "Ten o'clock. Do you do bottomless mimosas?"

I texted Dan as we walked to the Golden Spork. Just a basic *How's it going?*

He eventually responded: *Fine. Just signing some forms*

I half-expected him to ask me to join him wherever he was, but no. I imagined there wasn't anything for me to do but provide emotional support. If he wanted it, he'd ask me.

We scored a patio table, in the shade. The first of many mimosas arrived, and I held my dainty tulip glass up and out.

"It's all gone to shit, Rikki."

"Yes, it has," he said, his glass touching mine.

"To hell with it," I said.

"To hell with it," he said.

I mentioned Gil being outbid for the Knights Errant. "And, so there's that, as well."

"It's too much. Let's shift gears."

We tried, but things just ended up back at the shitheap, odor lines rising like in a cartoon strip. Maybe Dan would want to continue as a solo act, Rikki suggested. I didn't think so, but maybe that was just my shitty attitude: *who I am getting in the way of who I could become.*

Now what? The looming question as always. I had phone calls to make: Gil, Oliver, Jessica at NBC, my dad. It was too much. Dan would probably need help making arrangements for a memorial service. Abe hadn't communicated any of this sort of stuff to me. It was all in his spiral notebook that I imagined was still sitting on the side table by his bed. The thought of it gave me an idea.

"Bottoms up, Rikki," I said. "Let's go before we drink ourselves off the edge of the earth."

We headed toward the Haugenberry's house. Still no update from Dan. The door was unlocked, and I went straight for the notebook, putting aside any question of ethics.

Abe had serial killer handwriting, and I struggled to read it. This was page one:

Dan,

Sorry to have died on you. I hope I didn't make too much of a mess. As mom told me several times, you're kind of a fag when it comes to cleanliness!

If you can't find a way to steal my body and feed it to the vultures, then just do cremation.

Public gathering at Norm's.

Afterparty at the farm.

Have Floyd's BBQ cater. No potluck bullshit. No bowls of Jell-O and marshmallows, no disgusting casseroles, scalloped potatoes, none of that shit.

Three kegs should suffice.

Bernfeld said you can mix ashes into vinyl and press records with it. Do that. Give them out to anyone who needs one. Sell the rest at Oliver's shop. Sell all of my shit that you don't need or want: truck, rental house, whatever else.

Good luck with the farm and all of dad's junk. See if AJ can help you with an estate sale.

I think you should sell it all and move to the Denver house for good. The farm is a waste of your talent and time. We don't live long, us Haugenberrys. Quit dicking around out there and mix it up in the city where you belong. We both should've done that long ago. You could probably get hooked up with an art gallery—

Dan pulled up right then. I placed the notebook back where I found it, shut the front door, and Rikki and I snuck out to the alley. It seemed a bit juvenile, and it probably wasn't necessary, but we were both a little drunk.

We continued down the alley, and toward Rikki's house. I recited what I could remember from Abe's notebook. I'd only seen page one, but there were at least two more pages left to read.

"It sounds like he covered most of the big stuff," Rikki said. "*Three kegs should suffice.* That's crucial, first page material."

Dan called, just as we made it back to Rikki's porch. I asked where he was. "Just got home."

I asked how he was doing.

"I don't know," he said.

"Maybe I should come over."

"Maybe so."

When I arrived, Dan met me on the porch and we hugged. He looked completely spent.

"Have you been drinking?" he asked.

"Mimosas," I said. "I slammed the first two, and mostly sipped the third."

"Alright then," he said, before heading for the kitchen. The opening of aluminum cans echoed through the house. He returned with a pair of Pabst beers, handing one to me.

"I don't have a goddamn thing left I need to do today," he said, sitting on one of the porch chairs. "How about you."

"Nothing."

"I called my four people," he said. "I called Norm, and the BBQ guys. That's enough."

I asked if he needed any help with other arrangements.

"I'd like you to emcee the service," he said. "I think most everything else will be taken care of."

"I'd be honored."

"Don't be afraid to take jabs at the locals."

"I can do that."

He'd talked to Bernfeld that morning about turning Abe's ashes into records. "Did you know they did that?"

"That's perfect."

We sat quiet for a while. Dan asked what I wanted to listen to. I couldn't think of anything and was fine with nothing. He walked inside. Some old-school country music began to play from the TV speakers. I couldn't identify the singer, but I guessed the title of the song was "It Was a Good Year for the Roses."

Dan returned to the porch, figeting in his chair. He needed a distraction. Sitting still and contemplating wasn't going to do.

"Rikki and I cleaned up his entire yard this morning," I said. "Weeded, pruned, raked. It was very therapeutic."

"Hm."

"Just an idea."

And without even a second of though, he said. "I think I'm going to sell everything out east and move here permanently."

I liked the sound of this and told him as much.

"Just can't get excited about going back," he said. "Can't even stomach it, actually."

"I get it."

"And I wonder, sometimes, why I stayed out there for so long to begin with."

"Family obligation, perhaps?"

"What else? Anyway, now that *that's* gone..."

He walked to the front door, placing his hands on the doorjamb, leaning inside. "Goddamn, this place needs a lot of work still."

Now we were getting somewhere. "What can I help you with?"

"I'll bet we can get this living room painted before dinnertime."

And that's what we did, while taking turns playing music

from our youth on the streaming service. We were only two years apart in age, but his choices were consistently ten or fifteen years ahead of mine—songs and artists you'd never admit to liking as a teen where I grew up. I mentioned this several times, hoping for a deeper interrogation, but he deflected in every case, impulsively singing a harmony, playing air guitar, or pointing out some detail in a song I'd never previously thought to appreciate. I let him go with it, and after a while, the glam metal I kept returning to gave way to the mellow gold.

We finished painting the walls and ceiling, and hit a stopping point that was obvious to both of us. I offered to buy dinner, but Dan just wanted to shower and go to sleep. Understood. With both his parents gone, and no other family remaining, he'd just endured one of the most difficult days of the rest of his life. The last of the worst, or close. Time for me to leave. We hugged.

"Consider me on-call from here on out," I said, walking out the front door, and down the steps. "Oh, and one more thing. I can get kegs at wholesale. How many do you think we'll need?" I already knew the answer, but I just wanted to hear him say it.

"Three should suffice."

Charlie did most of his beer and liquor orders for the bar on Monday mornings, so I called him first thing to put in my requests. It was Labor Day.

"Okay," he said. "But this'll be my final order."

I asked what he meant by that, and he told me his plans to close the bar. "It's gonna be a drink-up-what's-left kind of week around here," he said.

This was happening much sooner than I expected.

"If you want to do a last hurrah, tonight's the night," he added. "I don't imagine there's going to be much left by the weekend. Last day is Saturday, no matter what."

I wondered if I hadn't called, when he planned on telling me this stuff. He didn't fuss with social media, so it's not like I would've found out that way. Over a decade of dealing with Charlie's quirks and bullshit came to a boil. I was pissed. *Pissed.* Time to cut the cord.

"You know what," I said. "Forget the kegs."

"Are you sure?"

"And you can keep the sign."

I hung up, and that was the last I ever heard from Charlie.

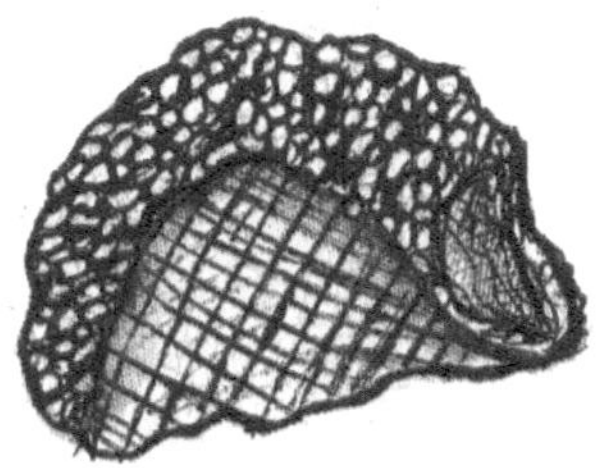

King Soopers. Tuesday night. Frozen foods section. A near-Dan Fogelberg experience. I turned a corner with my cart and encountered Professor Becker. He looked up from the pizza box he'd been inspecting.

"AJ!" he said, delighted. "I've been wondering about you."

"You and me both," I said.

He mentioned the mock obituary for *Lewd & Learned* that I'd posted on Facebook the previous day. "The end of an era."

"It ran its course."

"We missed you in class," he said. "The students enjoyed your deconstruction of Camus and *The Myth of Sisyphus*. If one of my undergrads turned that in, I'd fast-track them for grad school. Brilliant."

"Thanks. I've had twenty years to stew over that essay."

"What happened to you? You just disappeared."

"Oh, you know the old cliché."

He thought about this for a moment. "You had to drop out of Existentialism class because life got in the way. That could almost be a Steven Wright one-liner."

"Almost," I said, dismissive. "I'm looking for the last of the Choco Tacos," I said. "They discontinued them. You ever had one?"

"I don't believe so."

"The perfect proportions of chocolate, crisped rice, ice cream, and sugar cone in every bite. Perfect from end to end."

He didn't seem the least bit interested.

"I think, with a bit of revision, your Sisyphus essay could be publishable," he said. "I'd be willing to work with you on it. I'm thinking *McSweeney's*, *The Atlantic* maybe."

"The second your teeth cut through the sugar cone taco shell into the ice cream—that's the moment the Buddha was talking about. The past and future melt away. That is living in the present."

"I believe it," he said. "I'll have to try one of these Choco Tacos."

I scanned the ice cream shelves, slowly making my way down the aisle. He told me to contact him if I was interested in discussing my essay further, and I gave him a half-assed positive response. It didn't need refining or revision. It was what it was.

By eight o'clock Saturday morning, Dan and I were headed east on I-70. Three kegs, a guitar, and clothes for the weekend. Our first destination was the old farm to gather photos of Abe for display at the service.

We stopped for gas and coffee on the eastern edge of the city. The giant golf balls of Buckley Air Force Base were in clear view as we left the truck stop.

"What are those things anyway?" Dan asked. "Doppler radars?"

I said I didn't know. I grabbed my phone and began a search. "Rikki likes to think they were repurposed after the Cold War to detect and track homosexuals in the region."

Dan laughed. "I'm good with that. I don't need to know the truth."

He asked what I had prepared for the service, and I told him the basics: I'd do an introduction, then have others come up and talk, then a toast at the end. I had a song picked out to play.

"I think you should go last," I said. "The grand finale."

He thought for a moment. "Okay. Good plan. That way it won't peter out. Everyone looking around at each other, passing the buck."

I asked if there was a PA system at Norm's. Dan assured me there was. It was ancient, but there was a mic, amp, and speakers at least. I needed to plug my laptop into the system but didn't have the right cables and adapters with me. I had no cables or adapters whatsoever, actually, so I called Rikki and he agreed to bring his tackle box of A/V accessories.

We exited at Byers, and you guessed it, the flag peddler was open for business. Dan turned off the pavement onto the dirt and headed for him, stopping the pickup awkwardly close to the peddler's tables, then inching forward until the bumper came into contact with one of them. He rolled his window down.

"We're back," Dan said. "Which way to Lost Enemas?"

"Where?"

Dan turned up the radio and shouted over it. "Las Animas."

The peddler pointed south.

"Great. Thanks!" Dan said, putting the truck in reverse. He backed out slowly and headed for the crossroads. Instead of turning south, he turned north.

"Last call for most things," he said as we passed a farm and ranch supply store, motel, gas station, and a small grocery. I didn't need anything, so we kept on.

There's a bend in the highway just north of Byers that shoots you directly east. Once we were past this, Dan announced that we'd arrived at "the fun part." By this, he meant we were now going to be traveling at a hundred miles an hour.

It added an element of excitement, sending my thoughts to places inaccessible at regular speed. Marc's letters from the afterlife and his speed-of-light orgasms crossed my mind, at the very moment Dan asked me what I was thinking about. I told him, straight up.

"If I didn't know you, I'd think you were crazy," he said. "Some of the shit you say."

"Should I take that as a compliment?"

"Why not."

Four or five dots on the map later, we slowed and turned north onto a dirt road. "That was the old bus stop," Dan said. This meant we were getting close, I assumed. Not really. We drove another three miles before arriving at the farm. A ranch-style house, an old wood barn, a huge metal equipment shed, and an assortment of smaller shelters, lean-tos, livestock pens, and whatnot. Large evergreen trees lined the perimeter. The rest of the land was covered in corn, which a neighbor tended to.

The house definitely looked not-lived-in. Weeds and overgrown bushes, a curtain rod in one of the front windows had come unfastened. "I'm just grabbing some photos," Dan said. "Otherwise, I'll get distracted, and we'll never get out of here."

He left the truck running and went inside. I got out, stretched, and took a quick walk around the old barn. It hadn't been used in generations. A rope swing hung from a cross beam in the center of the barn. Bird nests, old hay, unused bags of seed and fertilizer, junk metal, the typical old barn scenery, all of it covered in bird crap.

Dan tossed a box of framed photos into the bed of the truck and shouted for me. I jogged back to the truck, and we were off.

Norm's is an old schoolhouse that sits on the west edge of a five-building town, in the middle of a grass field with no obvious parking lot or driveway. Someone mowed and maintained the place, but there were no tire ruts or other signs of regular use.

Two Buicks were parked by the front doors. Dan knew who they belonged to and why they were there. We parked next to them, and I followed Dan into the building. There were two long rows of tables set up. A pair of elderly women were unfolding chairs and placing them. Dan said we'd do the rest, and they stopped, looking relieved. We had a couple hours to spare, and not a whole lot to do otherwise.

Dan began placing some of the photos on a table near the front door. "Are we supposed to have a guest book or something?"

"I wouldn't worry about it."

"I'm sure we're forgetting all sorts of shit," he said.

"Most likely."

I finished with the chairs, and Dan started hauling the PA system out of a back room. The amp and speakers were covered in sparkly blue padding, upholstered like booths in a fifties-style diner.

"The ol' Kustom 300," Dan said, stepping back to appreciate the amp in all its glory. "Tuck-and-roll, motherfuckers!"

I watched as he hooked up the cables, microphone, and turned it on. A god-awfully loud mess of static and feedback came out of the speakers for a few seconds, until Dan got it under control. He began singing, testing the microphone:

> *Blinded by the light, wrapped up like a*
> *douche...*

"We're in business," he said. "This PA is probably ten years older than both of us. Still kicking ass. Built for eternity, or until a tornado rips through."

The Floyd's BBQ guys arrived in two trucks and trailers. Dan went out to meet them and started unloading bags of ice from the back of one of the trucks. A large metal watering trough sat on the north side of the schoolhouse. Dan placed the kegs in it, and I helped with the ice. Dan tapped the three kegs and served up a blue Solo cup of Pabst foam.

That was all that needed to be done. Not even a half-hour of prep. It seemed like maybe we had cheated somehow. We moved a couple chairs out to the small concrete porch and sat, waiting for guests to arrive.

An old man in a rusty 1970s Ford pickup parked in a random spot in the grass. "That's Norm," Dan said. "We call him Poopdeck Pappy."

I had to ask where the nickname came from. It was Popeye's dad, from the old cartoons.

We went to greet him. He made excuses for his early arrival, assuming we'd need help setting up.

"We're all set," Dan said. "We've been here since the asscrack of dawn. It's a huge production. You know how it goes."

Dan extended his hand, and they shook. This eventually turned into a brief hug. "I'm sorry, Dan," Poopdeck said. "It's been a rough year."

"It has," Dan said. "And it's only September for fucksakes."

Dan introduced me as his manager. "She almost got us on the *Tonight Show,*" he began, before explaining all the highlights of the previous months. Poopdeck was impressed.

"Are you gonna keep playing?" Poopdeck asked. This was something I wanted to know as well but hadn't asked.

"We'll see," Dan said. "I don't think lighting myself on fire and kicking my own ass would have the same magic."

Poopdeck caught him up on the local goings-on. They hadn't seen each other since George Haugenberry's memorial service the previous April.

"The cows got pink eye," Poopdeck said. "They painted new stripes on the highway in June. If you're looking for much else, I'll be happy to disappoint you."

Other vehicles began turning into the field, and Dan quickly became surrounded. A few more introductions were made, but I was soon on my own, having to introduce myself.

Rikki and Oliver arrived in Rikki's car. We hooked my laptop up to the PA and put on a classic country station. Gil showed up, to my surprise, since he had a big show at the ballroom that night. He said he could only stay an hour or so. I realized that he and Oliver had never met, and I remembered Oliver had been the first to warn me about him. They hit it off quite well, actually, dropping names like competing flower girls. Bernfeld arrived. All my people were there, my found family.

At some point after noon, but before the official start time, I counted ninety people, and then stopped. Ninety looked to be about half of everyone. I interrupted Dan's conversation to ask him if we needed to wait for anyone. No, I could get started if I wanted, he told me.

I stopped the music, picked up the microphone, and announced the start of proceedings. The guests sauntered in. Dan took a seat close to where I stood.

"I met Abe and Dan only three months ago..." I began, telling a brief account of their first Lo-Ball gig, and the story about George Haugenberry, the cow, and the Bee Gees.

"Right then, I decided I was going to make these guys famous," I said. "It almost happened."

I talked about the *Denver Post* article, the Purgatory gig, the state fair gig that didn't happen, and the *Tonight Show* appearance that didn't happen. Many of the guests looked like they couldn't believe a thing I was saying. I mentioned the album, and that we'd play it after the service was over.

The obscene roar of Harley-Davidson motorcycles interrupted everything. They turned off the highway into the parking field. Probably twenty of them. Everything just stopped. A mass eye-roll occurred, and we waited until the last of the engines had shut down.

"And then *that* happened," I said. It got a few laughs.

I asked for volunteers to come up and speak. Poopdeck was the first to take the mic. Various people shouted "Poop" and

"Poopdeck" as he walked slowly toward me. He grabbed the mic and inspected it. "I bought this PA back in Detroit, in 1968," he said. "All the Motown folks used it at one time or another."

Gil and Oliver's eyes lit up. There was going to be much conversation in Poopdeck's immediate future.

He talked about the brothers and their sidewalk performances in front of George's auto parts store.

"I never understood their taste in music," he said. Bernfeld and the rest of my crew laughed. "I'll never understand it. But I'm just an old metal guy. What do I know."

I wanted to adopt Poopdeck at this point.

He began wrapping things up and urged Dan to continue performing. "You have the gift," he said. "Don't waste it."

Bernfeld was next to speak. He introduced himself as the brothers' audio engineer and mentioned where he lived, twenty miles south of Burg. This got some laughs.

"That's the edge of the earth," someone shouted.

"I read somewhere online that the earth is flat," Bernfeld said. "I'll need to watch my step."

He paused, and shifted into serious, professorial-mode. "Ladies and gentlemen," he began. "I had the great fortune of spending some one-on-one time with Abe a few days after he learned of his prognosis. We talked about the threshold he'd just crossed.

"Abe looks up at the ceiling, rubs his eyes and says, 'I'm desensitized. I'm not afraid of a goddamn thing. It doesn't even occur to me...I'm like seasons, Herb. I'm like the wind and the sun and the rain.'

"'Is that Shakespeare?' I asked him. 'Walt Whitman, perhaps?'

"'So close, Herb. So, so close,' Abe says. 'Blue Oyster Cult.'"

Whoops and amens from the bikers.

Bernfeld continued. "Another notable quote from that all-too-brief conversation, 'Growing up with Dan, every day was a near-death experience.'"

More whoops, laughter, and amens.

Bernfeld then spoke about Jewish funerary traditions. He turned to Dan. "Take your full seven days," he said. "Surround yourself with friends and family. Reconnect. *Only then* should you start thinking about moving on."

Dan nodded.

"And, you probably know this already. If not, I'll save you the reading. There is no such thing as *closure*. Don't go wandering aimlessly grasping for it. Just know that things will get easier. Or, less difficult, if you want to be contrary."

Dan nodded, smiling, and thanked him.

A few other locals came up and shared brief memories. Nothing too revealing, mostly goofball events from their school days. One of them mentioned the brothers "going off to college."

This would need further explanation. I took a quick turn at the mic and called Dan out. "You never told me you went to college."

"Oh yeah," he said. "We both had academic scholarships to CU Boulder."

"What? Why didn't you ever mention that?"

"Neither one of us finished. What's there to brag about?"

A couple other folks took brief turns at the mic, then Dan took over. He put his guitar on and sat on the edge of the table with Abe's photos. He thanked everyone for coming.

"You'll be pleased to know that Abe was full of shit to the very end," he said, before looking over at me, and then the crowd. "Can I cuss up here? Is it okay to swear?"

"We'd expect nothing less," Bernfeld said.

"You got that from your mom, by the way," Poopdeck shouted. This got many laughs.

Dan tuned one of his guitar strings. "About three weeks ago, a doctor and a chaplain sat down with Abe and gave him the talk. They said, 'You have six to eight months, if we choose to be aggressive.'"

There was much whispering among the crowd.

"He woke up the next morning and dictated this little number to me. Told me which chords to play and sang along the best he could."

He sang a rehearsed, refined version of the first song he played for me over the phone that day:

This is my ticket out of this town
    My days are numbered, no more time for messin 'round
    'Cept that's all I've ever known to do
    Need to get my affairs in order
    Like the doctor told me to

This is my ticket out of this town
    I may come back some way, but this is all for now
    I'm tired of always living on the fringe
    And I'm tired of looking back
    Cuz every time I do I cringe

This is my ticket out of this town
    Got a few final things to say right here and now
    Which I've forgotten, it would seem
    Just tell all my stupid dreams
    It's their turn to follow me

This is my ticket out of this place
    So much forgiving to do, sorry for being late
    I should take a little time to vent
    But I feel like I'm at a corner store
    Loitering with intent

This is my ticket out of this town
My fool's golden ticket, lickety freakin' splicket
Kinda like the thought of never hangin' 'round
Good lord, take my ass and kick it
Out of this town

Half the crowd were already standing, but all the sitters were now on their feet applauding. He took a bow, then set his guitar back in its case. He had more to say, and when the applause faded, he picked up the mic and stood silent, head bowed, eyes closed.

"I'll just tell it to you straight," he began.

One of the bikers shouted "Preach it, brother."

"I'm gonna miss the hell out of the guy," he continued. "The funniest sonofabitch I ever knew. Dad was funny, Mom was funny, but Abe....nothing and nobody got past him."

More amens. Apparently, the all-Caucasian biker horde had grown up in the call-and-response tradition of the Black church.

He recounted the conversation with the doctor about vultures. "I'm pretty sure that lady doctor wet herself," he said, looking over at me. "Am I right, AJ?"

"She had dew on the lily," I said.

"I was the older brother, but he was always the funnier, smarter, more talented of us. I knew this early on, and that's probably why I tortured the shit out of him when we were kids. The oldest is always the more-responsible one, but not so in our case. With us, it was more like who was the *less-irresponsible.* I'll leave that up to you to decide.

"He bailed a lot of guys out of jail, drove a lot of drunk dudes home from the bars. He talked at least two people out of killing themselves. A few of those people are amongst us today. You know who you are. You probably still owe him one. Pay it forward, as they say."

He was right on the edge of tears. "Just an all-around good dude," he said. "The man had no demons. I had to turn thirty before I told myself, *Fuck it. Just let yourself look up to the guy.*"

More amens from the bikers.

Dan looked at Bernfeld. "I'm going to take my seven days," he said, before turning to the rest of the crowd. "I'll be out at the folks' old place. Gimme a call. Come by and see me. We'll find something to do. There's a curtain rod needs fixing. Thanks again for coming. Food is served."

He turned to me. "Any final thoughts, AJ?"

I stood and took the mic from him. "Get your beers filled or grab a soda," I said. "We'll do a final toast in ten minutes."

The crowd dispersed. Rikki had set up a projector and began playing footage from the Purgatory show on one of the walls. It was too much for me, so I stepped outside and got in the keg line. Dan followed me. Three of the bikers were performing their civic duty, running the taps.

"How'd I do," Dan asked.

"It was perfect," I said. "How'd you manage to hold it together that whole time?"

"I have an uncanny ability to detach myself from difficult situations."

"Compartmentalization," I said.

"Yes," he nodded, aloof. "*Compartment-izational.* That sounds like a word I'm gonna have to look up."

Gil and Oliver had Poopdeck sequestered by the porta-potties. I could hear the dropping of names: Diana Ross, Stevie Wonder, Michael Jackson. Something about a charity event in 1972. It was my turn in the keg line, and had to turn away, missing out on some prime eavesdropping. Gil and Oliver would have to catch me up later.

I walked back into the old schoolhouse, and approached the table and PA. The Purgatory footage was at a good pause point, so I stopped it, picked up the mic and asked the crowd to reassemble for the final toast.

A minute or so passed, and most everyone was back inside, with a few stragglers still at the kegs. They could see and hear me through a side window, at least. Dan noticed my hesitation and nudged me.

"Just go for it," he said. "You can't wait for *everybody*."

"How are you folks at reading dusty old novels?" I asked, not waiting for a response. "I rinsed off a copy of John Steinbeck's *The Grapes of Wrath* a few days ago. Toward the end, Tom Joad makes a famous speech before leaving his family. If what I have to say sounds similar to that, then I'll know you've watched the movie, at least..."

"Where is Abe going to be?" I said. "Abe will be everywhere. Wherever there's a vulture having a hot flash, Abe will be there."

Amens from the bikers.

"Wherever there's a fanny-pack of whoop-ass that needs unzipping, Abe will be there."

More amens, from everyone now.

"Wherever someone needs a ride home from a bar, or needs to be talked down from the ledge, Abe won't be there. They'll have to call Dan now."

I lifted my blue cup of Pabst. "To Abe, to Dan, to life. And for the one Jew in attendance, *l'chaim*."

Rikki knew to put on the song right then—Bette Midler's performance of "One More for the Road" from Johnny Carson's final episode of *The Tonight Show*. I'd just asked for the song, but Rikki played the video as well. I hadn't seen it since it originally aired, and it destroyed me. My tear ducts had an orgasm at the speed of light.

If anyone over forty-five showed up that day thinking they'd leave without crying, they were fucked. If anyone under forty-five had similar thoughts, they too, were fucked. It was a dam burst.

When the song was over, Bernfeld took the mic and introduced the Haugenberry's album. "Abe requested—demanded, rather—that his ashes be turned into vinyl records," he said. "It'll be a few months, but if you want one, get in touch with Dan."

The song "Dew Drop" started playing, and this too was more than I could take. I walked outside and did a toe-touch and a trunk-twister. Bernfeld approached and we hugged. He complimented me on my "air traffic control."

Gil and Oliver were at the back of the line for BBQ, so Bernfeld and I joined them. More hugs.

"Immortality is a fun thought-experiment at best," Bernfeld stated, random and unprovoked. "Something to do while you're at the DMV, or waiting for a slow gas pump."

"Something to do when you're fifteen, stoned, staring at a black light poster," Oliver said.

"No serious philosopher even bothers with the idea," Bernfeld said. "Just think how boring it would get. *Immortality.* I'm trying to picture myself on a street corner with a sandwich board hanging off me. It reads, *Hi, I'm Herb Bernfeld. I've seen and done everything imaginable with no real consequences. I'm never going to die.*"

"I'd toss you a dollar," Oliver said.

"If you had one," Bernfeld said, his index finger extended.

"Half a cigarette, at least," Oliver said.

I spotted an elderly woman walking through the crowd, carrying some sort of dish covered in a towel.

"Guys guys guys," I said, getting everyone's attention. "You probably don't know this about me, but I have x-ray vision."

"Is that so," Bernfeld said. "Who knew?"

"That lady over there," I pointed. "I don't know her name

or where she's from, but I do know this: under that towel is a glass punch bowl, and in that bowl are baby marshmallows suspended in Jell-O."

Oliver asked what color of Jell-O.

"I don't know," I said. "X-ray vision is just black and white, but I'm going to guess green."

"Yellow," Gil said.

"Red," Oliver said.

It was Bernfeld's turn, but he hesitated.

"C'mon, Herb," I said. "There's a lot at stake."

"I'm guessing pasta salad."

I made a game-show buzzer sound. "Wrong."

And thus began an afternoon of random conversations and encounters. Bernfeld was the man to be around, full of philosophical zingers, reflections on death and dying, the meaning we create out of nothingness.

We got our brisket sandwiches and sat at a table near the PA system. The Haugenberry's cover of Dave Edmunds' "Never Been in Love" began playing. Herb went on and on about how the song can now, finally, be a hit. "There is no time like *too late*," he said. The guy put bells, whistles, and glitter on everything.

I spotted the elderly woman's dish sitting on a small table at a far corner of the room, all lonesome, still covered by the towel for whatever reason. I stood from the table and went for it. I lifted the towel enough to see what was inside the bowl, then carried it back to the dudes and set it down.

"Read 'em and weep, bitches," I said, lifting the towel swift like a magician.

Green Jell-O and baby marshmallows. The bowl seemed to have generated an aura.

"Oh, c'mon," Oliver said, looking offended. "You had to have known."

"X-ray vision, dude," I said. "It's a thing. You just have to let it happen."

We stared at the bowl, silent for a moment, as though we were looking at some long-lost cultural artifact, or looking death in the eye, whichever you prefer.

"This dish was brought to you by Robert McNamara and Dow Chemical," Bernfeld said.

"It's so beautiful," Oliver said. "You almost don't want to break the surface."

One of the Harley dudes tapped me on the shoulder, asking if he could use the mic. The last song on the Haugenberry album was over, and we were just listening to random Mellow Gold. Sure, I told the Harley dude. I paused the music and let the guy talk.

"In Harley culture and tradition," he began. "When we lose a brother, we do what's called a rev fest. A final send-off for our fallen comrade..."

And so on.

All the Harleys started up and rev-fested. Deafening, obnoxious, ridiculous. I wished Calvin from *Calvin & Hobbes* would come pee on the whole thing. A few seconds in, Oliver gave me the I'm-gonna-go-have-a-cigarette gesture. I joined him, on the side of the building opposite the pack of Harleys.

He handed me a cigarette—a pricey, boutique brand I'd never seen before.

"Loud pipes save lives," he said.

"It's not the gun, it's the individual."

"Don't tread on me."

"Coexist."

"Ask first before hunting and fishing on private land."

"Ooh," I said, teeth clinched. "That's a good one."

The rev-fest finished three-quarters of a cigarette later. Oliver and I walked back into the schoolhouse. The noise had sent many of the older folks packing. The line for BBQ was gone. There was one dude at the kegs. Everything seemed to be winding down. Gil gave me a hug and left.

Dan eventually joined us at the table, looking spent. Ollie and Bernfeld were boring deep into esoteric, autism-spectrum musical strata.

"I just paid Poopdeck an extra five hundred," Dan said. "We can leave whenever."

It was only three o'clock, and I'd planned on being there at least three more hours including wrap-up-clean-up. I'd assumed we'd stay til the last of the last, the whimper.

"Say your goodbyes," he said. "We're gonna have to sneak out of here."

I was surprised to hear it, but it was his day, so I went with it. I said my goodbyes to the gang, grabbed my laptop, and followed Dan to his truck. I asked about the keg and tap deposits.

"Fuck 'em," Dan said. "Poop can take 'em out to the shooting range."

One of the biker chicks tugged on my sleeve as I opened the door to Dan's truck. She asked if I watched *Downton Abbey*.

"What the fuck does that have to do with anything?" I said, completely unhinged and bitchy. The biker chick gave me the side-eye and walked away. It was a legitimate out-of-context question from a well-meaning stranger, and my response was admittedly harsh and uncalled for. I was beginning to turn. Dan's instinct to leave was spot-on. If I were a banana, the brown speckles were upon me, and the bottom of a dark freezer was in my future. I hopped up into the passenger's seat of Dan's truck, and we were off.

Not a mile down the road, Dan spoke up. "It's early," he said. "Should we just go back to Denver?"

"Whatever you want to do."

"That's a wide berth. You sure you want to go there?"

"As long as there's no rape, or death-by-a-thousand-cuts, I should be good."

"We need some music," he said.

I asked what he wanted me to play.

"Slayer, please."

I'd dated a Slayer enthusiast for a couple months, back in the days of Monica Lewinsky, and was familiar with their menu. It was Dan's day.

"Slayer," I said.

"Slayer cleanses the palate. A huge breeze comes through every time."

I asked him which album, and he named a few. We settled on *Decade of Aggression.* "Hell Awaits" is the first song.

We listened for a bit. "These dudes seem preoccupied with all sorts of shit I'm not concerned about," I said. "But, I like it. Something weird about it."

Dan laughed. "Marry me," he said.

I got flush in the face. "I don't get married," I said. "If you would've asked back in the late-Clinton era, I might've had a different answer."

"Marry me."

"Did you ever read *The Grapes of Wrath?*"

"That was Dad's favorite book," he said. "I tried. Couldn't get past the vernacular. Simple-minded folk saying simple-minded shit to other simple-minded folk. My fifteen-year-old brain couldn't handle it. Maybe I need to take another crack at it."

"You remember Ma Joad, at least?"

"Sure."

"She said, 'A man lives in jerks, a woman lives in flows. A man gets a job, loses a job—that's a jerk. A woman has the whole world in her arms.'"

He laughed. "A man lives in jerks. That reminds me. Do you know what that sonofabitch did?"

"To which sonofabitch are you referring?"

"Abe decided to have some semen preserved," Dan said.

"What?"

Dan looked me straight in the eyes. "Yeah. I just said that."

"Why?"

"Nothing about it makes sense," he said. "I think it was his final prank on big brother, if you want to know the truth. There's a *storage fee* that I'm expected to pay."

We contemplated for a while.

"I would like to know *when* and *where* this preservation occurred," Dan said. "It must've taken an hour, at the very least."

This wasn't the kind of detail I was expecting to veer toward, so I asked why he thought it would've taken Abe so long to do what he did.

"This is going to get personal," he said.

"I can handle it," I said. "I've been to Georgia on a fast train."

He shifted in his seat. "So, we're big dudes, obviously. Things are big, if you know what I mean. The problem is our prostates aren't up to the task. It's like putting a push mower engine in a super-duty pickup. You'll get to the end of the driveway, it'll just take you all morning."

This answered as many questions as it raised. I decided to share some personal information of my own to balance things out. "I'm pretty sure I was never able to have kids," I said. "I never had a pregnancy scare. Not even once."

"Is that right."

"Not that I ever *tried* to get pregnant," I said. "But, you know, bad choices get made, operator error, equipment malfunctions, OSHA regulations don't get observed."

"Huh."

"I'm too old to even think about it now," I continued. "I have no tits and there's a nationwide baby formula shortage.

That ship has sailed, my friends. Headed for an iceberg near you!"

"Marry me AJ," he said. "You can have the big room upstairs. Your own private patio."

"We don't need to go that far, Dan," I said. "But, I could get interested in the big room."

WANDERING AIMLESSLY, grasping. Bernfeld said not to do it, but it's impossible. I walk the Sand Creek Trail every Saturday morning. *Meditation on the Abe*. There's exercise involved, semi-fresh air. It's not the *Tonight Show*, but what do you do?

I'm not aggressively looking for corpses. I'm also not *not* looking for corpses. I keep an eye out for scavengers and vultures.

Speaking of vultures: Marc's estate sale. There were fifty plus standing in line when I opened the front door on the first day. Dan and Rikki helped. I didn't budge on prices, especially on the cheap stuff. Little things I knew I could sell online for five bucks, I put a two-dollar sticker on. Old ladies and obvious antique-store dealers haggled all three days over the low-dollar items, and most of them left pissed, shaking their heads over pocket change.

Go shit on your legs, I thought to myself.

My apartment lease was up at the end of September. Rent was jacked a couple hundred a month. I moved into the big room upstairs, with the patio. A no-brainer.

Marc's bookcases of signed first editions are up there with me, as is the stereo system. When the Haugenberrys' album finally arrives, we're going to crank it on a two-armed, five thousand dollar record player.

You don't tell a novelist what to write, you don't tell a song-writer what to sing, you don't tell an artist what to paint, or draw. I know this.

It's the times we're living in.

I walked downstairs, high as fuck. Dan was at his drafting table.

"Dan-d-d-Dan-Dan, Dan-d-d-Dan-Dan," I said.

He looked up from his drawing, glassy in the eye, also high as fuck.

"I'm thinking a square canvas, seven feet one inches by seven feet one inches."

"Okay."

"Working title of the piece: *AJ Washburn's Lonely Hearts Club Band.*"

"Okay."

"You, Abe, and me behind the big drum. Bernfeld, Rikki, Oliver, Gil, Josh on the flanks."

"Poopdeck?" Dan said.

"Of course, Poopdeck," I said. "He's front row material."

"Exactly eighty-nine Buddhist monks, Michael Landon, Dan Fogelberg, Seals & Crofts, Lightfoot..."

"I've gotta put Mom and Dad in there."

"Front row. Put the cow in there, too. Put the bowl of green Jell-O and marshmallows in there. Put Kleethith in there. There'll be room."

"*Kleethith?* Who or what the fuck is that?"

No actual photos would be used, distinguishing it from the famous Beatles album cover art. He could do anything with the faces. This was crucial.

"Make us all look like we've just heard the most devastating news of our lives."

The author wishes to acknowledge the generous support, encouragement, and expertise of:

Jan & Maj, Courtney, Soapy Argyle, Dynamaux and the Prairie Futures project, Charly Fasano, Marty Moran, Kate Lind, and Lea Deforest

ZACH BODDICKER is the author of *The Essential Carl Mahogany.* He lives out by the airport, and occasionally writes, records, and performs songs with the band 4H Royalty, among others.

www.ingramcontent.com/pod-product-compliance
Lightning Source LLC
Chambersburg PA
CBHW031255120726
47906CB00003B/750